HOW TO OUTWIT A WIZARD

SEVEN SUITORS FOR SEVEN WITCHES BOOK 2

AMY BOYLES

LADYBUGBOOKS LLC

HOW TO OUTWIT A WIZARD

What happens when magical enemies wind up in a real-life Freaky Friday?

Witch Blair Thornrose has spent her life working in her family's magical bookshop. But when the magic begins failing, the only thing that can save it is for Blair to marry. The one way that witches know how to do that—throw a witchy ballroom dance to find the most eligible suitor.

But Blair has a power that makes most men run for cover—all of them except the brutally handsome and terribly arrogant Devlin Ross, that is.

Wizard inventor Devlin Ross has never gotten over Blair Thornrose. The two dated in high school, but things ended badly between them. When he discovers that she must find a husband, Devlin's jealous. He wants Blair badly, but there's a reason why they can't be together—a secret that Devlin refuses to share.

When a magical spell goes terribly wrong and Devlin and Blair switch powers, Blair is furious. But Devlin makes her a deal—he will help her win the man of her dreams if she helps him build his latest invention. This is too big an opportunity for Blair to give up. But will Devlin reveal the secret that tore them apart, or will he push Blair into the arms of another man and give her up forever?

Start reading to find out!

A series of magi-notes written and passed between Blair Thornrose and Devlin Ross while they were in high school, which was at least ten years ago, though neither would like to admit that so much time has passed.

Blair hates to think that high school was way back then, because for the past ten years she's been wondering what she's been doing with her life, and Devlin doesn't want to focus on the time gap because that means he's spent ten years without Blair.

Blair: I aced that potion theory test. What about you?

Devlin: When you say "ace," what exactly do you mean?

Blair: I mean 100. Read it and weep. All around the world magical fireworks have been set off in my honor. ✺

But I must be humble. So this is the only time that I will make you feel inadequate in my supreme presence.

And what about you? What'd you make? Don't worry, I won't gloat. Too much.

Devlin: 102.

Blair: I hate you. 😊

Devlin: Is that so? Do you promise to take all that hate out on my mouth later?

Blair: You are the devil.

Devlin: 👿 See you at our usual time? Usual spot?

Blair: You mean behind the bleachers of the witch ball pit?

Devlin: Most romantic place on earth. 😊

Blair: 😏

Devlin: Blair Thornrose, I do believe that I could kiss you forever.

Blair: Don't say things like that.

Devlin: Things like what?

Blair: Things you don't mean. 🌚

Devlin: I'm not sure if you've noticed, but you own my heart.

Blair: Hmm. A unique thing to be in possession of. I've never owned someone else's heart before. What do you think those go for on the black market? How much could I get for it?

Devlin: You are truly diabolical…in the best way possible. 🖤

Blair: But I do know what you mean. 🖤

Devlin: Do you now?

Blair: Stop smiling like you've won.

Devlin: I don't know what you're talking about.

Blair: Always so smug…listen, there's something I need to tell you.

Devlin: You've already mentioned how handsome I am. As much as I love hearing it, you don't have to tell me every day.

Blair: This isn't a joke.

Devlin: Then what is it?

Blair: Not over magi-notes. In person. It's personal.

Devlin: So serious. What you do to my emotions, Miss Thornrose. 😍 Can whatever this thing is that you need to tell me be done while kissing?

Blair: Maybe when we come up for air.

Devlin: Blasphemy. But, I can't wait to find out what it is.

Blair: I destroyed that warding exam.

Devlin: You did better than me. I didn't study.

Blair: Why not? And don't say it's because you don't need to. I know that you look over material. You might be brilliant, but even brilliant minds have to study every now and then. So what's up? Why didn't you do good?

Devlin: It's nothing.

Blair: Which means it's something. Is it about…?

Devlin: No, it doesn't have anything to do with that.

Blair: You sure?

Devlin: More than sure. Promise. Look, I won't be able to meet between fourth and fifth today. I've got some stuff going on. But see you tomorrow?

Blair: Sure.

Devlin: I'm so sorry.

Devlin: Blair?

Devlin: Blair?

Devlin: ????

Blair: Exactly what are you sorry for? That you were sucking on her face, or that you told me that I owned your heart? Which one, Devlin? What are you sorry for?

Blair: ???

Devlin: I'm sorry that you had to find out that way.

Blair: Find out THAT way? By seeing you with her in the same spot where you take me? You didn't even have the decency to hide it. You are scum, Devlin. SCUM.

If you'd wanted OUT of us, you should've told me instead of going behind my back.

Devlin: I'm sorry. It's all I can say.

Blair: What's worse is that I trusted you… How could you say that?

Devlin: Say what?

Blair: You *know* what.

Devlin: No I don't.

Blair: Whatever. I hate you, Devlin Ross. From this moment forward, I will hate you forever.

*M*agic lives in a well—one so deep that you can't see the bottom for how full it is.

If you drop a bucket into that well and pull it up, it's overflowing with power—shiny, shimmering magic that sloshes and slurps over the sides and spills onto the ground. Power that's ready to be harnessed and used.

But what happens if a well doesn't have a spring to replenish it?

That well goes dry.

Just like my family's magic is doing now, and there's only one way to replenish it—for my sisters and I to marry.

It's antiquated, right? Totally makes *no* sense. But magic, like life, is always in a state of flux, and in order for it to replenish, a new cycle must be birthed, and for me, that means marriage.

Yes, in the twenty-first century.

Which brings me to today.

Castleview Books is my family's magical bookshop. Everywhere I look, there are shelves and shelves of books. The spines span the colors of the rainbow, and they're lined up perfectly, alphabetically, the surfaces dusted and the wood polished to a bright sheen. The whole place smells of paper, glue, leather and magic.

Oh yes, you can't have a magical bookshop without that, now can you?

Glancing out of the lead-paned windows, I spy the blue witch lights flare, signaling that a customer's about to enter the store.

I drop my cleaning rag on the counter and ready myself—shoulders back, chin up, slight smile, nothing too bright, nothing forced. Because whenever I force a smile, I look constipated.

Right on cue, the door blows open and in steps a witch wearing a long ebony coat, flowy black slacks, and red stiletto boots. Her eyebrows and lips are penciled to severity with the thanks of makeup, but Mrs. DeWalt is a pussycat—as long as you don't cross her.

Which can be said for pretty much any witch, I suppose.

"Mrs. DeWalt, are you ready for your monthly visit *into* a book? I've got some great stories for you to choose from," I say with a knowing pump of my eyebrows. "I know how much you like romance."

Her sharp gaze sizes me up as if she's surprised to see me, which of course, she shouldn't be. I'm here every month. I literally see Mrs. DeWalt all the time. We are best buds. I know what she likes, and I line up a curated selection of books for her every thirty (sometimes thirty-one) days. Today I've got some sweet romances for her.

Because you see, in Castleview Books, you can live out whatever story you'd like. Just jump into a book and spend the next several hours becoming your favorite character and living out their story.

But before Mrs. DeWalt says a word, she glances over my shoulder to the back of the store where my sister, Addison, helps another patron. "I'm sorry, Blair, but I was hoping to see Addison today."

"Oh." Without a word she slides past me, beelining for my sister, which makes my next words come out as a pathetic whine. "But I can help you."

The only indication I receive that she hears me is a flick of her hand, a clear sign of dismissal.

Yep. This is how it's been for the last several months. Ever since word got out that my sister can pick a person's perfect book to read, most of my regular customers have been ditching me for Addison.

I'm not angry. I'm not jealous.

Okay, maybe I'm a little jealous.

But the truth is—I love Addison and I love watching her succeed.

But even that doesn't stop my excitement bubble from popping, and it certainly doesn't stop a little bit of my soul from crumbling into the abyss.

But that's okay. I'll nab the next customer. Addison can't help everyone. She can't take every single customer who enters the shop.

My wish is granted when the door opens again.

"Mr. Patel, great to see you." I charge forward, intent on helping him. "What book would you like to enter today?"

His dark eyes do the same thing that Mrs. DeWalt's did—landing on me before skating to the side and finding my sister.

"Sorry, Blair, but I need to see Addison."

Maybe I was wrong. Perhaps Addison *can* take every single customer.

I step aside and gesture for Mr. Patel to take a spot right behind Mrs. DeWalt.

"Traitors, all of them," my sister Chelsea whispers, sidling up to me.

I bite back a laugh. "Stop it."

"I don't really mean it." She fluffs the ends of her long blonde locks with one hand. "But I *sort of* mean it."

Chelsea smells of vanilla and lavender, like she's fresh from the oven—in a good way. She leans back on the counter and stretches her feet up onto the shelf in front of us.

I smack her leg, and she rolls her eyes before setting her feet back on the floor. I grab my rag and continue wiping down surfaces. If nothing else, it's a great distraction from my lack of helping customers.

Chelsea, I notice, doesn't lift a finger to assist me. Instead she bends over and searches the shelf for something. It's cluttered down there, full of books on hold for people, pens, notepads, balls that children have abandoned and never claimed.

My younger sister comes up for air holding a black slip of paper. I pretend not to notice it. In fact, rubbing a circle into the counter seems an appropriate response.

Chelsea clears her throat dramatically and reads (really thickening up her natural Southern accent in the process):

"You are cordially invited to a witch ball in honor of Blair Thornrose. February 1st. 112 Castleview Lane. White tie required."

She drops the invitation onto the counter, and I stare at it, hoping it'll burst into flames. But it does not. Not that destroying it will change anything.

"So. You excited for tonight?"

"Nope." Hoping the conversation is over, I turn my attention to the front door. But from the corner of my eye, Chelsea watches me for a ridiculously long moment. "Did you want me to say more?"

"Maybe."

"Okay, then."

A group of teen girls—probably werewolves if their long, dark hair is any indication—stop to peer into the windows of the store. *Please come inside. Save me from this conversation.* But to my disappointment, they move on. Our town has all kinds of supernaturals—all are welcome as magic is out in the open. Humans know our kind exist, and they mingle with us. However, they are not allowed to own property in Castleview, and that's the way things are.

My sister is still waiting for an answer, so I say, "I'd rather hide under a rock for all eternity than walk into another witch ball where people are just going to gossip and whisper about me behind my back."

Before my family got into this situation, this whole having-to-get-married thing, I *thought* that I wanted to marry, but when I started meeting eligible supernaturals, old feelings of inadequacy—*my* inadequacy—got dragged to the surface.

Chelsea shoots me a sympathetic look. "An 'I'm not ready for the ball,' or 'I am ready,' would've been just fine an answer, too." I scoff as she elbows me. "You're being too hard on yourself. Maybe our family's magic will be okay."

At that very moment, a young woman pops out of a book, her cheeks red, hair tangled. She blinks and looks around, confusion and frustration etched in tiny little lines all over her face. "What? No, no, no. I was supposed to have a full hour. It's only been..." She glances at her watch. "Forty minutes."

"Right," I mumble to Chelsea. "Our magic will be okay, you say?"

It will very much *not* be okay.

My sister jumps up. "I'll go smooth things over with her."

As she walks away to deal with the frustrated customer, I shake my head. No matter how much we may want to believe otherwise, our magic is failing. People being thrown from books before their allotted time's up isn't a new occurrence.

And it's only going to get worse until we can't put people into books at all.

And then we'll be done for.

I just wish...I just wish that the men at those balls didn't look at me the way that they do—eyes glittering with hope until the whispers start.

And they always start.

The door opens again, and I plaster a huge smile on my face just so it can drop, because in walks Catherine Farber, aka Chatty Cathy, and her besties.

The three women are dressed in faux fur coats and warm wool hats tugged down to their ears. They're giggling when they enter, but when Cathy sees me, the laughing stops. She whispers something to her friends, Sadie and Cherie, and the three burst into another, even louder fit of cackles.

Heat floods my cheeks, working all the way down my neck to my hands, which I curl into tight fists.

"Cathy, you here to jump into a book?"

She drags her gaze from Sadie to me. The three stalk forward, looking very much like they never left high school, like they're ready to terrorize anyone that steps into their path.

Cathy rubs the golden bangles on her left arm. "Jump into a book? I was thinking about it."

"Great," I lie. "What's your favorite genre? I can help you."

"What's a genre?" Sadie whispers to Cherie.

Oh gods. It takes all my willpower not to roll my eyes.

It's Cherie's turn to whisper. "I thought we came because of the witch—"

Cathy snaps her fingers, and Cherie's lips pin shut. The poor woman tugs at her mouth, but whatever spell Cathy's cast, sticks. The minion can't part her lips.

"Going to the ball tonight?" Cathy asks, her voice dripping

with poison. Not literally, of course. But if poison could have a sound, it would be Cathy's Disney villain voice.

"A better question is, are you?" I throw back. Of course I'm going to the ball. She knows that. It's being held in my honor.

My high school nemesis sneers. "I am. Daddy's bought me a beautiful new gown. Had Daisy make it."

Daisy's the town tailor and is awesome at her job. "How nice for you."

She bats her lashes innocently. "I'm so looking forward to it, but of course, I'm always worried."

Chatty Cathy was the biggest mean girl in high school. I hardly ever see her now, but whenever she does rear her ugly head alongside her Doublemint Twins, I don't back down from the meanness.

Never let the bullies win.

And it's obvious that she wants to play. Well then, let's play.

"What do you worry about?" I ask innocently.

"Well"—now she's twirling a platinum strand of hair around her finger—"I worry that there's no point in going, that you'll get there and use your power to steal all the eligible men."

The heat of anger that had been licking down my skin dissolves into barely restrained fury. "I don't know what you're talking about."

"Don't you? Don't you remember what happened in high school? With Devlin?"

My jaw tightens so hard I'm surprised it hasn't cracked. There are a myriad of replies that I can make, from *I don't know what you're talking about* to *what do you mean?* But all of those vanish from my mind, leaving me with, "I didn't do anything to him."

Which is just as good as admitting that I *did* do something to Devlin.

And of course, this is what Cathy's been waiting for.

She tsks. "It's a powerful thing, being able to influence someone into falling in love with you. It's good that he got away from your *freakazoid* magic before it was too late."

Sadie laughs. Cherie tries to but can't. She taps Cathy's shoulder, and the bully looks back at her, giving a dramatic eye roll before she snaps her fingers and Cherie's mouth becomes unglued.

"I never magicked Devlin," I growl.

"So you say."

"So you say," Cherie mocks.

Cathy shoots a nasty look over her shoulder, and Cherie's gaze drops to the floor. "But what really bothers me," Cathy continues, "is that you might pull something like this on Storm Grayson."

Wait. What? "Storm Grayson?"

She fans herself as if it's hot. It's freezing outside, being winter and all, and it's warm in the shop but nowhere near baking.

She tsks. "Haven't you heard? Storm's attending the witch ball. The whole town's talking about it. I guess if you had friends, you'd know."

She starts to turn away, but I grab her wrist. She twists around and glares at my hand, but I don't drop it. "You're sure?"

She scoffs. "Do you think that I'd lie about something like this? A famous magical inventor and billionaire comes to our town to meet the women in it, and I'd lie about that?"

"You might," Sadie says, thinking it over. Cathy's jaw drops and Sadie quickly backpedals. "Never mind. You wouldn't lie about it at all."

"No, I wouldn't. I mean, not only is Storm Grayson a crazy rich supernatural, but he's handsome, and no one, from what I hear, knows what *sort* of magical he is."

All of this is true. The man is one of the most famous

8

magical inventors of our time, a celebrity, well-known for being outspoken and extraordinarily handsome. The most intriguing part of all is what Cathy said about his magical status—no one knows what sort of supernatural he is. It's kept under wraps, with Storm himself claiming that he is what he is and that's the most important thing.

Which of course has made the rumor mill run wild with theories. Is he a half vampire/werewolf hybrid? Is he a wizard/werewolf? Is he part human?

No one knows.

And Storm Grayson's coming here.

Cathy blows me a kiss. "Good luck, *freak*. Oh, and don't get in my way."

"Excuse me?"

She tips her head, looking at me as if I'm a sad little puppy who doesn't understand. "Storm Grayson might be coming to the ball to meet you, but he's going to be mine."

Our gazes lock for a long moment. "Get out, Cathy."

She tosses her head back and laughs. "I didn't want to jump into a nasty old book anyway. No telling how many times they've been used and what diseases they carry. I like my toys brand-new and shiny."

Her minions cackle as they turn on their heels and walk out the door, releasing a blast of cold winter into the store.

I shiver against it, and when the door is shut firmly behind them, I exhale the breath that I've been holding.

Holy cow. Storm Grayson. Coming to the ball. Does my aunt know? She's the one who always puts the balls together, so of course she knows. Why didn't she tell me?

I'm irked, but my head's still spinning. It's said that Storm Grayson once magicked an entire team of doctors to a South American village because the children were getting sick. I could faint at all that goodness.

If there's one magical who could make me even remotely

excited about the ball, it's him. Not only is he filthy rich, handsome, totally brilliant and completely eligible, but he's also the magical rival of one—

"Devlin Ross," Addison says.

I blink. "What?"

My older sister, who's somehow managed to pull herself away from the tentacles of needy customers, places a hand gently on my arm. Auburn hair tumbles over her shoulders, and brown eyes peek out from under a glossy curtain of bangs. When did she escape from her fan club?

Before I get a chance to ask, she says, "Devlin Ross ordered some books. Since you need to get ready for tonight, I thought you could leave early and drop them off on your way home."

I choke on a gob of saliva and pound my chest until the coughing stops. "Devlin ordered books?"

"Yes. I'd ask Chelsea to take them, but she's staying until closing."

My gaze dashes to Chelsea, who's still talking to the customer who was tossed early from a book.

"Addison, I don't... I mean, Devlin should come and get them himself." She knows that just seeing that man makes me want to grab the nearest fork and jab it into his hand. "He's got two legs and his own flying skillet. He probably owns an army of them. Besides, it takes forever to do my hair—"

She shoves the books into my arms and grins. "I appreciate it. I'd say we could put it off for another day, but he's been waiting almost a week. Thank you so much. Oh! I gotta get back." She clicks her tongue impatiently. "People need me to find books for them."

Before I can blink, I'm bundled up in a coat with a scarf wound around my neck all the way up to my ears, and I'm standing outside holding a stack of books, my body pointing in the direction of Devlin's house.

Let's get this over with.

It's a short walk to his ridiculously big mansion that's three stories and topped with a thatched roof like the rest of the homes in Castleview.

The place is so wide that it takes up three lots. It's also got huge windows which of course don't have curtains, so that the neighbors can have a front-row seat to whatever debauchery Devlin partakes in with his revolving door of girlfriends.

Not that I care. Why would I care that he dates as many women as he desires while I'm shoved into marrying some guy I may or may not want? Probably *won't* want. Perhaps that's for the best.

In fact, it is for the best. What has love ever gotten me?

Heartache for starters.

Besides, I don't have to love someone in order to marry them, and I certainly don't have to fall for Storm Grayson.

I can thank Devlin Ross for ruining all men for me.

I ring the bell and exhale a slash of bangs from my eyes. A lifetime too soon, the door swings open.

My breath lodges in my throat at the sight of him.

Devlin's full head of dark golden hair is tousled as if he recently rolled out of bed. He cocks his head and sighs, obviously annoyed that I'm here. *Well that makes two of us, buddy.*

There's a dark smudge of soot under his right eye, which makes him look like he just finished partaking in some really manly work that involved chopping wood.

As if he can hear my inner thoughts, Devlin lifts an arm and raises it over his head. His bicep strains against his sweater, threatening to tear the wimpy fabric in half.

He wipes a hand down his face, passing those hazel eyes before caressing his strong cheeks and finishing at his chin, where there's a cleft (as if to prove he's all masculine energy).

The air crackles (or is it just me?) as his voice rumbles. "Why, Blair. It's been a while. To what do I owe the honor of your visit?"

Just hearing his voice stops the drool from falling out of my mouth. Devlin Ross is the worst person in the world, and the last man on earth that I would ever be caught dead with.

And to punctuate that point, I shove the books right into his stomach.

2

DEVLIN

5 minutes earlier

I'm screwed.

Irrevocably, completely, totally screwed.

But maybe I'll be lucky enough to survive the explosion.

"It's going to blow!"

In front of me hovers a pulsing, basketball-sized, golden mass of magic. It stretches like a balloon about to burst.

"Find cover!"

A pair of white-gloved, disembodied hands that are currently resting on the table jump to the floor and scurry to safety.

"Hang on!"

I throw up a force field as the mass implodes, sucking the air from the room like a vacuum, pulling me along with it. My shirttails threaten to get sucked into the vortex, but I hit the mass with another blow of magic and the balloon deflates, falling on the table in a lifeless heap of golden threads.

I glare at it for nearly destroying my home and say sarcastically, "And here I thought we had the spell *that* time."

Hands (both of them—they always act together) jumps back onto the table and glowers at me.

Yes, hands can glower.

I rub a palm down what I assume can only be my very tired-looking face. "You're the one who wanted to add milkweed."

Hands shakes, telling me that I'm not so easily forgiven for throwing around sarcasm like a pair of tossed-aside underwear.

"Look." I scoop up the mess and drop it into a trash can. "I told you it wasn't going to work." Hands's fingers sag over the palms of his body in shame. "It's all right. You're forgiven. It's nothing that a bottle of water and a new set of hands can't solve."

He does not look amused.

"I'm only joking." I chuckle and head from the lab into the kitchen, which is pristine—everything in its place. I run a palm over the smooth marble counter, dance my fingers to the edge and open the refrigerator. "I wouldn't give you up for anything. You know that."

Once a bottle of water is in my grasp, I shut the door and lean on the refrigerator, taking a large gulp. Hands walks his way into the room and jumps onto the counter.

He signs and I nod. "I'm aware that sometimes milkweed can work, but I told you that it wouldn't, and before you ask, no, I haven't seen *it* yet."

Hands stares at me blankly.

"Staring at me doesn't make my visions come any quicker. I will see the one we need. Trust me, it can't come soon enough," I mutter under my breath.

He signs, *Maybe you should have some fun to get your mind off it.*

"What would I know about fun?" Hands twitches his

fingers. Hint taken. Yes, I like the company of women, and no, I don't like to get emotionally involved.

When you can see the future, sometimes it's not a future that you want to know about.

Hands teeters over to a slip of black paper and lifts it.

"That's not funny." I snatch away the witch ball invitation and toss it to the other side of the counter, where that pest can't get to it. "Yes, I know Blair Thornrose is up for grabs. Well aware, thank you, and no, I have no intention of going to that ball. What do you think, I want to torture myself?"

You went before, he signs.

"That was before it was her ball. *For her.* For Blair to be married off. No. I'm not going, and that's the end of it." He waits a moment, which is Hands's annoying habit of suggesting that I really want to attend that dance. "I know we had something in the past, but I've explained all that."

But explaining it doesn't change anything. If there is a ball and I know that Blair will be present, it has been my habit in the past to go. But I shouldn't have. However, I am what you call a glutton for punishment. I simply can't stop myself from dancing with *that woman* every chance I get.

But good grief, she's going to be getting married. I can't keep flirting with her, which is what I would do if I went tonight. Flirt shamelessly and drink it up while she verbally flambés me.

Such a turn-on.

No. She is trouble. Too much trouble. Distance between us is good. A lot of distance. So much distance that I don't even know she exists, and so that she continues to believe the lie that I cheated on her.

Yes, it's a lie.

It's all for the best, because whenever I see her, it feels like someone's putting their hand through my chest and squeezing my heart. I can't keep doing that to myself.

Decision made—I'm not going to the ball, and I'm sure as hell not going to flirt with her anymore. From now on I'll be stone-cold.

A stone-cold fox.

Hands stares at me. *Right*. We were having a conversation. "I'm not going to that ball, and I'm not pursuing Blair. If I hadn't—"

The doorbell rings.

"You expecting someone?"

Hands shakes a *no*.

"I wonder who it could be."

The trek from the kitchen to the front door is a showcase of every invention that I've created. All of them hovering on shelves or bobbing up and down, suspended by nothing more than magic.

There's the pocket cauldron, my first successful creation and the one that put my name on the map. Then there's the warmer in a bottle. Just uncork it and every time a witch has to dance naked under the moonlight, she won't freeze to death in her birthday suit. Then there's my personal favorite—instant eye of newt. Just one drop on anything and it becomes eye of newt—a key ingredient for many potions.

The doorbell rings again. "So impatient." I lift my hand, and magic slinks out, creeping over the polished marble and to the door, where the handle turns and opens it.

And there she stands—Blair Thornrose.

It feels like I've been punched in the gut. Or perhaps it's just the wintry air entering the house.

No. Not the air. It's definitely my body's reaction to this woman.

She is the most beautiful creature on earth, even now as she glares at me with chocolate-colored eyes full of hate. Her pouty, sensuous lips are puckered in displeasure (what those

16

lips could do on my skin), and she's tapping her foot like she'd rather be anywhere but here.

She's making my knees freaking weak.

There is no one like Blair Thornrose. I have never, ever gotten over her. Trust me, it's not for a lack of trying. There have been many women (too numerous to count), but no one has ever even come close to outshining her. No one else understood me like she did, could make me laugh like her.

And then it ended because of me.

My heart lurches from my chest, and it takes all my will not to slide my hand up the back of her neck, wrap my fingers in her hair, drag her into my house and do all the things to her that I've imagined over the years. Oh, we would play for hours, days, weeks.

If I were a werewolf, I'd mark every inch of her skin with my razor-sharp canines, even the delicate bits.

Though I want her, she's staring at me as if she's deciding whether it would be better to throw me off a bridge or set me on fire.

"Why, Blair. It's been a while. To what do I owe the honor of your visit?"

Without a word, she shoves a stack of books into my gut. Hard.

I double over and grunt in pain.

Good thing she didn't aim for the crotch and crush the family jewels.

"There. Take your stupid books."

What?

She's already walking away, her backside swishing hypnotically. I *should* let her go. I *should* walk inside and return to my experiment. There are a lot of shoulds that I *should* do.

But apparently I am an idiot.

"Wait." I'm down the steps, ignoring the cold as it bites into my face and neck, and grabbing her by the arm, which of course she yanks away as if I'm made of fire. "I didn't order any books."

She barks a laugh, and steam rolls from her mouth. "Right. *How to Impress Witches with Magic Tricks?* Come on, Devlin. That title has you written all over it. Sure, you didn't order books."

What?

I glance down at the spines, and sure enough, not only is there a book by that title, but there are two others, *A Way To a Witch's Heart* and *Wash Your Face, Wizard.*

What sort of self-help magical hell did someone order for me?

"Have a nice life," she says, strolling off.

"Wait, wait, wait." She stops, twists back toward me. Not only is this embarrassing, it's a downright joke. "Look, Blair, I didn't order these books."

Her beautiful mouth quirks. "Like I said, I don't judge, Devlin. What you read is your business. But I thought you didn't need any help in the romance department."

She says it with a little lilt to her voice, like it's a challenge.

I smirk. "I assure you, I *don't* need any help."

"Oh, I know." She folds her arms. "I've seen all your women."

It's my turn for a brow to lift in question. "Have you been looking through my windows?"

She gestures toward them in frustration. "Everyone looks in there. You don't have curtains. We're all witness to your exhibitionist behavior."

"I have a bedroom." It comes out seductively. Can't help it. It's my go-to voice.

"One that I'm sure will give someone herpes as soon as they step foot inside."

With that, she starts to walk away again, and I can't help but be both ticked off and completely turned on. But this woman isn't getting away from me that easily. She's like a rare bird. Once I've seen her, I must have more than just a glimpse. I want to own her.

"Now, hold on a minute."

She pauses. "What do you want? I have things to do."

What do I want, Devlin? What can I possibly say that will keep her in my presence for two more seconds? "What if I don't want the books?"

She clicks her tongue. "Well, I'm not taking them back. There's no telling where your hands have been."

I chuckle. Oh, Blair. If she's *not* joking about STIs, then she's joking about STIs. "Where would you have *liked* my hands to have been?"

Her face turns red. "I'm leaving."

I scamper to catch up, and man, can she walk fast. "Sorry. That was a bad joke. Just so you know, my hands haven't been anywhere bad. I've been working on an experiment."

She lifts a palm, giving me the stop signal. "I don't want to know the details. Whatever it is, it probably involves copious amounts of lubricant and penicillin."

The fact that she's insinuating my experiment involves sex is downright insulting, maddening and giving me a boner. "For your information, I wasn't *telling* you any details."

"Good. Because I don't want them."

I don't know what makes me say what comes next. I really don't. Probably my whole glutton-for-punishment thing that I need to talk to a psychiatrist about. Or maybe it's the fact that she's walking away and this could be the last time I see her before she's engaged to someone else. A man who's better for her, who's right for her, who won't give her a life of misery.

A man who's better than me.

But even that thought doesn't stop me from word vomiting, "Your ball's tonight."

She stops again. Turns around. Cocks her head and stares

at me with fire burning in those perfect chocolate-colored eyes. "Why would you say that?"

"Why wouldn't I?"

She sucks in her cheeks and juts her hip out. "You're not going to that dance." It is a statement that sounds like a warning.

I throw attitude right back at her. "I wasn't planning on it."

"Good."

"Great," I snap.

"Fantastic. Because Storm Grayson's coming, and I don't want you screwing things up for me."

"That's even better, because I don't want to—*wait*. What?" The world stops, tilts. I fall off it and into the abyss before I'm somehow spit out and placed back in front of my home. "*What did you say?*"

Now her gaze flits around, worried that she's said the wrong thing. It lasts about half a second before she shoves back her shoulders, defiant.

"Storm Grayson. You hate him. I know that. The whole world knows it."

My spine tightens into a steel rod. I do hate Storm Grayson. She's right about that, but it's not for the reason most people think. Storm Grayson is not what the world believes he is.

Blair walks away, and this time I let her.

When I'm back on the front porch, Hands is in the doorway, holding the invitation. Little bastard's been spying this whole time.

I take it and stare at the black paper stamped in golden ink.

Storm Grayson is going to be at that ball.

He's making a play for Blair.

And there's no way in hell I can allow that.

No, I can't have her.

I don't want her.

I don't need her.

My body might go nuts when I'm in her presence, but there is no way that the two of us will ever be together.

And there's also no way in hell that I'll allow Storm Grayson to have her. She could have anyone, *anyone* in the world besides him.

And I'm going to make sure of that.

"Get my tux, Hands. I'm going to a ball."

3

"*W*here's Aunt Ovie?" I demand, throwing myself through the front door of the house.

My dad looks up from where he's sitting in his recliner, smoking a pipe and reading *A Dragon's Quotidian Life,* a book about dragons that *he* wrote.

Dragons are his favorite subject. Don't get him started on them because he can talk for hours. Even though I like those creatures, the last thing I'm interested in is a long-winded explanation about their mating practices.

Trust me, I've heard it all—especially about how dragon courting rituals put werewolves' practices to shame. If you think the biting between wolves is risqué, you ain't seen nothing until you've studied how dragons go about mating. There's biting—*everywhere.* And also some scandalous fire breathing that I would rather not think about.

My father looks up from the book, startled, his thinning blond hair falling into his face. "You're looking for Ovie?"

"Yes. Is she here?"

"I'm not sure." He points to the ceiling. "She might be upstairs getting your sisters ready."

Mama walks into the room. Her hair's piled high on her head in swirly curls, but she doesn't have on her gown yet. "What's wrong?"

"She's looking for Ovie," Dad says over his shoulder.

She frowns. "Blair, listen, there's something I need to tell you—"

I cut the air with my hand. "I already know all about it, Mama."

She peers at me curiously. "You do?"

"I do and I'm going to talk to Ovie."

"You sure about that?"

"Yes, I'm sure," I snap, then quickly apologize. "Sorry. It's just been a stressful day."

"Tell me about it," Dad says, looking upstairs, seeming to refer to having a house overflowing with women getting ready for a ball. I'm sure it's a headache for any man.

Mama nods. "Try upstairs."

"She better be there," I reply, exasperated.

No, I'm not exasperated by the fact that I've just seen Devlin. He doesn't get the privilege of doing that to me.

Ever.

A growl rips from my throat as I storm up the rickety steps that line the wall, being sure not to smash my shoulder against the collection of family photos that are hung there for all the world to see.

You know how most families showcase the nice school photos of their kids? Not mine. They like to frame the rowdy pictures, the ones where we put rabbit ears behind each other's heads. Or worse, the ones where we pretend to pick our noses.

Oh, my family's got some kind of sense of humor all right.

And the funniest part is that Ovie is MIA. "How can she be missing when she invited Storm Grayson and didn't tell anybody?" I grumble.

Not true. Somehow Chatty Cathy found out. That horrible woman knew about it before I did and it's *my* ball.

Needless to say, Ovie is in big trouble.

"Ovie," I call.

The second floor's a mess of dresses. Beautiful frilly gowns are either lying on the floor or are suspended from hangers hooked onto the tops of doors, as my younger sisters fight over who's wearing what.

"You said that I could wear the pink gown," Finn argues.

Dallas twirls a piece of her short brown hair around her finger. "And you said that you'd loan me your silver shoes."

"Have y'all seen Ovie?" I ask, stepping between them.

Finn's eyeing Dallas, but she's talking to me. "I think she's downstairs, getting the ballroom ready."

Fine. So on we go.

"Where're you heading?" Dallas asks. "You're supposed to be getting ready. It's only an hour till showtime."

I drop my chin onto my chest. "Fine. I'll get ready. What am I wearing? Some hideous purple explosion of flowers?"

Normally I like flowers, but ever since we started doing these balls, whoever is in the spotlight always wears some sort of traditional gown, and when witches talk about tradition, they mean big ugly dresses with tentacles coming off them that look like spider legs.

No, I'm not joking.

So it's hard for me to get excited about a witch ball gown.

Dallas shoots me a wide grin. "Your dress was dropped off earlier. Come and see."

They guide me to my room. Spread across my bed is a strapless silver dress made of velvet with a white fur bolero over it. Probably not real fur. No one here wants to kill animals. But the fur is soft, very soft, and nice. I push it aside to get a better view of the dress. It has a sweetheart neckline and a full skirt that's covered in tiny pearls.

I release a low whistle. "Holy cow."

"Holy cow is right," Finn says, seeming to have forgotten her argument with Dallas. "Get into it. We've been waiting all day for you to put it on."

Emory appears at the door. Yes, in case you haven't guessed, all of us girls are named alphabetically, in order to how we were born. There's Addison, me, Chelsea, Dallas, Finn, Emory, and Georgia. Whew. It's a mouthful.

Emory's dirty blonde hair hangs in barrel curls that cascade down her back. "You're here. Oh, do you love that dress? I had a feeling you would," she adds with a wink.

Emory is empathic, so of course she had a feeling about how I would react to the dress.

"Well, everybody's here except Georgia," I say. "What'd y'all do with our youngest?"

Finn thumbs the doorway. "We made her go on a scavenger hunt for her dress."

My hand flies to my mouth and I laugh. There's no one like my sisters to put me a in a good mood. They know exactly how to melt me.

As if on cue, Georgia appears, gently pushing Emory out of the way so she can see. "Do you love your dress? I wanted to wear it so badly that I almost stole it."

I chuckle. "No one's stealing this. Come on, y'all. Help me get dressed."

It's not until my sisters have finished fussing with my hair and the dress that they let me get a good look at myself in the mirror.

I can hardly breathe at the sight. The dress hugs my curves perfectly, and the silvery color complements my olive skin. Finn took her time curling my hair, and she pushed a mother-of-pearl comb into one side, sweeping it up.

"You look so beautiful," Georgia says. "I bet Storm Grayson proposes tonight."

My eyes narrow. "You knew about Storm."

My sisters, all four of them, stare at their feet. *That's it.* Everyone knew but me. Ovie kept this from me. On purpose. What else is she keeping from me? Is the Prince of Neverland going to show up? If such a person exists, I want to know about it beforehand. I don't need Cathy and her minions having the upper hand.

"I'm going to find Ovie," I tell them. "Thanks for making me look beautiful." And I mean it. I really do. "I'll see y'all downstairs."

The ballroom is in the back of the house. Actually it's the parlor, and with magic, my family turned it into a big, beautiful room filled with marble floors, tall windows, grand chandeliers, mirrors, and a cozy fireplace—you know, just in case all the dancing makes someone cold, you can light a fire and warm up (insert eye roll here).

The musicians are setting up when I enter, and I know my aunt has to be here somewhere, making sure that all the preparations are ready to go.

I scan the room and see her. She's standing in the corner talking to a woman whose back is to me.

"Ovie, why in the world didn't you tell me that Storm Grayson is coming?"

Her gaze flicks up to me and my aunt, who is like a miniature Kristin Chenoweth on steroids, grimaces. "Well, Blair, if you'd like to know why, it's because I didn't invite him."

"Then who did? Mama? Dad?"

"I did," comes a commanding voice. The woman standing beside Ovie turns around and my knees buckle. "I invited Storm Grayson, and what are you going to do about it, kid?"

Standing in front of me, wearing a brocade dress and high heels, with her silver hair twirled into a tight bun, is my nana.

My *dead* nana.

I scream, and Ovie grabs me before I faint on the floor. I right myself and exhale a deep breath. "Nana?" My gaze flicks to Ovie. "What is going on?"

My grandmother clasps both hands in front of her. "My dear, what's going on is that you and the rest of your sisters have to marry, and I've come back to make sure that it happens. I'd like to say something along the lines of 'over my dead body,' but it looks like I'm already dead."

Then she throws her head back and cackles, while my stomach churns like I'm about to vomit. Somehow this night has gone from bad to worse.

And guess what? The evening's just getting started.

his is bad. This is extremely bad. Nana coming back from the dead isn't just unexpected. It's unprecedented.

When I screamed earlier, it brought Mama to the ballroom. She took one look at Nana and said to me, "I thought you knew about Nana. That's why you wanted to talk to Ovie."

"I didn't know about her," I yelled.

She sighed. "Let's go talk in the kitchen."

So we left the ballroom and headed to the kitchen to chat about the fact that my dead grandmother has come back from the grave to ruin my life.

Yay, me.

As soon as we're settled in our cozy kitchen that for some reason has five wooden mug trees that are all filled with cups with printed catch phrases like, LIFE IS BETTER AT THE LAKE and MISSION ACCOMPLISHED, my mother slumps into a chair and gives my grandmother a worried glance before saying, "I know how this looks."

"It looks like I've come back as a ghost," Nana says proudly.

Not only is it bad, but Nana seems to have forgotten how bad this is.

"Blair! Where are you?"

Chelsea appears in the doorway, now dressed for the ball in a black gown with long sleeves. "Oh, there you ar—" Her gaze lands on Nana, and she screams right before slithering unconscious to the ground.

Ovie shakes her head. "If this keeps happening, we won't have any Thornroses at the ball because they'll all have fainted."

I crouch beside Chelsea and pick her up by the shoulders. "Who else?"

"Me," Mama says, giving Nana an eyeful while my grandmother just shrugs innocently. "I fainted."

Nana sniffs. "I do have that effect on people. Hey, it's better than not having any effect, right? What if folks took one look at me and just kept on walking? That wouldn't be any fun."

I slap my forehead.

Chelsea shifts in my arms, slowly waking back up. Her eyes flutter open, and her voice is wobbly. "What happened?"

"I did," Nana tells her.

Chelsea passes out—again.

"Must be the power of the undead," Nana whispers proudly.

"You ain't undead," Ovie snaps. "You're just a ghost who's come back to make our lives hell, is what you are."

Mama shoots Ovie a hard look. "Let's try to calm down."

"How am I supposed to calm down when my mother's returned from the dead to do God knows what with the ball I've organized?"

"If you weren't so busy with that good-for-nothing husband of yours, I wouldn't have to come back," Nana spits.

Oh wow. This has gotten really ugly, really fast. But it is

true that my aunt has an awful husband. Spends all her money, leaves for months at a time on gambling binges and only returns when he's out of cash—which Ovie always gives him.

None of us can stand Charlie, but no matter how much I assume that my mother has talked to my aunt about it, Ovie keeps taking him back.

"Mother," my mom says coolly, expertly pulling the conversation away from Ovie, "it's wonderful that you've come back, but other people won't think it's so spectacular."

"We've got to keep you hidden," Ovie says.

"I will not hide," Nana says in her regal voice. "The world should know that I'm here."

"No," my mother and Ovie say in unison.

"Nana," I start, keeping my voice as gentle as possible, "have you forgotten what it means when someone returns from the grave?" No point in waiting for an answer. "It's bad luck. It means the family has done something wrong. Things have gone so far south for them that one of their ancestors had to return to straighten things out. If people catch wind that you're here, you can forget any chance of getting me married. No one will want to be with me because they'll think that we're ruined before we even get started."

Nana grimaces. "I didn't think about that."

Ovie and my mother exchange a look. "Probably because you were dead," Mama says.

"The beyond does make you think about things other than life," she explains.

Shocker. Being dead makes you not care about the banal existence of life? Who would have ever guessed?

"So what needs to happen, is that you must stay out of sight," I tell her.

Nana looks surprised. "Baby didn't come all this way to be put in a corner," she says, referencing a line from *Dirty Danc-*

ing. "God, I loved that Patrick Swayze. You know, I looked for him in the afterlife and couldn't find him."

"Probably because he passed on peacefully and had no intention of haunting his family," I mutter.

My mother places a hand on my grandmother's transparent shoulder. "We're not trying to cast you aside, but we don't want anyone to know about you, either." My grandmother shoots her a hard look, and Mama adds, "Not because we don't love you, but how it will reflect badly on Blair and the rest of the girls. If people start gossiping, no one will come to the balls."

"But I'm only trying to help."

"Of course you are. But you can help by staying out of sight."

Nana doesn't look happy about that. "No."

We all stare at her. "No?" Ovie says.

"No," Nana tells her. "I didn't come all this way, traveling interdimensionally, to be cast aside like a two-bit hooker."

Yes, my nana has a way with words that would make even the highest of society ladies blush.

From under my arms, Chelsea stirs. "Oh my gosh. I had the worst dream. I dreamed that I saw Nana. That she was here, with us."

"Chels, it wasn't a dream."

My sister's gaze flicks up and lands on our grandmother, who taps her foot impatiently. "Don't tell me that you're going to faint again."

"No." My sister shakes her head and slowly gets up on her feet, me behind her, making sure that she doesn't fall. "I'm not going to faint; I'm just going to find an exorcist who can send you back to wherever you came from." She glances at Mama. "Does her being here give me bad luck? Like, will a cinder block randomly fall on my head?"

Ovie tsks. "See, Mama? Everyone knows *you* are bad luck. You need to just scurry on back to where you came from."

But Nana's not one to go easily. She folds her arms. "Not until Blair's married. I won't return until she's successfully wed. If I return at all."

Then, for some reason, all gazes turn to me. "What? Do I look like I have a ring on my finger? It's not like I'm not trying, here. I just haven't met anyone yet."

"Yeah," Chelsea adds. "It's not Blair's fault that all the men think she's going to mind control them."

Mama shoots Chelsea a hard look and my sister winces. "Sorry, Blair."

"It's true. No point in being sorry."

Nana claps her transparent hands. The action doesn't make a sound, which is surprisingly not the weirdest part of any of this. "That's why I've invited Storm Grayson. He's the most eligible bachelor in the country. The whole world will know he's here, and that will bring a lot of attention to you, Blair."

No pressure.

"And I'll be watching every move you make," Nana adds with glee.

"No, you won't, Mama," my own mother gently tells her. "If folks catch wind of you—"

Nana waves her away. "Fine. I won't watch every move. Such superstition. Witches and their old wives' tales. There's nothing wrong with me being here."

Ovie rolls her eyes. "Yes, there is. How many ghosts do you see walking around? Pretty much zero, which means that folks will be freaked out by you and all your hovering. The less that you're around Blair, the better."

"I'll do what you ask, but if I see that things aren't going the way that they should, I reserve the right to act."

Ovie sucks her teeth. "What does that mean?"

"It means what I said. As this family's matriarch, I reserve the right to help move things along."

"Um, Nana, you aren't the matriarch anymore," Chelsea delicately points out. "That's now Mama's role."

Nana lifts her chin and pushes back her shoulders. "I'm sure Clara won't mind sharing."

From the sour look on my mother's face, yes, she will mind sharing.

But even so, there's a certain twinkle in Nana's eyes that means trouble is definitely brewing. Great. This is just great. Exactly what I need, for Nana's ghost to be a big fat bad omen hovering over my head like a bird looking for a place to poop on.

While Mama and Ovie usher Nana from the kitchen, Chelsea sighs, resting her shoulder on mine. "This is going to be awesome, isn't it?"

"Nope."

We both laugh and my sister adds, "This might not be so bad." I shoot her a look and she shrugs. "It could be worse."

"How?"

"Hm. Let me think about that."

The truth is, it really couldn't be worse. If anyone sees Nana, then tongues will wag. People will say that the Thornrose women are cursed. They'll say things like, *See? Even their grandmother had to come back from the dead to help them get married. You don't want to be part of that family.*

Yeah, ghosts are a terrible thing.

From the hallway Ovie yells, "Blair! You've got ten minutes until guests start arriving!"

"Yeah, Blair," Nana calls out. "Get ready to be presented to all of Castleview, and Storm Grayson! Man, is he a looker. If I was still alive…"

Her voice fades out. Thank goodness. I have no interest in

knowing what Nana would do to Storm Grayson in private if she was still alive.

I exhale an ocean of air. Maybe Nana showing up is the worst thing that'll happen tonight. Maybe things won't get any more harried.

And maybe the bad stuff is only just beginning.

5

*O*ices hum from behind the double doors. My heart pounds against my ribs. It feels like it's threatening to throw itself out of my chest.

Calm down, Blair. Calm down.

The doors open and light floods into the dim hallway. The ballroom is full of witches and wizards, werewolves and vampires.

They're all looking at me.

A wizard doorman to my right clears his throat. "I present Miss Blair Thornrose."

I step into the room, and the sea of people part, nodding and smiling as I make my way past them. I should dance. I really should. But my nerves are all bunched up, so I murmur a few hellos and rush past the men looking at me with anticipation to find my aunt, who is hiding in the corner.

"Well, this is going to be fun, isn't it?" I say to her, turning toward the crowd. "We get to hide Nana, attempt to get me married and have a successful ball. Think we can do it?"

Ovie downs a glass of punch, which I'm pretty sure is

straight alcohol, judging by the pinched and overly tense look on her face.

"I just *hope* we can get you married," she replies tersely. "And that you don't sabotage a relationship before it starts."

I clear my throat, a sure sign of guilt. "What are you talking about?"

Ovie scoffs. "Blair Thornrose, I *know* you. You've been asked out by several men in the past few months, but you haven't gone out with any of them."

"Ovie"—I drop my voice so that no one can hear—"you *know* what I'm up against. When they find out about my power—"

"They run." She shoots me a cold glare. "I realize. But you haven't even tried, Blair, and this family needs you to try."

Time to change the subject. No, I don't want to think about how Ovie is right. Yes, a wizard and maybe a werewolf have asked me out in the past six months, but what was the point? Once they found out about my curse, the relationship would end up dead on arrival.

"So, does anyone else know about Nana?" Seems like a perfect topic change.

"Addison," my aunt says, watching the crowd.

I balk. "Addison? She never said anything."

"Nana asked her not to. Probably so that she could stir up trouble without any of us knowing."

"Oh, you mean with like the whole Storm Grayson thing."

"Exactly."

Nana stirring up trouble sounds just about right. In fact...I bet she's the one who ordered those books for Devlin. She probably even asked Addison to have me deliver them.

Why, those two sneaks. Next time I see Addison, she's going to hear about this—in a friendly, sisterly manner, of course.

Chelsea approaches, swinging a glass of punch. "So where's

Storm Grayson? Isn't he coming? Oh, look, Nana's trying to eat food." Her eyes slide to Ovie. "I wish someone had bothered to tell me that my grandmother was back from the grave and has more attitude than every hornet in a hornet's nest."

I snort. "At least you didn't get *the talk* about how you're disappointing your family."

My sister clicks her tongue. "Shame on you. The night's still young. My talk could happen any minute now."

A laugh bursts from my mouth. Ovie drops her voice to a tense whisper. "It looks like I'll be spending my entire night hiding my mother. I'll be back."

Ovie storms off to the refreshment table, which is surprisingly empty, where she appears to talk sternly to Nana, doing a lot of discreet pointing, while Nana shrugs and looks around like she's an innocent lamb. That makes Ovie's face turn bright red as if she's about to explode. My aunt taps her foot and gestures to the back door. My grandmother's shoulders sag as she realizes she's been busted and has to leave the ball.

They both exit and Chelsea laughs. "This might be the most excitement we've had in forever."

"Just wait till Storm Grayson arrives. Every woman in this room will throw themselves at him."

She sighs. "Hopefully he'll only have eyes for you."

I scoff. "I could be so lucky."

The doors to the ballroom open, and my heart leaps to my throat. Maybe it's Storm!

Then the announcement comes. "Devlin Ross."

Against every bit of my better judgment and common sense, my gaze searches him out.

He steps inside wearing a black tuxedo, white tie and with a white scarf draped around his neck. Nestled on his head is a black top hat.

A top hat.

Of course. I'm surprised he doesn't have a black walking

stick to go with it. Maybe he'll burst into "Putting on the Ritz" and start tap dancing.

Oh, that would be fun. I would pay to see that.

Devlin vanishes his scarf and hat while surveying the room.

Even from this distance, he looks ridiculously yummy with his dark golden hair combed back, his chiseled jawline looking all *chiseled* and those hazel eyes scouring the crowd for whomever he's searching for.

Which hopefully isn't me.

Just to be safe, I hide behind Chelsea.

"What are you doing?"

"Hiding."

"Why? Oh, because you don't want Mr. Hot and Sexy asking you to dance."

"Nope. That's not why. I just...want to hide."

"Miss Blair, may I have this dance?"

I glance up and do a double take. Devlin, who had been on the other side of the room only seconds ago, now stands in front of me, smirking with that stupidly handsome face of his.

Chelsea moves out of the way, completely revealing my location. Traitor.

"May I?" he repeats.

I'm about to say no, to say *hell no*, I don't dance with skeevy jerks, but just as I'm about to do that, the doors blast open like they've been hit with a tornadic wind.

Everyone in the room turns, because how often do doors blow open at a witch ball?

And there stands a man who must be six-two with silvery-white hair, cheekbones chainsawed from stone, dark eyes and a physique that could rival Devlin's.

Yes, Devlin's built, okay? I just don't like to think about it very much.

"Storm Grayson," the doorman announces.

The entire room goes silent. Everyone, and I mean everyone, is staring at him, wondering what he'll do. Does he walk like a normal person? Laugh like one?

Storm's gaze slashes across the room, searching, looking for something. Then that gaze lands on me, and a fiery inferno of heat works its way from my core and flares out across my entire body.

This man has come here for me, to meet *me*, and what better way to make an entrance, to get his attention, than to dance with another man?

Oh, I am evil, aren't I?

I nod to Devlin, who rips his gaze from Storm and settles it back on me. The inventor is Devlin's biggest rival, and it must be bothering him something fierce that the billionaire is here.

"Yes, it would be a pleasure to dance with you," I force out in a sugary-sweet voice.

Devlin frowns because he knows that I'm never this nice. He shoots an annoyed glance to Storm.

"On the contrary," he rumbles in his deep, masculine voice, "the pleasure's all mine."

He leads me to the center of the ballroom, and as soon as our hands touch, electricity snakes up my arm, sending a shiver licking down my backbone. I bite down the feeling and pull away slightly so that I'm only touching him where it's necessary. Even the fingers of my left hand are barely brushing his shoulder.

The string quartet begins, playing something fun, light-hearted, quick-paced.

Basically a song that'll have me sweating and smelling like an ogre in no time.

Devlin holds me gently, as if I'm made of porcelain. I get a whiff of his cologne, and I'm suddenly taken to the center of a forest, where the scents of pine and earth mingle in perfect harmony.

"You're dancing with me because of Storm."

"I don't know what you're talking about."

Devlin smiles. It would be an absolute lie to say that he doesn't have the most dazzling smile that I've ever been blessed to see. He really does. It sucks you in and makes you feel like you're falling off a cliff—one with spikes below that you impale yourself on.

That was just a reminder of how I feel in case you were unclear or forgot or suffered from amnesia because Devlin's so attractive.

He cocks his chin. "At least you picked the most handsome man in the room to make Storm jealous. Good choice."

"You—do you even know how conceited you sound?"

"The truth can't be conceited," he purrs.

"That's even *more* conceited." I shake my head in frustration. "You know, this is why you've never had a serious relationship."

"Oh, I've had a serious relationship."

And the way he looks at me makes goose bumps jump up on my skin and run away. His eyes are scorching, and suddenly his hand feels sweltering and sweat sprinkles across my back even though it's cool in the ballroom.

The look in his eyes suggests that Devlin is begging me to ask him about the serious relationship, as if he's hinting that what *we* had was serious.

No way. I'm not falling for it. Devlin is a player, a conceited, cocky *player*, and I'm too smart to be pulled into his whirlpool of death.

"Whatever," I say, sounding more like a sulking child than a debutante who doesn't have time for his games. "The words 'serious relationship' and 'Devlin Ross' don't go together."

"No," he admits (surprisingly), "they do not." He glances down at me (not that I'm looking) and frowns. "How am I supposed to lead if you're barely touching me?"

"With mind control?"

He sighs. "I'm afraid that I don't have your remarkable gift, and it is remarkable, as I once told you a long time ago."

My eye twitches. Dancing with Devlin was a terrible idea. Horrible. Worst idea ever.

As if to prove it, he takes hold of my hand and squeezes. All the distance that I've put between our white-hot palms vanishes. I want to jump out of my skin, and at the same time I want to soak up his heat.

What is wrong with me?

"How many men have you danced with so far tonight?"

"One thousand," I say tartly. "How's your string of a gazillion girlfriends?"

He chuckles and glances down, which makes his thick lashes brush his cheeks. Or, at least that's what it looks like. Disgusting that he can do that, isn't it?

"I thought you'd know all about my love life from spying through my windows."

"I don't spy," I nearly shout. Then I realize that folks are looking over, so I drop my voice. "I don't spy on you," I whisper hatefully. "I have better things to do."

"Like?"

"Like, work at the bookshop."

"No potion making?"

I frown. "No. I haven't done that since high school."

"Why not?"

"I don't know. I guess I just forgot about it."

He spins me and the skirt of my dress swishes around me gracefully. "You forgot about your passion?"

"No," I reply, annoyed. "I didn't forget. I've just been busy."

"Finding a husband?"

I huff out a frustrated breath. See what this man does? He annoys the bejesus out of me. "No, I haven't been busy finding a husband."

I just want to kill him.

"I had asked about your girlfriends, if you remember. You know—the many. The slimy. The STD filled."

His eyes narrow. "Well, from the looks of how many men you were dancing with before I asked you, which was *none*, I'd say my nonexistent girlfriends are going about as good as your epic crusade to find a husband."

I. Hate. Him. So. Much. "Shouldn't you be tied up with a rope and blindfolded while getting robbed by your latest conquest?"

He chuckles. "Oh, Blair. You do know how to carry a friendly conversation."

"Only with you. So. Why'd you come?"

He looks down and his golden-green gaze hits me like a spear straight in my heart. "I came to torture you, obviously."

"I don't need to be tortured by you. I was tortured enough in high school by your presence, don't you think? Our breakup wasn't exactly nice."

He gives me a mock-startled look. "Wasn't it? I thought we ended things all peaches and cream."

"Hence why I hate you now."

"And why you should keep on hating me."

I want to explode. Every muscle in my body is wound tight. I'm half a second away from screaming. It takes every bit of restraint to whisper and not scream my next words at him.

"Then why are you here? You just said yourself that I should keep on hating you, yet every chance you get it seems like you want to dance with me, remind me of what you did. I don't get it. What do you want?"

His hand squeezes mine, and I want to jerk away, but smiles! Storm might be watching! "Perhaps I want to call a truce."

I laugh. Oh, that's pure gold, right there. "A truce? You've had years to do that."

"I've apologized."

My jaw falls. "The only reason why you apologized is because I caught you. If I hadn't caught you, you never would have said sorry. Ever. You are a playboy, Devlin, through and through. You absolutely destroyed me and had no problem watching it all play out. I hated you then, and I hate you now."

I expect my bold words to shock some sense into him so that he'll stop torturing himself and *me* by asking me to dance.

But instead he stares into the crowd and nods. "You have every right to hate me, Blair, and you should."

That's it. That's all he says. He doesn't say, *Of course you hate me. Perhaps I should find a new dance partner.* Nope, he doesn't do anything normal like that. Devlin just keeps right on dancing.

"I don't know what you're up to, but I will always hate you, Devlin Ross," I bite out. "You've proven yourself to be despicable, absolutely lacking in any morals."

"Thank you."

That's even worse. Why doesn't he fight back? There's something horrible about telling someone off and they don't argue. Instead they accept the tongue-lashing.

But Devlin looks almost sad for some reason. Doesn't matter what it is. I don't care.

I'm about to keep telling him off when Nana slips through the crowd.

No no no! Not again!

My eyes widen and Devlin follows my gaze. He squints. "Is that your nana?"

"No."

His gaze swivels from her to me. "Yes, it is. Why's she—" His eyes flair and he tips his head back, giving me an ample view of his thick neck and manly Adam's apple. "Things *are* bad, aren't they? None of y'all are married except Addison, and now your nana's showed up."

"You've got it all wrong." As if I'm going to tell him the truth.

His eyes shine with mischief. "She's looking for you."

It's true. Nana's eyes are scraping over the crowd. I catch Chelsea's gaze and jerk my head toward Nana. My sister spots her, and her face immediately goes pale. She slips through the witches and wizards and finds Ovie. The two of them quickly corral Nana and whisk her out the back door before anyone else can see her.

Whew.

Crisis averted.

"That's bad luck, you know."

"I know it's bad luck," I snap.

A slow, delicious smile curls his lips. "She's come back because you're not marrying off fast enough."

"No comment."

He tips his head back and laughs. It's a rich, velvety sound, a skein of silk unraveling down a walkway. "So I'm right. Not that it bothers me." He takes my hand and points it at his chest. "I, unlike most of the other magicals here, do not care for old wives' tales. I don't believe in bad luck."

That might be the best thing I've heard all night. It tells you how terrible my night has been when the best thing comes out of the worst person's mouth. At this point my standards are well below sea level.

He lowers his lashes as he peers down at my dress. That fringe of dark velvet makes his eyes look smudgy, with the corners just begging to be traced by my finger.

"You look…um, nice tonight."

Wow. Devlin sure isn't so great at the compliments. "Thank you." *I guess.*

"You actually look nicer than that."

"I'm not sure what that means."

"It means saying you look nice is a small comparison to how beautiful you actually are."

Now I'm tongue-tied. Before I can reply, the couple next to us gets so close that they bump into Devlin, and he brushes against me.

I should pull away, but the heat from his skin is so welcoming, it's so wonderfully delicious in the chilly ballroom air that I stay exactly where I am.

He's looking up into the room, and his jawline, no, his entire face looks like it was sculpted by a Greek artist. No, Michelangelo, for sure. That's how gorgeous he is.

And he smells like heaven—like cedar and musk. It's so intoxicating that I want to roll around on top of him and wipe his scent on my flesh.

His gaze snaps back down, and I glance away, annoyed that he caught me staring.

But his beauty doesn't matter, because I still hate him.

"May I cut in?"

I jump back, surprised by the intrusion. It's the first time I'm hearing his voice, and it sends a shudder pulsing down my spine.

To my right stands Storm Grayson, and he wants to dance with me.

6

*T*his close, Storm's eyes are lighter than I first thought. They're gray, actually, and gorgeous (just like him), with flecks of brown.

His hair is silvery, but it doesn't make him look old. It makes him look unique, hard-edged, as if he's really lived life. Like maybe he was once lost in the mountains during a snowstorm, separated from the rest of his family, and the only way that he could reunite with them was to weather the cold, harsh, deserted mountain, climbing the icy sheets with his bare hands. The wind being so fierce that it burned his sk—

"Storm, good to see you," Devlin says like he's biting off pieces of steel from an airplane.

"Same to you, Devlin." Storm places a hand over his heart like he's sincere. Well, at least one of them is. "Will you be dropping any new inventions soon?"

A tight smile, a smile that's holding back fury. "I hope to. Got one right on the edges of my mind, but you'd know all about that, wouldn't you?"

One side of Storm's mouth tips up in a half smile. His lips

are thin, I notice, but not so thin that they can't take hold of mine and claim them for himself.

"Would I know about your invention?" is all Storm asks.

We stand there for a long, awkward silence. Devlin must've forgotten what's going on, so I clear my throat and glare at him. His eyes snap from Storm's back to me.

"That's right. You were cutting in. Well, Grayson, that's usually not how these things are done—"

"Yes, you can have me," I declare like a heroine in a bodice-ripping novel. *Have me? Did I really just say that? Why don't I wrap myself up in a bow and show up at his hotel room later? That would look less desperate than I sound right now.*

Also, Ovie would die if she heard me throwing myself at Grayson. Or would she? She does want me to marry, after all.

Before Devlin can embarrass himself by arguing about the etiquette of Storm cutting in, I unhook my hand from his shoulder and tug the other one from his grasp.

At first he doesn't want to let go, but one sizzling look from me and he releases his hold.

I turn to Grayson and smile. There are other people on the dance floor, and the music has shifted from the tempo of *sweat bath* to one that's more like lounging in a pool float on a summer's day.

Perfect for getting to know Storm.

Devlin slinks away like a hyena who's stolen his latest meal, while I beam up at my new dance partner. Even though he's tall, I'm not overextending my elbow joint in order to rest my hand on his shoulder, and I'm not looking up his nostrils and seeing his brain. This is a good start.

Also, his hand is warm, not sweaty, and when he begins to dance, he's easy to follow. One gentle touch from Storm and I know which way that we're moving, as if it's instinct.

Not trying to get ahead of myself here, but this might be a perfect match.

Better rein in that enthusiasm. At least for now.

"Blair Thornrose," he purrs. "I'm Storm Grayson."

I've never been properly instructed on how to introduce myself to a celebrity. Are you supposed to pretend like you don't know who they are? Or are you supposed to say, *I know exactly who you are.* Sounds kinda desperate and way too fangirl for me.

So I just go with, "It's nice to meet you."

He quirks a brow in intrigue. "You mean, you're not going to ask how I know who you are?"

Time to flirt this up. An innocent shrug seems appropriate. "I assume you asked and someone told you. After all, the ball invitations have my name on them."

He stares down at me, and a little shiver of excitement threads throughout my body. "They do. But there are plenty of other eligible bachelorettes here."

Why is he talking about them? "But you're not dancing with them."

"No, I'm not."

I grin. "So you did seek me out."

He smiles, and it's like seeing the heavens part. Nothing like the arrogant smiles that are Devlin Ross's forte—you know, how one side of his mouth becomes lopsided like he's totally innocent of all wrongdoing when it's obvious that he's Satan himself.

My body certainly responds to him like he's the devil.

Stop thinking about Devlin and focus on Storm.

"I did look for you," he confesses.

From the corner of my eye, my grandmother edges to the rim of the ballroom, watching us with the intensity of an eagle about to steal a meal from a hawk.

Can someone please stop her?

Just as I'm thinking it, Ovie spots Nana and tries to drag

her away, but it's impossible to move what cannot be budged by physical strength.

Nana makes a face and tries to argue, but Ovie convinces her to go on.

I release a breath that I didn't know I was holding. And another crisis averted. For now.

Nana's hell-bent on ruining this for me. If wind of her presence gets out, my chances will be ruined. Stop. Do not pass go. Do-not-collect-$200 ruined.

"Tell me about you," he says.

And just like that, my attention is back on the handsome Mr. Grayson. "What would you like to know?"

"Whatever you think I might enjoy learning."

Not sure if the sentence was supposed to sound seductive, but it did. Heat crawls along the back of my neck. "I work at my family's bookstore."

"Ah yes, Castleview Books."

"That's the one."

"What do you do there?"

"I help put readers into the stories that they adore." My heart swells because it's something that I love. Or loved. Used to be, people loved having me help them, but now my presence is obsolete—like I'm a horse and buggy compared to that new-fangled invention they're all calling the horseless carriage.

The car.

"You're an inventor," I muse.

"I am." He spins me out, and I come back to him, falling against his chest. Storm catches me expertly, and we stay in that position one, two, almost three seconds (while my blood sizzles, by the way) before he gently pushes me out and I take hold of his shoulder once more.

"Any new inventions on the horizon?"

"There's one. There's always one, but from the way that Devlin's looking at me, it seems he'd prefer I didn't have any."

What?

It takes a moment to find Devlin, and when I do, he's staring fiery spears at Storm.

He is not going to ruin this for me.

As Storm spins me in a different direction, I glare at Devlin until he catches me looking and begrudgingly glances away.

Good. Keep it like that.

"Don't worry about Devlin. He's just jealous because your inventions are great."

That catches Storm by surprise. "You think so?"

"Of course." What has he invented again? *Think, Blair!* "I've used Magical Messages for ages, and you came up with that when you were, what? A teenager?"

He looks completely impressed with my knowledge of his pubescent life. "Fifteen. I was fifteen when I invented that, but to be honest"—dramatic, woe-is-me sigh—"it's really a bit prehistoric in terms of inventions, at least compared to what I'm doing now."

I chuckle because of course it's prehistoric. He's in his thirties. Isn't he?

But when I laugh, Storm's eyes narrow hard and fast on me. I clear my throat in embarrassment. "Well, it seems that of course anything you created when you were younger would probably be juvenile compared to your talents now," I explain.

"Yes," he agrees, sniffing and glancing into the crowd, "they would be. You're right. I'm always so hard on myself."

Is he opening up to me? Like, opening up and we've only just met? Yes, Storm Grayson is being vulnerable. I might cry tears of joy.

"I know what you mean. When I can't give a reader a great experience, it really weighs on me. Even though it may seem so small and simple, it's funny how I take it personally."

He sighs. "It's like that with my inventions. Not everything I create will be for everyone. But for those whom I have made something for, I want the invention to touch them deeply, affect them, change them from the inside out."

"So profound."

"Thank you."

The music stops. Abruptly I might add. There really should have been more of a fading-out sort of thing instead of a quick halt.

I take a step back from Grayson, and he does the same. "I'll be here for the week," he explains.

"The week?"

He smiles shyly and pushes away a few strands of hair that have fallen into his eyes. They really are a gorgeous shade. "There are outings. That's what I was told."

Outings? Now is not the time to act like I have no idea what's going on. "Wonderful. I look forward to seeing you, then."

Without warning he takes my hand and bows, pressing his lips to my flesh while tipping up his gaze to me. "The pleasure," he growls, "is all mine."

A bolt of lightning sweeps down my back, nearly knocking me to the floor.

Holy cow.

I manage a smile as he releases my hand. With a nod and my heart thundering against my chest, I walk back into the throng of guests, searching for Chelsea.

Oh my gods! I can't believe what Storm Grayson said to me!

I'm floating on a cloud. He wants to see more of me this week! He's interested! Woo-hoo!

And best of all, he doesn't know anything about me. He doesn't know that I'm a magical—

"Think you got yourself a man, don't you, *freak*?"

I stop and spin around.

There stands Chatty Cathy with Sadie and Cherie. This is *my* ball. Mine. Other witches are invited, of course. It would be rude not to have them come. But the event is held in my honor.

Unfortunately that's not how the other witches always see it.

Cathy's blonde hair is pinned up, and her face is pinched like she's experiencing constipation pains.

"What did you say to me?" I snarl.

She jerks her head back toward the floor. "I said, good luck with Storm Grayson. Try not to influence him into falling in love with you, like you did with Devlin. It would be a shame if Storm found out about your little ability too soon."

I am not going to be intimidated by this little tool. With my shoulders back and my spine straight, I cross over to her. The look of surprise in her eyes is almost soothing.

"If you tell Storm Grayson about me, do you know what he will think of you?"

"What?"

"That you're a scheming gossip, and no man likes a gossip."

She frowns. "*I* like a gossip."

What an idiot. "Then go ahead and tell him what I can do." *No, don't! Don't really tell him.* "But if you do, he won't be interested in you."

She thinks about that. I can practically see her brain working behind her eyes. Cathy seems to decide that I might actually be right. "Fine. I won't tell him…for now. But just so you know, I want him for myself."

"Shocking." Sarcasm drips from my voice. Obviously she wants him. Cathy might as well have the words GOLD DIGGER stamped on her forehead, she's so obviously interested in him. "Well, good luck."

I start to walk away, but her voice stops me. "Is that a challenge?"

The hairs on the back of my neck soldier to attention as I turn to face her. "A challenge?"

"Yes. Are you challenging me to seduce Storm Grayson?"

No. I want to say it, I really do, but I just can't stand Cathy, and Storm asked me to dance with him, and we had chemistry. The sparks practically knocked me across the room! So against all my common sense, I say, "Yes, Cathy. May be the best witch win."

Her eyes sparkle with malice. "You just sealed your doom, Thornrose."

Oh, am I supposed to be intimidated because she called me by my last name? I'm not. "We'll just see about that."

She folds her arms and sneers. "By the time I'm finished with Storm, I'll have him wrapped around my little finger and he won't even remember your name."

"Oh yeah?" I drop a hand to my hip. "Because by the time I'm finished with him, he's going to be down on one knee, proposing."

She laughs. "As if. You haven't gotten anyone to marry you yet. You'll never get him."

Anger burns through me in big, long ropes. I want to grab Cathy by the hair and toss her into a mud pit. But in spite of that, all I say is, "You're on. May the best woman win."

athy's words keep playing in the back of my mind. *Try not to influence him into falling in love with you, like you did with Devlin.*

Like I did with Devlin.

My stomach churns in anger. It's the same old cut, opening the same festering wound. When Devlin dumped me, he told the entire school that I'd influenced him into caring about me.

I'd never been so humiliated in my life. It felt like a knife had been plunged into my gut, then twisted, pulled out, shoved back in and twisted some more before being pulled out again, put back in...you get the idea.

That wound didn't heal overnight. Not sure if it ever healed, now that I think about it, and whenever I see Devlin, it's hard not to remember how he betrayed me on so many levels.

It wasn't so hard to forget when you were dancing with him.

Shut up, self.

I would never, not ever influence someone into liking me. What a horrible thing to do to another person.

I attempt to shake off those old memories and focus on

something else. From where I'm standing, I've got a great view of everyone and everything in the ballroom. Witches dance with werewolves. A few fae are here, too, talking to guests. I inhale, and the smell of spicy cologne mixed with floral perfume permeates the air. At the buffet table is an arrangement of petit fours and fruit.

I might not influence someone into loving me, but that won't stop me from getting someone to bring me a plate of food.

Yes, it's lazy. Yes, it's using my power. But right now sugar is what will make me feel better.

I spot Chelsea standing off to the side, and I decide to give her a little nudge.

That's what I call it—*nudging*. Nudging a person in one direction or another. I've never tried influencing anyone into doing anything huge. It's merely a suggestion, one that they either accept or reject.

But mostly they accept.

I push through the shield around my mind and toss out my power like a lasso. Though I've never seen myself when I do this, my sisters have told me that my eyes turn black the moment that my power is used. Then just as quickly as they turn black, they become normal again.

A hard snap tightens in my stomach, and that's the sign that I've roped Chelsea with my power.

Very gently I send over the idea of me and cake. Next thing I know, my sister has a plate of dessert in her hand and she's bringing it to me.

She has a funny look on her face, almost like she's laughing at an inside joke. "If you'd wanted cake, all you had to do was ask and I would've brought it. You didn't have to nudge me, because of course I want to know all about your dance."

"I shouldn't have done it. It's wasteful."

She shrugs. "Sometimes you have to be a little wasteful."

I chuckle as she places a glass plate that holds pink-icing petit fours in my hand. "Thank you, and dancing with Storm was amazing. He's very considerate and we hit it off."

She squeals. "Really?"

"Yes!"

"Oh, I'm so excited for you!"

Dallas walks up, tucking her short brown hair behind an ear. "I don't know about y'all, but I've spent the last fifteen minutes keeping Nana busy in the back. Even though she swears that she's not interested in the ball, she keeps trying to sneak out here."

Chelsea rolls her eyes. "That's the last thing we need."

"Why couldn't she have just stayed in heaven?" I muse.

Dallas checks her nails. "I'm beginning to wonder if she was in heaven at all."

We stare at each other before laughing. Then Dallas says, "What's Storm Grayson like? Have you found out what supernatural he is? I've been watching who he talks to, to see if there's a hint there, but he seems to fit in with all of them."

In unison, our heads turn in his direction. Sure enough, Storm's talking to a werewolf and a vampire that I recognize. There's even a wizard hovering nearby.

"I think he's got the blood of all three in him," Dallas says, rather boldly, I might add.

Chelsea folds her arms. "Impossible. There's no way. Maybe he's part werewolf. I can see that." She wiggles her brows at me. "Be sure to let us know if he bites."

I nearly choke on the petit four. "Oh gods. Stop it. We only danced once."

Dallas sighs. "Don't worry. According to Nana, there's an entire week of activities."

I blink. "Yeah, Storm said something about staying for the week. What's going on?"

"Nana's finished with Ovie only scheduling one ball, and

told her so. If Storm Grayson's here, then he's here for a whole witch-courting session."

My stomach opens, and I think that I'm going to vomit. *No pressure.* This is good for me, but it also means that Cathy has more face time with Storm.

I'm gonna have to be on top of my game.

"Uh-oh," Dallas murmurs.

"What?"

"Looks like our old friend Cathy's on the prowl."

My stomach tightens as my gaze floats to the dance floor, where a frilly skirt swishes past. Cathy's dancing with Storm. Sometime between talking to other supernaturals and me taking a bite of cake, Cathy dug her claws into him.

My stomach sinks.

"If you're not careful, that one will steal your happiness," Chelsea whispers. She pauses for a moment. "You don't think she's telling him about you, do you?"

I shake my head. "No. I already warned her not to." But still, that doesn't make me feel any better.

"Maybe you should nudge her into not liking him," Dallas suggests.

"You know I can't do that. It's completely immoral." Watching Cathy dance with Storm isn't my idea of a good time. "I'm going to get some air."

Chelsea reaches for me. "You want us to come with you?"

"No, no. Stay in here." I force a wide grin that feels as fake as a silicone breast implant. I mean, I *imagine* it feels fake. I wouldn't know. "I'll be right back."

My mind's swirling as I push through the doors that lead into the garden. I inhale deeply and throw myself against the railing, studying the hedges that have pools of moonlight dripping on them.

Even though it's winter, the garden is all four seasons, even blooming in the cold like it is now. After the frigid day, a warm front has moved in, making the temperature bearable. But still, I hug my arms to fight off a chill that's settled on my skin. However, this cold is more from Cathy than it is the actual weather.

I inhale the comforting scents of gardenias, roses and lilies. The fragrance is heavy in the air, and it clings to my skin.

I sigh and drop my head into my arms. I must get married for my family, but every which way there's an obstacle. Besides Cathy, there are my own mental blockades. Storm can't know about my power. The last man that did dumped me, and it shattered my heart so badly that it's never fully recovered.

Isn't that dumb? Even though what happened with Devlin was years ago, it still destroyed me.

Most people would say, get over it, but the repercussions of him telling the school about my curse continue to haunt me to this day.

I'd be better picking a guy off the street and proposing marriage *to him* than I am going to fancy balls.

Stop it, Blair. Stop beating yourself up.

I'm so lost in my own self-doubt that a scraping sound takes me by surprise. My spine snaps to attention, and I spin in the direction of the noise.

"Sorry to startle you," Devlin says as he steps from the shadows.

"Great. Just great. I come out here for a break, and you're already tainting the place."

His jaw tightens. Yes, I can see it. Moonlight cuts across his face, making his beauty seem almost ethereal.

Not that I noticed.

"I'm sorry that I'm such poor company."

I scoff. "Don't try to make me feel bad. You've made me feel plenty bad in this life. You can take a little of it now."

He drops his chin to his chest. Does the great, arrogant,

cocky Devlin Ross feel guilty about something? Does he have feelings?

"You're right. I have made you feel bad." I suck in a breath and he chuckles. "Surprised that I can apologize?"

"No. I'm surprised that you can admit when you're wrong."

His head lifts and his eyes search me, looking for something, I don't know what, but it feels like he's got X-ray vision that's sinking through my skin and looking at my bones, turning them over to see what's on the other side, what I could be hiding.

Then he rips his gaze away. "I never should have come."

He starts to walk off, and there's something so vulnerable about him that I can't stop myself from asking one more time, "Why *are* you here?"

He slips his hands into his pockets before turning to me. "I wanted..." He shakes his head. "I don't know what I wanted."

"To make Storm Grayson jealous? To ruin my chances with him?"

Devlin looks surprised like I punched him in the gut. His recovery is quick as he narrows his eyes and says in a hateful voice, "If you don't want me here, why don't you *make* me leave?"

I stop breathing.

He's suggesting that it would be okay to use my power in such a way. As it sits now, my power is always simmering under the surface of my skin, rolling and boiling, waiting to be used, prodding me to release it. It begs to be harnessed. So every so often, like I did tonight with my sister, I give in and use it for trivial things. My sisters are accustomed to fetching things for me, even if I don't do it that often.

But using my magic to force Devlin into doing something against his will is an insult.

Anger blisters my insides. "I would never use my power

like that. You know that. But of course you want everyone to know what kind of mutant I am—for their own protection."

He shakes his head. "I don't know what you're talking about, Bee."

Bee. The nickname he gave me all those years ago. Just hearing it makes flames lick across my skin, it's so infuriating. What makes Devlin think that he has the right to call me by a name given out of love?

I step forward defiantly. "You don't get to call me that. You don't get to pretend like you care." It's all so maddening. I plow my fingers up the sides of my hair, pulling it out of the comb and no doubt ruining it. "Gods, all of this is ridiculous. My power. All of it is because of my power. What I wouldn't give to not have it."

"Your power?" he growls. "You don't know anything about having a power that's a curse."

"Like you do. All you care about is getting laid."

"Stop. It."

Devlin's eyes are brimming with rage. I don't think I've ever seen him so angry. He's always annoyingly charming.

Oops. Perhaps I have pushed him too far.

But I don't care. "Why should I stop it? You're the one who shows up to social engagements with two dates."

"I didn't tonight."

"Wow. One time. Big deal. Is that the worst problem you have? Try living life as a magical freak."

He shakes his head in disgust. "You think your power is so bad?" he grinds out. "You can do what? Some mind trick on your unsuspecting victims? Use *the force* on them?"

"How dare you—"

"Yes, I will dare, Blair. I will dare, because you don't know what being cursed with power is."

"And you do?"

"Yes." Pain flares in his eyes before he quickly looks away. "I do."

During this time we've been stepping closer to one another, like we're tugged into the other's gravitational pull. I don't notice it until now, when I'm only a few inches from Devlin and am staring at his bow tie.

It's silk, perfectly tied. He probably used magic to do that. Wouldn't it be nice to waste magic on things other than getting your sister to deliver a plate of dessert? To have so much power that using it for something as simple as tying a bow is okay, instead of feeling like every time you burn up magic, you're being irresponsible and pushing your family closer to the brink of extinction?

He clears his throat, and I look up at him. Moonlight cuts his face into all sharp angles and high cheekbones. The urge to touch his cheek and let my fingers brush over the coarse stubble makes my fingers twitch.

He stares down at me, and I've forgotten where I am, what day it is, what we were even talking about.

That's what Devlin Ross does to me. He makes me forget my own name, makes me forget what I was about to say. His good looks steal my breath.

His throat bobs and my gaze tracks up to his eyes. There is pain in them, something that I don't understand.

Right. We were talking about his power.

I want to speak, but my throat's thick. I lick my lips, and his eyes flick to them. My words are barely more than a whisper when I say, "What could be so bad, Devlin, that you seem to think you've got it worse than me?"

He rips his gaze away, giving me a view of his amazing profile. "Let's just say that you don't have the monopoly on magic that harms more than it helps."

Did this have something to do with his parents? They'd

died when he was young, a plane crash. But that's all I know about them.

Either way, the air on the balcony has shifted, changed, become more intimate, and I don't like it.

"There are things you could do with your power, Blair."

I scoff. "Hilarious. Like what?"

"You see the bad in it. But there's so much good you could do." He glances back through the window into the ballroom. "See that wizard over there? The one who's staring at that little blonde?"

"No," I tell him, not bothering to look.

He points. "Right there."

"I still don't—"

He grabs me by the shoulders and pulls me against him. I'm now overly aware that I'm touching his torso. That there are only a few layers of clothing between us.

Devlin doesn't seem to notice because with laser-beam focus he says, "Him. Right there."

The only thing worth paying attention to right now is the fact that our crotches are lined up. But somehow my gaze tracks to where he's pointing. "You mean the guy who looks lonely?"

"Exactly. You see he wants to dance with her." He points to a petite blonde.

"How do you know?"

"Watch." Sure enough, the wizard keeps glancing her way. "See?"

My face is pressed against Devlin's rock-hard chest. "Yes," I say, my cheek smooshed. "I see."

Every few seconds the wizard glances up shyly, but when the blonde tries to make eye contact, he looks away.

Devlin drops his mouth to my hair and runs his hands down my shoulders to my elbows. He murmurs in a voice that makes chills wrap around my spine, "With your power you could give him a touch of confidence, Blair, just enough so that he'll ask her to dance. You could nudge him into believing in himself."

His hands tighten on my elbows. I'm overly aware of how we're pressed against one another, how I haven't touched him like this in years.

Pressure builds between my legs, and he exhales into my hair. He starts to slide his hands down to my waist, but I pull away.

The spell of Devlin is broken. "But that's forcing my power on someone I don't know. It's wrong."

He blinks like he's waking up from a dream. It takes him a moment before he slides a hand down his cheek and shakes his head. "You'd be offering that man a gift. Maybe something that would change his life forever."

"Yeah, right. This power doesn't work like that."

"Have you ever tried?"

"That's not the point."

He throws his head back and laughs. "That's the whole point."

"It's a curse," I argue. "I would give anything to wish it away." I drop a hand onto the railing. "Since you hate your mystery power so much, maybe you can wish yours away, too."

He doesn't laugh. Instead he tips his head toward the sky as if he's actually contemplating it.

And it's sexy as hell. It's been too much—the physical contact with him, the dancing, the *talking*. Most of all the talking.

I need to get out of here. I take a step back, but his hand shoots out, grabbing my wrist.

"Oh!" Surprise unravels inside me, sending a pulse of energy ripping up my spine. "What?"

Devlin nods to a star. "Make a wish. Anything you want. Make it, and I'll do the same."

Has he gone nuts?

I don't know because his expression is unreadable. It's all clouded and shrouded in dark Devlin energy. It's kind of alluring, actually. I might like this dark Devlin.

Snap out of it, Blair! Devlin is the devil. All you gotta do is rearrange the letters of his name, throw out the N and it's right there staring you in the face. D-E-V-I-L.

I haven't said anything, so he glances at me with those hazel eyes of his, the gold flecks in them shining. My body becomes a puddle.

"Make a wish," he commands gently.

Right. He's my mortal enemy. It's best if I remember that. "Fine."

"We'll say it at the same time, and maybe it'll come true."

I laugh because it's ridiculous. He doesn't laugh. Devlin's still holding my wrist, his fingers burning imprints of heat into my flesh, imprints that I know will last well after he's released me.

"Are you serious?"

"Why not?"

Why not? My gaze shifts to the star, a single star that's winking at me from up in the heavens.

"Fine." Anything to get out of here and get back to the ball. Chatty Cathy probably has Storm Grayson pinned up against a wall and is trying to get pregnant via osmosis or something so that she can trap him and steal all his money.

"Ready?" he asks.

"Ready."

"I wish—"

"I wish—"

"That I'd never—"

"That I'd never—"

"Been born with this power," we say in unison.

From out of nowhere, a fierce gale rips over the balcony, picking up my skirt and blowing it toward the ballroom.

Devlin's still holding my wrist, but a wave of heat pulses from his hand and shoots down my arm, making it feel like I've been set on fire.

I screech and he drops me.

The fire shoots up to my shoulder and dives into my stomach, where it coils up like a snake before the power explodes out of me. As soon as it's gone, a new force pushes in—a beam of energy traveling a thousand miles per hour. It slams against me and I stumble back.

Devlin does the same. There's shock on his face. He stares at his hands, pats his chest, then looks at me.

"Did you feel that?"

"Of course I felt it. What was it?"

I feel different, strange, as if a part of me is gone. That power of mine which is always simmering is simply silent, like it's vanished into thin air.

What the hell?

My gaze swivels around as if I can find answers out in a garden overflowing with gardenias and hydrangeas.

That's when I see her.

My grandmother's standing at the door, her ghostly face pressed up against a pane of glass.

She's staring at us.

And she's smiling.

8

"What have you done?" I demand.

Devlin shoots me a harsh look before turning to my grandmother, who came outside as soon as we motioned for her to.

"It's good to see you, Rebecca," he says casually as if some weird magic hasn't just ripped through us.

It occurs to me—where are Nana's handlers? Where's my aunt? My mother? Who's supposed to be watching her? Who has left their post and is letting my grandmother run amok?

"It's not good to see her," I snap at Devlin. "She's a bad omen. Everyone knows that, so don't lie."

He slips his hands into his pockets. "I'm not lying."

Nana grins at me. "See? Someone's glad I'm here."

I just…can't. "What did you do to us?"

She lifts her palms to the sky and shrugs innocently. "What do you mean?"

"Do not play coy," I hiss. "What happened out here?"

"You mean to you?"

Oh my word. If this is how this conversation's going to go, I might throw myself on a knife. "Yes, to us."

"It looked like to me that the two of y'all were wishing on a star, and a beautiful one at that." She peers up at the sky. "What a magical night."

She can shove the innocent act where the sun don't shine. "We were wishing, but then some weird magic thing happened." I fold my arms. "What was it?"

"Not sure. You might want to ask the star."

"Not funny."

"Well, what did you wish for? Seems like the heavens may have granted it."

Devlin's eyes widen in surprise. "It was a joke. A casual wish. It wasn't anything that should have been taken seriously."

"Do I look like I rule the night sky?"

"No," I snap, "but you look like someone who might meddle in the affairs of others."

"Preposterous. I'm just an old dead woman. Look at me. I'm see-through." She lifts her brocade skirt to prove that yes, she is indeed transparent. "But if you're wondering about what happened, test your wish."

I laugh. "Test it? No. There's no way—"

Devlin's hand is on my skin again. This is happening way too much for my comfort. "Do as she says. Try your power."

"But—"

His jaw flexes. He's not joking.

"Fine."

What should I try? Get Devlin to dance by himself? Yes, that seems appropriate,

So I stare at him, willing him, nudging him to move toward the dance floor (that's still highly occupied with people, by the way).

But nothing happens. Like I felt before, the power isn't there. But in its place there's something else, a nugget of energy that I can't touch. Like it's sitting high on a shelf just out of reach.

Oh no. This is bad. I don't like my power, but I don't want to lose it.

"I...can't," I whisper.

Devlin shoots my grandmother a look that's unreadable, and the next thing I know, his eyes go black. I have an overwhelming urge to find out the time.

"What time is it?" I ask Devlin. He tells me and then I turn to Nana. "Do you have the time?"

"No, I don't."

The need to ask everyone in the ballroom for the time is overwhelming. I'm stalking toward the door when an arm snakes around my waist, tugging me back.

The desire instantly fades. I push Devlin away and point finger at him in accusation. "You've got my power."

"And you've got mine," he says darkly before turning to my grandmother. "Switch them back."

"I don't know what y'all are talking about. I had nothing to do with switching anything." She's speaking to us as if we're children and she's explaining why you shouldn't put a fork in a light socket. "As I've explained, the two of y'all wished on a star."

"Then why is there a twinkle in your eyes?" I accuse.

"Who, me? Like I said, I'm just a ghost."

Just a ghost, my foot. "What did you do?"

She shakes her head. Literally two hours ago Nana was fierce and in charge. But right now she's pretending to be a feeble old lady, unable to remember where she stored her false teeth.

I'm not buying it.

"Okay, Nana. I get it. This is the old switcharoo in order for me to learn some lesson. Lesson learned. I like my power. I want it back."

"Do you?" she asks, eyebrow lifted. "Are you sure that you don't want to see it gone? Think of all the baggage you won't have anymore. Think how you'll be free of it."

Her words sink into my bones. If I'm free of my magic, that means I'm not a freak anymore. So when Storm Grayson falls in love with me, he won't think that I used my power to make it happen.

Not being cocky, just acting confidently.

This is amazing! No one can question if I'm manipulating them into a relationship because I *can't.*

I can be free. For once I can be absolutely, completely free.

Nana clears her throat, and my gaze slides to her. Her eyes flick onto Devlin, and then my false high crashes to the ground like a burning rocket.

Devlin has my power. *Devlin.* The man who shows up to every single party with two women on his shoulder. When I had my power, I never abused it. I couldn't. There's no way that I would have used that gift to sway a person into doing something that would have harmed them—or me.

But Devlin?

"Switch us back," I command Nana.

"I can't, my dear." Now her voice sounds sad, as if she's seen the evil future that's in store for our town as Devlin loves and leaves every single woman in Castleview, beginning his evil crusade to bed the women of earth.

"Nana, I know you're behind this. Change. Us. Back."

She shakes her head sadly. "Whatever power caused this to happen, I'm afraid it will simply have to play itself out. It will have to work its way out of you."

"How long?" Devlin asks impatiently.

"I don't know. A day? A week? A month?"

"A month? Devlin could give the whole world herpes by then."

"I do not have herpes," he grinds out. "I don't have any

69

STIs, thank you very much." He shakes his head. "Rebecca, as good as it is to see you, and my own grandmother I'm sure would love to have a good long chat with you about the other side—"

"I'd love to see Lilly."

"I can arrange that," he says gallantly like he's the best gentleman in all the world. "But before you can go on your tour down memory lane, would you please excuse Blair and myself?"

"Of course."

And then Nana floats away with her shoulders lifted as if she doesn't have a care in the world. To her credit, she probably doesn't.

As soon as she's gone, I glare at Devlin. "Give me back my power."

He glances up at the sky and shakes his head as if silently asking, *Why me?*

"Just try," I explain. "I know that you can't figure it out, but let's just try. I don't want it back, gods know, but I can't have you running around town convincing every woman to sleep with you."

His jaw tightens. "Is that what you think of me? That I would use your power to have massive orgies?"

"Yes, I do."

He scoffs but says nothing. "How would you like me to give it back? Put our hands together? Maybe press our foreheads to one another and hope that it happens?"

"You don't have to be smart," I snap. "I just know that you can't be trusted with my magic."

"And you think that I want *you* having *mine?*" He touches his chest. "I barely want it myself. If I'd known this would happen, I never would have spoken those words."

His face contorts in hurt, but there's more than that—

worry. He's *worried.* The great playboy Devlin Ross is worried about something? Impossible.

"What is your power?"

He punches his hands into his pockets and rips his gaze away. A moment later he sighs. "Sometimes I have visions of things that are going to happen. They always come true, always, and right now I'm waiting on one that will help me decipher the next piece of an invention that I'm working on. I've been feeling it coming, but now..."

"But now I have your power," I murmur.

He drops his head for a moment and then glances at me through his thick eyelashes. "Yes, you do."

It takes a second for this to sink in. Devlin can see the future. His magical power is that he has visions. "You... No one knows this."

My tone makes it sound like an accusation, but there's more to it than that. I'm shocked, really. This knowledge not only surprises me. It's a blow. Devlin and I dated for months before I ever told him about my power, and he never, ever told me about his. I didn't even know he *had* a special gift until tonight.

"Some things people don't need to know." His playboy mask drops for a second, and I see the vulnerability in his eyes. "There are people who would use it against me and for their own gain."

His tone suggests this isn't a theory. It's a fact, one that's happened to him before, and against my working brain, the smart part of my head that tells me not to feel things for this jerk, an unexpected wave of sympathy overwhelms me.

"I'm sorry," I whisper.

"There's nothing to be sorry about except that you have something that I need back. Now."

And I can help that, how? "Maybe our powers will reverse tomorrow."

"I don't think so." He glances over his shoulder, out into the garden that's still bathed in moonlight. "You have to come home with me."

"What? You just jumped from zero to sixty with nothing in between. I'm not going home with you."

"But you'll have the vision."

I scoff. "What makes you think that I'll have it?"

"You will if you're near me," he states stoically, dragging his gaze from the garden to me. There's a fierceness in his eyes that sucks the breath from my lungs. It takes a moment before my body remembers how to breathe. "If you're with me day and night, you'll have the vision that I need."

"How do you know? You could be saying that so that you can get me to your house and unleash my own power on me, keep me chained up as your sex slave for days or weeks on end. I can see it now—you'll have me lashed to your bed so that you can play your sick games with me anytime you want."

He smirks. "Is this supposed to be *your* fantasy or mine?"

Heat immediately floods my cheeks. "It's yours obviously."

He drops his mouth to my ear and purrs, "Darlin', I don't need to use magic if I want you in my bed."

My panties are suddenly soaking wet. "There's no way I'd go willingly."

His eyes say, *We'll see about that*, but his mouth says, "I need you to help me, Blair."

"Whatever this curse is—and trust me, it's a curse—it'll have to work its way out by itself. I'm not going anywhere with you."

With that, I turn on my heel and walk back into the ballroom.

The first thing that hits me is the cool air. It washes over my skin like a wave, making goose bumps ripple on my flesh. I shiver off the feeling and then take in the scene.

There are a dozen couples on the dance floor, but the one

couple I see, the one that strangles my attention, is Storm Grayson dancing with...Cathy.

Still? What the hell?

She's smiling at him. He's smiling at her. Fury boils in my blood right then. Jealous, angry fury.

Cathy glances to her right and spots me. Her lips curl into an evil smile. She's won. That woman already thinks she's won.

"If you do this for me..." Devlin's standing beside me. When did he arrive? He leans down and whispers, his breath floating across my ear and causing me to shudder. "If you do this for me, stay around me, don't leave my side, then I will..." There's a very long pause here, as if he's trying to figure out what to say next. He inhales and finishes. "If you help me, then I will get Storm Grayson to marry you."

A pulse of excitement zings through my body. I turn my head, and Devlin's so close our lips are an inch away from touching. He immediately stiffens.

"How can you do that?"

He takes a position behind me, his mouth to my ear. His breath is a wave of electricity rushing over my skin, igniting me from inside and making every cell in my body shudder.

"You can't use my power on him. I forbid it."

Devlin chuckles. It's a husky, seductive sound. "No, I won't use your power on him. But I'll help you. Darlin', by the time these courting weeks are over, Storm Grayson will be begging you to marry him."

"How can you—"

"Trust me, okay?"

I shouldn't trust Devlin. I should run for the hills and not look back. But this is the man who has women dropping their panties for him like they're on fire. If anyone could get someone wrapped around their little finger, it's Devlin.

He can help me win Storm's heart. He can help me secure my family's magic.

My body is screaming at me not to do it. If Chelsea were here, she'd be telling me to think long and hard about this. Do I really want to be near Devlin Ross for weeks on end? Or until our magic switches back?

No, I don't.

But I sure as hell don't want Chatty Cathy to steal Storm. I want him all to myself.

I glance over my shoulder and, from the corner of my eye, see that Devlin's watching me closely.

"Devlin Ross, you have yourself a deal."

9

"**Y**ou have to what?" my mom asks, her blonde curls frizzing around her face as if she just touched an electrical outlet.

To be fair, I have just dropped a bombshell on her.

"Well, um…" Suddenly twisting my fingers into the skirt of my dress seems like the most intriguing thing ever! "Well, something strange happened with my powers, and they got switched with Devlin Ross's."

My father drags a tired hand down his face. "And I suppose that means something bad?"

Mama shoots him a look. "Phillip, we're trying to be supportive here."

My father shrugs. He's sitting in his favorite recliner in the living room with his feet up. I'd tracked both of them to this room after the whole *Freaky Friday* thing happened with Devlin. I think they were looking for a break from the ball. Surprise! Things got bad.

Mom's sitting on the love seat, her deep burgundy gown looking like a wave made of wine that surrounds her.

Dad stretches his arms behind his head. "I have the feeling you're about to pull an Addison."

"Of course she's not going to pull an Addison." Mama scoffs. "Boy, we don't need that happening again. Remember last time? We thought Feylin was going to throw her in a dungeon and never let her out."

Dad thinks about it. "That was on the worst side of what could happen. We knew he was smitten with her."

"Yes, and see how that unfolded." Mama smiles. "It worked out great. Now they're married."

My dad takes this as his cue to shoot me a funny look. "Are you and Devlin about to elope?"

I roll my eyes. "No, Dad. We're not eloping. Will you just let me explain?"

"We've been sitting here," he says.

I stop myself from reminding him about how they were both just waxing poetic about them good old days of Addison and Feylin's relationship. "Devlin and I have switched powers, and he needs me to be near him so that he can—"

Oh crap, I'm not supposed to tell anyone about his CIA clearance level of wizardry. Time to make something up, or at least hug the truth closely enough that no one notices that I'm not *actually* explaining the situation.

"I need her for a project that I'm working on."

Devlin's voice takes me by surprise. He stands in the doorway, looking all rumpled and gorgeous. He's plowed his fingers through his hair, and he's tugged down his tie a bit. He kind of looks like he just climbed out of bed and threw on a tux like he couldn't be bothered.

Well, he can bother me anytime.

Wait. Where did that come from?

Wherever that voice came from, it can retreat back down to the pits of hell where it belongs.

That's a big fat *no* to me and Devlin. No no no. I don't want love. I don't need love. All I need is to get married, and my perfect match is not Devlin Ross.

I will repeat—it is not Devlin Ross.

Dad perks up. "Devlin, good to see you; why don't you sit down? Cigar?" he says, pulling a box from his pocket like cigars are Tic Tacs that he carries around to keep his breath fresh.

Before I can explain that no, Devlin does not need a cigar, and no, we don't need to treat Devlin like royalty, he lifts a hand and shakes his head. "That's very kind of you, Phillip, but it's getting rather late."

Dad is crestfallen. He lives with a bunch of women, and he probably feels like his testosterone is swept up into a dustpan and thrown out the back door just about every day. So whenever there are men around, he makes it a big point to bond with them.

I really need this thing with Storm to work out so that my dad doesn't imprint on Devlin Ross. He can imprint his devotion onto Storm instead.

"But yes, I need Blair," he says, sidling up to me.

I instantly stiffen at his proximity. Did I approve this closeness? Not technically, no, but as long as he doesn't put his arm around me, we'll be fine.

He drapes his arm around my shoulders. The move is so sudden that I jolt. Devlin flinches, too. For me it feels like a thousand fire ants are biting my flesh. He must be experiencing the same thing. See? Not meant to touch. Fire ants are proof.

"As I was saying, I need Blair's help with a project. Her expertise with potions is going to come in handy."

"But can't you just hire someone?" Dad asks.

He's trying to help, I know he is, but for once can't my father just sit back, nod and say, *Okay, kids, go have fun. Don't burn down the house while you play chemist.*

"I wish that I could," Devlin explains. "But Blair has the sort of talent that you really can't buy."

I frown. "I do?"

"She does?" Dad asks. Way to have faith in me, Dad!

"Of course she does, Phillip," Mama says in my defense. Go, Mom! "Remember how she was top of her class in potions?"

"Oh, that's right. I was doing a lot of dragon chasing in those days. It's hard to remember."

Devlin's hand has found its way onto my shoulder like a tarantula trying to stow away into my luggage. I shrug it off as he says to my father, "I'd love to talk to you about those dragons sometime."

"Anytime," Dad says with an easy smile. "Stop by whenever you'd like."

Mama rolls her eyes. "But back to this whole thing with Blair."

"Yes." Devlin shifts on his hips. When he does, his body brushes against mine. And I take a small step away. "This particular project that I'm working on requires a full-time, twenty-four-seven helper. It's just for a few days."

Now Mama's eyes are big as plates. They scour my face, then his, then back to mine. "But what about the courting season?"

This is a big deal because this is the first time that my family is pulling out all the stops. They're not just hosting balls. There are also *events*. Old-fashioned events where the gents and ladies are chaperoned by the older witches, who all giggle, plot and bet on who's going to end up with whom.

There's even correct grammar like the word *whom* thrown around.

"She'll be at every event," he tells them.

"With you?" Mama asks.

"No," I say loudly. Devlin stiffens. "We won't be together. We're not together. I'm only helping him on this thing."

"But you're spending the night there," Mama says.

Oh, right. This looks bad, right? Like I'm shacking up with Devlin at night and then flirting with other men during the day.

"It's the nature of the project," Devlin insists. "I have no intention of defiling your daughter or laying any claim to her."

"Thank goodness," I murmur. Everyone looks at me. I shrug. "What? We're not together. I'm only helping him. Storm Grayson is here. I'm not going to lose out on the chance to get to know him."

Devlin nods. His body reminds me of a mountain—a hot, lava-created structure made of flaming coals. Heat wafts off his body and clouds around me like a fog. His presence can't be ignored because he's so big and...just...everything about him is too much.

In fact, it feels like the air is being sucked out of the room.

"Well, it's at a strange time," Mama murmurs.

"I know, but Devlin needs his own power for the experiment and I have it," I explain.

"Plus she does have other potion-related talents that I require," he adds, returning to his original point that I'm some sort of potion savant, which I am not.

I won't lie. There is a special place in my heart for potion making. A big one. It's been years since I was dumped in a lab with ingredients and given the chance to have at it. Even though Devlin's lying so that my parents approve of this arrangement, the urge to start mixing ingredients and seeing what happens makes my fingers ache.

Mom looks at Dad and he nods. Then she glances back at me, and her gaze is searching my face like a spotlight. She's trying to look into my soul to see if this is really what I want.

Of course it isn't what I want! But for the sake of this

family, I need Storm Grayson to love me. He has to fall for me, and if anyone can seduce a person, it's Devlin.

So unfortunately, that means I need him, too.

Finally Mama exhales a big sigh. "Well, if this is the only way for you to get what you need, Devlin."

"I wish it was any other way, Clara. I don't want to use Blair like this, but she does have my power, and like I said, I can also use her expertise with potion creation. But don't you fear—I'll have her at every single event, and on time, too."

"But you won't make it look like we're together," I snap.

Devlin's sharp gaze flicks toward me. He hesitates but says, "No, we'll arrive separately so that no one will suspect. The last thing that we need is for anyone to think that we're joined at the hip."

"Amen."

Devlin clears his throat and turns his attention back to my parents. "I promise that I won't keep her for any longer than I have to, but right now I do need her near me."

My dad shifts his attention to me. "And you're okay with this?"

It feels like my rib cage is hugging my heart so hard that it's about to be smothered. The world has literally been sucked away from me in the past few minutes. I'm going home with Devlin Ross. I have to help him see the future. I have to help him, period.

This isn't something that I thought I'd be saying. But he's going to help me, too. Devlin is going to ensure that I win Storm Grayson, the mysterious inventor. By the time this courting season is over, I will know everything about Storm Grayson, including what kind of supernatural he is.

All with Devlin Ross's help.

I steel my heart, which is screaming and tugging me by the imaginary sleeves of my dress in the other direction. It wants us to run away, and I don't blame it.

But I mentally lock it in a box. This is for the best. This is a business transaction. I help Devlin. He helps me.

End of story.

I smile widely at my mom and dad. "Am I okay with this?" I say, repeating my dad's question. "Of course I'm okay with it. Devlin needs my help, and I'm the one person who can do that."

Turns out, he's the one person who can help me, too.

Fingers crossed this works.

---

*a*s soon as I step into Devlin's home and the reality of this situation sinks in, I have one thought—*I am going to kill my grandmother.*

Even though she swears that she had nothing to do with this whole *Freaky Friday* situation, I don't believe her. The woman had her face pressed up to the glass and was staring at us, for goodness' sake.

"Make yourself comfortable," he says as I walk into his house, my bag slung over my shoulder like I'm a hobo about to jump on the next freight train straight out of town.

Boy, that is tempting.

Devlin's home is clean, and it smells like cotton sheets and Febreze. Like, it smells really good. And there are little knick-knacks sitting on shelves. No, not knickknacks, I realize on closer inspection.

"This is the pocket cauldron."

He steps back into the living room. His tie's now completely undone, and he's unbuttoned his collar by one, no, two buttons. He looks sex-rumpled. Like he jumped out of bed and straight into an underwear commercial.

It's unnaturally sexy.

So I look away.

But now he's standing right next to me, and his scent is filling my nose. It's all over this place. I can't escape it.

He picks up the miniature cauldron and turns it over before handing it to me, which I suppose that I'll just have to take since he's offering.

It's the tiniest little bowl and honestly looks like a kid's toy except that when you push a button, it explodes into something much, much bigger.

"The invention that changed my life," he murmurs.

"Not just yours. Every witch and wizards, too. You no longer had to stow a life-size cauldron in a bottomless bag. Those can get so heavy."

"I know. That's why I invented this. It's great for whipping up a potion anywhere, anytime," he adds, a spark in his eyes.

There's something about the way that he mentions the potion making that makes my heart pulse. The pocket cauldron came out soon after we graduated from high school, and I remember that I always complained to him about having to drag a big cauldron with me to competitions.

Then he created this.

There can't be a connection. No, I refuse to believe it.

"Do you have one?" he asks.

"Of these?" I try to give it back to him, but his hands are now in his pockets and he's leaning against the wall. "No. I never needed one, at least not after high school. No more potion making for me, remember?"

He frowns. "That's a shame. You always liked potions. I wasn't lying when I said what I did back at your house. I *do* need your help. I could use *you*"—he blinks, shakes his head— "I mean, your help, on my project."

It doesn't take a brainiac to know what Devlin was going

to say. Obviously the implication that he would use me had a sexual connotation. Duh. This is Devlin we're talking about.

Thanks to his little slip of the tongue, a million very naughty images are flicking unsolicited in my head. My cheeks burn. So that he doesn't notice, I look down.

"You press a button to get this to open, right?"

"That's right," he says quickly. "It's on the side."

He points and I wave his hand off. "I can find it. I have eyes."

"You do? I hadn't noticed."

"Very funny."

I press the button, and the cauldron immediately jumps to life, opening in a series of clicks and whirls, growing quickly, so quickly that I barely have time to put the thing on the floor before it explodes into a full-sized potion-making machine.

I laugh in spite of myself, because before me sits a huge cast-iron bowl just ripe for spell creation.

"That is very coo—argh!"

I jump back because out from behind the wall appears a set of disembodied hands. Hands clad in white gloves and nothing else. Not that they could have anything else on, as they are, um, *hands*.

Devlin slides in front of me, a frantic look on his face. He pats the air and says calmly, "Blair, I know what this looks like."

"Yeah, it looks like you murdered someone, stole their hands and enslaved them to do your bidding."

"That's not what this is. Hands, meet Blair Thornrose. Blair, this is *Hands*. Hands lives with me, and yes, he does help with my inventions."

The hands creep along the floor slowly, moving like Lefty, the Hamburger Helper mascot. Only Lefty had a face. These hands do not, which I'm thankful for. I don't think that I could take one more surprise today—first Nana, then the magic swap, and now Hands. *Hands.* Like, I just can't *even* with this day anymore.

The hands, both of them, bow over like they're greeting me. As much as I can't stand Devlin, I don't actually have a bone against the hands, or *Hands*, I suppose, so I say, "How do you do? Oh, sorry. You can't answer, unless there's a speaker in one of your fingers."

Hands shakes.

"No, no speaker, I guess. Sorry, of course not." Wow. This is just getting worse and worse. Time for me to shut up. "Well, nice to meet you, Hands."

He moves a few of his fingers, and Devlin says, "He said that it's nice to meet you as well."

My jaw drops. "You can understand it?"

Devlin nods to me. "Yes, and unlike another famous appendage, Hands is a *him*, so that you know his pronouns."

"Okay, got it."

Devlin rubs the back of his neck sheepishly. "Well, I suppose that I'll show you where you'll be sleeping."

"Yeah." The sooner I put this day behind me, the better. Maybe tomorrow I'll wake up and find that this was all a dream.

I follow Devlin through the house. The cotton scent changes into citrus and vanilla, very homey, very welcoming. And it's neat. Everything is tidy and in its place. I'd forgotten how organized Devlin is. I wonder if the women he beds appreciate a man who likes order? I doubt they're ever around long enough to think about it. I also doubt they have the brain cells to consider it.

I once overheard a date that he brought to a dance commenting on how the ballroom smelled like flowers, but she couldn't figure out why.

The *why* was that the room was filled with bouquets—they

were literally sprinkled on every table. The woman was standing right next to one, and she still couldn't figure it out.

Okay, maybe I'm being too harsh. Perhaps she was blind in one eye. Or both.

But anyway, I follow Devlin up the glossy wooden stairs to a second-floor bedroom. It's painted a light blue and looks lived in—what with books on the nightstand and a clothes hamper in a corner.

My gaze locks on Devlin's, and it hits me where he's brought me.

This is his room. No way. No how. No no no. See? This is all a ploy to get me into bed.

"I'm not staying in your room," I snap. "There's no telling what kind of stains a forensics black light would find on your sheets."

I spin on my heel and walk right on out.

I head down the hall, all the way to the end, and push open the door. What do you know, but it's another bedroom. This giant mansion is probably full of them. I bet if I started walking, I'd begin tripping over bedrooms without any problem at all.

I throw my bag on the mattress as Devlin enters, eyes narrowed, scowling. "You're not sleeping in here."

"I'm not sleeping in your love chamber. I don't even want to think what's on those sheets."

His jaw ticks. "They were just changed this morning."

"By whom?"

"Me."

I cock my head and stare at him. "You do things like change your own sheets."

He sighs. "Yes, and before you ask why I changed them, what foreign substance was on them, there wasn't anything. I haven't had anyone over in months."

"Oh, deciding your reputation has gotten the best of you?

86

Wanting to fool us all into thinking that you might pivot in your ways and instead of bedding two women at a time, you're going to bed three now?"

He slowly curls his hands into fists. "Not that it's any of your business, but there are things that are more important to me than getting laid."

I bark a laugh. "No way. Impossible."

Devlin exhales a long, low breath. "Have you ever considered that maybe I don't sleep with those women? The ones I take out?"

"Nope. Not for a moment. They look at you with too much lovey-dovey stuff in their eyes." I wave my hand around for emphasis on the *lovey-dovey*. "Even if you're not sleeping with them, they're expecting it."

He leans against the doorframe of my room. *My room.* That's right. I'm not budging. And to prove my point, I start fluffing the bed pillows, showing that I've already claimed my territory. I feel like a lioness.

Or a puppy begging for scraps. Yeah, more like the puppy. Will not let Devlin know.

"I don't sleep with them."

I bark a laugh. "Yeah, right."

"Do you really think I sleep with two women at a time?"

Is that a trick question? "Isn't that every man's fantasy?"

He crosses one ankle over the other, looking way too comfortable in my room. "Maybe. But not mine. I don't want those women. There's only ever been one woman I really wanted."

His gaze is laser focused on me. The air in the room thickens, crackles with energy, and the edges of my vision blacken as everything else slips away except for Devlin.

It's just him and me right now, and I don't particularly like his tone.

"What are you talking about?" I say in a sorry attempt to diffuse the air.

"I've just told you. There's only ever been one woman for me."

Oh gods. The way he's saying it makes me think that he means...nope. Not me. There's no way.

But good grief, why is his voice so rumbly, and the light's hitting his back just right, showing off his wide shoulders, and why is my mouth dry?

Danger! Danger, Will Robinson!

Right. Devlin dumped me. He cheated on me. If he'd loved me, he wouldn't have done that.

I click my tongue. "Well, that's nice."

It's a terrible comeback, but it's all I've got.

But Devlin does not seem deterred. My lioness prowess must not be working. Perhaps ignoring him will work. So I open the bag and start pulling out clothes.

There's really not much to put away—some panties, jeans, a couple of sweaters. But I make it look very interesting, as if it has all my attention.

And yet Devlin steps into the room, completely oblivious to how busy I clearly am. "I need you to sleep in my bedroom."

"No. Way. In. Hell."

I look up from the bag, and he's got his arms crossed, a beautiful scowl on his face. Nope, not beautiful. Dangerous. No! Dangerous suggests he's hot. It's not dangerous, either. It's just a scowl, a really small twitch of his lips and hardening of his sculpted jaw that makes him look ALL THE THINGS ALL AT ONCE ALL THE TIME.

He sighs and sits on my bed. I glare at him, and he then lays back and puts his arms behind his head.

"What are you doing?"

"I'm getting comfortable. If this is where you're going to sleep, it's where I'm sleeping, too."

I've got to get him out of here. "I fart. A lot. At night. It smells very bad. You won't want to be in here."

Now he looks amused. It makes him look even prettier. It's just sickening that from every angle he looks gorgeous. Why am I cursed with having to spend time with him?

Oh, right. *Thanks, Nana. You're in deep shit next time I see you.*

"I'll create a force field so that the smell stays on your side."

"Argh! Will you just get out of here? I'm sleeping under your roof; isn't that enough? There's no telling what I'll be subject to see, much less hear, in the next couple of days, or however long it takes for this to go away. Can't you just give me this one thing?"

"No."

I want to pull every single hair out of my head one at a time. This is already torture. Why is he making this so much worse?

"Blair—"

It's so sexy when my name rumbles from his mouth. *Stop it, Blair!*

"I wouldn't be doing this if I didn't have to."

"I doubt that."

"I wouldn't. You don't *want* to be here, and I don't want you to *have* to be here, but what I'm attempting to build is important, and to make sure that I have the vision, we have to be together twenty-four seven."

"Why?" I ask while folding a T-shirt into a piece of origami. It just keeps getting smaller and smaller.

"By us spending all our time together, that will make sure that I'm the subject of your vision."

"It's all about you, isn't it?"

"No, it's not at all me." He sighs and pinches the bridge of his nose. "Forget it. If you want our powers to be switched for the rest of our lives, go for it. But I can promise that you won't like mine very much."

Oh, the bitterness is palpable from this one. So much so that I put my T-shirt giraffe down and say, "Why not?"

He closes his eyes. "I could have saved my parents if I'd known about my power."

My heart instantly drops. In that moment I forget all about my Asian artwork and the fact that I hate Devlin. I quietly sit on the edge of the bed. "What?"

He pauses for a long moment, and I wonder if he's going to shut down the conversation. And surprisingly, I find myself not wanting him to stop talking. I want to hear this, know this. The great Devlin Ross can feel pain? Hurt? Regret? He has a human heart?

It takes a long moment before he starts talking, and when he does, I'm holding my breath. "It was the first time that my power ever came in." His eyes remain closed, and he's so still that I don't want to move and disturb him. "They were going on a trip across country. My father wasn't a wizard, so they often used human means of travel, so this wasn't strange. But what was strange was that the night before they left, I had a vision of them boarding the plane and of it exploding after takeoff. I was only five, and I didn't know what to make of it, so I didn't tell anyone. I just thought it was a dream.

"My grandmother and I took them to the airport and said goodbye. Then we went to the observation deck to watch the plane leave." He opens his eyes and lifts his arm like his hand is riding an air current. "The plane lifted into the air, and right before our eyes, it exploded, just like in my vision. I could have told them, Blair. I could have stopped it."

During the speech I obviously suffered some sort of brain damage because I'm now stretched out across the bed, facing him, feeling my heart breaking for him. I know, I know. The brain damage is worse than originally thought.

I lick my lips. "I didn't know that."

"That's because I've never told anyone. Well, Hands knows."

"But it's not like Hands is going to spill the tea."

He turns his head to me. Our gazes latch and we each laugh. Why am I laughing with him?

I don't know, but it feels good.

When the laughter dies down, we glance at one another again, and the air between us has changed. It's no longer crackling with anger. It's simmering with something else.

He speaks first, quietly, as if talking too loud will shatter whatever this is between us. "I was going to tell you when we were in high school, but the time was never right."

"It's okay," I murmur. "I understand why you didn't."

He just nods, still keeping those hazel eyes on me. I don't think there's any air in my lungs anymore, but strangely they keep right on working.

"I wanted to," he confesses. "But then…the time just wasn't right, and I blamed myself for what happened to them."

Without thinking, I grab his hand and squeeze. His fingers are warm, and they squeeze back.

And now I'm stuck holding his hand. How am I going to get out of this?

Best to pivot. "You were only a child when it happened, and it was the first time that your power ever showed itself. You didn't know what was going on."

"No, I didn't."

He's still holding on to my hand.

His fingers send pulses of heat wrapping around my forearm and tightening on my elbow. I can barely think. We're facing each other. We're touching. We're talking about something intimate.

And then he shifts toward me, still holding my hand. And I shift toward him. Involuntarily, obviously, because the bed dipped when he moved.

And we're still touching.

"I gave myself a lot of grief for that. A lot of blame."

"But you were just a child."

He nods. "I know that now, but I didn't then."

It hits me why he's telling me this. "And the vision that you want me to see, it's important?"

His eyes brighten. They're already bright, like gold and emerald stars, but now they're shining. "This is the most important thing I've ever made, and as long as I can keep it under wraps and no one gets wind of it, it will change the world."

"More than the pocket cauldron?"

He smiles. "More than that. A lot more."

We're both quiet for a moment until I say, "That's why you need me."

"That's why I need you," he murmurs.

Our glances catch again, and he's studying me openly, his smug smirk gone, and emotion flits through his eyes. Too much emotion.

It's the kind of emotion that happens before two people kiss, before they start telling each other that they've always loved one another and that they never stopped pining for each other and oh, why did they ever break up in the first place?

My heart, which had been soaring, crash lands back on planet Earth.

Devlin cheated on me, and then his rumor ruined me. It also ruined me for love. I don't want love. I don't need love. I just need someone to marry—and it's not Devlin Ross.

Keep telling yourself that, Blair. Stay strong.

I clear my throat and pull my hand away. "And you think that by me sleeping in a different bedroom, we won't be in each other's orbit well enough."

"I think the vision will come faster if we're in the same room, yes."

Why am I doing this, again? I exhale a resigned sigh. "Fine. You can sleep in here. On the floor."

He smirks. "My bed is bigger."

"On. The. Floor."

"You drive a hard bargain," he jokes. Then he jumps up. "I'll be right back."

As soon as he's gone, I pull off my dress, jump into jammies, brush my teeth and get under the covers.

A couple of minutes later Devlin knocks.

"Come in."

He enters in low-slung cotton jammy pants, the lined muscles of his hips openly being flaunted and so sexy that I look away. "I'm making a palette," he tells me.

"Have fun."

He makes said palette at the foot of the bed and sighs before he slinks under the covers. I assume that's what he's doing. I don't look. Not interested.

After he settles in, I expect him to say good night, but instead he says, "Tell me about the first time you got your power."

I turn onto my side and slide a hand under the pillow. "Oh, are we sharing tonight?"

"*I* told *you.*"

"So it's only fair?"

"I like to live life fairly and dangerously."

We laugh, and when it stops, I say, "Since it's only fair."

"I wouldn't expect anything less," he remarks flirtatiously, which I ignore.

I clear my throat because all good stories begin with a solid throat clearing. "It all began a long time ago in a galaxy far, far away."

From the foot of the bed, a pillow is launched at me and hits my hip. "I'm being serious."

I toss it back to him. "Fine. Okay." I sigh. "The first time my power came in, I was a teenager. I was thirteen with acne, braces and glasses."

"You wear glasses?"

"Used to. Magic fixed that problem. But I still had to go through braces and zits."

"I'm sure you were beautiful just the same."

Being called beautiful makes my heart jump, even if it does come from my nemesis. "Anyway, Chatty Cathy was a terror even when we were thirteen. For some reason that year she decided that I would be the target for her evil. So every chance she got, she taunted me, telling me that I'd wake up with braces growing into my gums, or that I'd have a zit on my face so big that when I popped it, my face would explode."

"Jesus."

"Yep, you know, just the usual kid bullying. But when magic's involved, bullying takes on a whole new meaning."

Over the years I've tried not to think about how awful Cathy was back then, and for the most part it's been easy to put out of my mind.

"Until one day," Devlin says in his velvet voice, "you had enough."

I bark a laugh because it's true. "One day I did have enough. The words she said to me were so filthy that I thought she should put something filthy back into her mouth to make it even. We were outside the school. I was walking home, and she was just going on and on about how stupid I was, all of it. I saw a pile of dirt and just thought how much I wanted her to eat it. Next thing I knew, something took over my body, a force that I'd never experienced, and she had stopped talking. I looked at her, and Cathy was kneeling on the ground, digging into the earth. She shoveled a handful into her mouth like it was nothing. Some kids were horrified. Some laughed at her. *I* was scared because I felt that desire inside of me. It terrified me so much that the spell broke and my power fell away. Cathy was humiliated and ran home, crying.

"She later realized that she'd been influenced by magic and put two and two together, that it had been me who made her eat dirt. After that, she eased up for a while, but she's never truly left me alone. Even still, I made a promise to myself never to use my power to harm ever again."

Slow clapping comes from the foot of the bed. Devlin laughs. "Bravo, Blair! There are only a few people I can think of who are more deserving."

"Like whom?"

"Nobody in particular," he says pensively.

I sit up. "Nope. No way. You can't just say something like that and not tell me."

I peer over the bed to see him lying on his back, his hands tucked under his head. His gaze darts up to me and he smiles. "There are some things that should be left to mystery."

I drop a pillow on him. He catches it with one hand and tosses it back onto the bed. "If you want a pillow fight, I'll give you a pillow fight."

My body lights up from the inside. Pillow fights lead to arms and legs getting tangled. Tangled limbs lead to kissing. Kissing leads to other things.

"Nope, that's okay," I chirp.

I fall back down on the bed and for a moment feel guilt that I'm making Devlin sleep on the floor. Not that much guilt, but a bit.

"Blair?" he says, sounding tired.

"Yes?"

"I'm glad you made Cathy eat dirt."

I laugh. "I'm glad that you shared your story with me, too."

"You're welcome." He sighs. "Good night."

I flip off the lamp. "Good night."

I thought that I wouldn't sleep a wink with him in the

room, but when I wake up the next morning, I've slept like a baby.

The water's on in the bathroom, which means Devlin must've gotten up and decided to use *my bathroom*. Pretty sure we need some ground rules here about who gets to use whose toilet.

The water turns off; the door opens. I open my mouth to say good morning, but then Devlin walks out, completely naked, his pecs popping, his abs looking like a stone wall, his cock looking all...glorious.

I clamp my eyes shut and yell, "What are you doing? Why are you naked?"

There is literally not one smidgen of regret in his voice as he replies, "I always sleep naked."

"Why are you sleeping naked now? While I'm here?"

"It helps me solve problems when I sleep."

"What kind of problems—never mind. I don't want to know. Can you...just put on clothes?"

"I don't know...*can I?*" he says, making a completely inappropriate grammar joke.

"I'm going to kill you. This is not the time for an English lesson. Just do it!"

"As you wish." A moment later he says, "There, you can look."

"Do you promise?"

"I promise," he murmurs.

I open my eyes, and he's standing in his pants. He rubs his hands together and winks. "Hurry up and get ready. Hands will have breakfast for us, and after that, you've got some wooing to do."

11

DEVLIN

I've lost my mind. That must be it. There's no other reason why I would've asked Blair to essentially live with me.

Oh gods, the way she smells. Like honey and rain. It's all over me. I don't know how she managed to make her room smell like her in one night or how that scent jumped from her to me, but it did.

I don't want to wash it off. But I must.

Hands didn't have breakfast ready, can't tell you how disappointed I am at that. I really wanted to see Blair with her hair all messy à la Julia Roberts eating a crepe (or was it a pancake?) in *Pretty Woman*. But since my messy hair fantasies went up in smoke thanks to a set of hands that I should look into replacing, I came to my room to clean up and think a lot about Blair—about how pouty and sensuous her lips are. They puffed out when I told her that she needed to stay with me, and I just wanted to nibble them before I slowly made my way down her neck to her breasts and then between her legs.

I'm giving myself a boner. Best to stop thinking about her, but that's impossible.

How am I supposed to endure the days or weeks it takes for her to have the vision?

I'll just have to close my eyes when I talk to her, I guess. Or better yet, I'll wear nose plugs.

The more I remember that this is a business transaction and nothing more, the better off I'll be. Blair wants to marry Storm Grayson and she *deserves* to marry someone else, someone who can take care of her, 'cause gods know that I can't.

I regrettably take a shower. The whole time my mind wanders to what it would feel like to trace my finger over her collarbone, what she would taste like if I nibbled her flesh in that spot and how wonderful it would be to hear her gasp my name.

I am lost.

I'm so lost. Somehow, someway I've got to get my head screwed on straight.

A knock comes from the door. "Come in."

The door creaks open and Hands waddles in. He shuts the door and stops, both hands facing me.

"What?"

He signs, *What are you doing?*

"Waiting for you to have breakfast fixed. Is there a reason why it's late?"

I couldn't sleep last night.

I bark a laugh at that. "You don't sleep."

Besides the point. Again—what are you doing?

I sigh. "I hope this isn't about Blair."

This is definitely about her.

I slip on a crisp white shirt and roll up the sleeves. "What I'm doing is making sure that I get the vision to help me solve the problem that you haven't been able to help me fix."

Hands drums one set of fingers on the floor impatiently. *And how's that?*

"Our powers got switched. Her grandmother, who's come back as a ghost—don't tell anyone." Not that Hands would. His social circle consists of me, me and me. "Her grandmother switched our powers. Blair's got mine and I've got hers."

You're not going to use it to bed the whole town, are you?

"What is it with everyone thinking I'm a man whore?" I snap. "Yes, I've dated several women, and yes, I've often taken two to a party on more than one occasion. But I haven't slept with anyone since…"

Since before the winter solstice. Since I last danced with Blair at the ball held by Feylin, the king of the fae. I'd asked her to dance with me plenty of times before then, but that was the first time that she had said yes in years.

And it ruined me for everyone else.

Gods, that was a year ago. I must really have it bad.

"I haven't slept with anyone in a long time," I correct as I button up my shirt.

Hands pauses for a long moment. Oh no, here it comes. I brace myself, because when Hands decides to get real, he doesn't mince words.

Are you going to tell her the truth?

"I wasn't planning on it."

But now she has your power. Surely you can see the problem.

"No, I can't."

Hands does a series of acrobatic jumps, catapulting himself on top of the dresser so that we're eye to…um…hand.

But now she has your gift.

"I know." Where is this going?

She might see what you saw.

Oh, that's where this is headed. "I doubt it."

I don't. She'll see exactly what you saw, and she'll put two and two together.

My rib cage becomes a steel trap, grabbing my heart in its

tines and closing down hard. "She won't have the same vision. Blair won't have my power long enough for that to happen."

But don't you think that you should just tell her about—

"No, I don't," I snap. My house is big, but it's not so big that Blair won't hear our conversation, so I drop my voice. I place my palm on top of the dresser beside Hands. "Yes, Blair and I dated a long time ago. I'm not with her now, and I'll *never* be with her again. Do you understand?"

But it could be that the vision will still happen.

"It won't," I growl.

I've worked too hard to make sure that it doesn't come true. I forced myself to give up the one person that I wanted, all to keep her safe. It's nearly killed me these years, and it's damn well likely to kill me now as I help give her to the one man I hate. But she's better off with him than she is with me.

Is she?

Yes, she is. Storm might be a lot of things, but he won't hurt her.

Even if all I want to do is bury my nose in her hair, run my fingers down her legs and fill her up with my—

A smart knock comes from the door. Better put my hard-on away before Blair sees.

"Come in."

Blair pushes open the door. She's got her witch face back on. I guess our little heart-to-heart last night hasn't changed her feelings about me.

She runs a hand down her thigh, showing off tight jeans that hug those luscious hips. The jeans pair well with a fitted sweater that makes my mouth water. I can just imagine peeling her clothes off her, one piece at a time. It takes all my self-control not to wolf whistle at her.

I smile. "Looks like you beat me. I'm almost ready."

Her gaze zeroes in on my chest. I haven't closed all the buttons of my shirt yet, and she licks her lips. The hunger in her eyes matches the hunger that I feel. But before she gives herself a moment to let it sink in, she blinks and quickly snaps her head in the opposite direction, focusing on Hands.

Her witch look is back. "Good morning," she tells him.

Hands bows.

"I got a message from my aunt," she tells me.

"Oh?"

"We're meeting in the gardens behind the house for a game of spell ball."

"Spell ball? This should be fun."

"Yep," she says sharply. "You ready?"

She's still looking at Hands, who jumps down, clearly ready to go.

"Not you, big guy," I tell him. Hands's fingers sag. "Next time you can come. Don't worry, we won't be gone long. Just long enough to get Blair married to her dream man." I close the last button. "Now I'm ready. Would you like to head over? We can grab some toast on our way out the door."

"Yep," she replies quickly, still not looking at me.

"Then let's go."

12

*W*hat do I care if Devlin doesn't want to be with me? I don't, because I don't want to be with him either. He destroyed me in high school. Yes, I know that I'm beating a dead horse, but sometimes I just want to keep beating it until it's dust.

So why is it bothering me so much what I overheard him say to Hands? That he'll never be with me again? And why does my chest ache now?

It doesn't matter. I hate him, too. We're only doing this whole stupid me-living-with-him thing so that I can be with Storm. That's it. End of story.

The ride over to my house (yes, Devlin wanted to drive, so I insisted we park a good block away so that no one would see us get out of a car together), I'm silent. So silent.

He's not talking, either, which is no surprise since he doesn't want to be with me.

I've got to stop thinking about this.

Fine. I will. It will be easy.

It's just that last night, when he opened up about his parents, I felt a connection with him. Yes, it was unwanted, but it was still there, and I thought that maybe, maybe Devlin isn't who I've been thinking he is.

Well that went up in smoke this morning. First thing.

Thank the gods it did, because I need to be focused on Storm Grayson. Beautiful Storm Grayson, the man of my dreams.

The garden is brimming with people when we arrive. Someone has spelled the area to block out the cold and make it feel like a late spring day. I peel off the coat I'm wearing and toss it onto a bench.

After that I spot Chatty Cathy and her hoard of minions, so I steer clear and go find my sisters.

Chelsea and Dallas are lugging out a set of mallets and hoops.

Chelsea sees me and smiles. "Be glad that you're not at the house. Nana was trying her fiercest to watch the game."

"But Ovie and Mama both said no," Dallas says with a sigh. "However, I fully expect Nana to escape and wind up hanging out in a magnolia tree."

I glance up, suddenly worried that my grandmother will swoop down and startle the guests, revealing herself, and then everyone will know that she's haunting us.

I can see it in the Castleview Gazette now—FAMILY MATRON RETURNS TO SAVE GRANDDAUGHTER FROM SPINSTERHOOD. ALSO AT RISK—FAMILY'S FAILING MAGIC.

No one will care about the magic. All they'll see is a spirit haunting us to death.

Chelsea drops the spell ball set onto the grass and brushes off her hands. "Yep. Keep an eye out. You never know what that dead lady's bound to do. But now that you're here"—her eyes sparkle in a way that I don't like—"what's going on with Devlin?"

"Oh, um, nothing."

Dallas smirks. "Doesn't look like nothing. He's staring at you."

I whip around, but Devlin's turned away. Good. He doesn't need to look at anything that he doesn't want.

"Nothing is going on," I say sternly to end the conversation. "He needs help with something, and I'm helping him. That's pretty much it. Oh, and he has my power, too, so I'm ultimately keeping the women of our town safe by making sure that he doesn't influence them into his bed."

"There are worse things than winding up in Devlin Ross's bed," Dallas says.

Chelsea laughs.

My face burns hot. "No, there aren't. He's an awful, terrible person. Trust me, I'm saving lives here. And a lot of them. Lives of women who will be thanking me subconsciously even if they don't know consciously what I'm doing for them."

Chelsea and Dallas exchange a look.

"What?"

"Keep telling yourself that." Chelsea pats my shoulder as she breezes past me. "Come on. Storm Grayson just rolled up. Ovie's going to be pairing us together soon."

My sisters walk away, leaving me fuming, and that's when I take a good long look at the spell ball set.

Oh crap. This isn't normal spell ball, which is similar to croquet. This is *magical* spell ball, and I'm terrible at it.

"Something wrong?" Devlin's beside me.

When did he slither up?

"No. Yes. I'm awful at magical spell ball."

"Here. Let me give you a quick lesson."

I start arguing that no thank you, I don't need his help, but he's already gently pushing a hoop into the earth and grabbing a mallet and ball.

"No, really, that's okay."

"Just trust me. All right. Show me how you hold the mallet."

He puts it into my hands and I show him.

"Now hit the ball."

As soon as I start to aim, the hoop jumps up and wiggles. This is what I hate about this version of the game. The hoop won't sit still. It's all cartoonish and leaps out of the way before your ball can go through it.

I always come in last place when I play against my family. Even Addison, who used to not have any magic to speak of, can beat me.

I hit the ball, and of course it misses the hoop, landing in the bushes.

"I see your problem."

Before I can tell Devlin that he's my only problem, he places his hand atop mine and presses his chest into my back.

Oh. My. God.

I think I might faint.

He smells like the ocean, like waves beating against the sand. He moves the hair off my neck, and of course while doing so his fingers brush against my flesh, sending a shiver cartwheeling down my spine.

His voice is low, husky. It sounds like sex. "When you aim, you have to anticipate where the hoop will move. It gives you a hint in how it dances. See? It's wanting to go left."

And I see it. The hoop doth dance too much, methinks. It wiggles and wobbles, looking very much like a croquet hoop that ended up in cartoon land.

Devlin, for some reason, is still behind me. His chest is still pressed to my back, and his mouth is dangerously close to my ear. Not exactly sure why that's dangerous, but it *feels* dangerous. Risqué. Like his mouth could slowly make a play for my ear and begin nibbling it.

In public.

"Lightly tap the ball, and it'll go in," he murmurs so close to my skin that the hairs on the back of my neck soldier to attention.

His hand is still on mine, and heat sears my flesh. It feels like he's branding me, like we've suddenly become conjoined twins and there's no way to separate us.

I tip my face toward his, and his mouth is right there. Beside me. Next to mine.

I whisper, "Like this?"

Before he can answer, I hit the mallet against the ball, aiming just slightly left of the hoop. The ball flies across the lawn and plows through the hoop just as it wiggles left.

"Very nice," Devlin says, still holding my arm, still with his back against mine, still cradling me in public.

"Storm," someone shouts.

The announcement takes me by surprise, and I jump, elbowing Devlin in the gut in the process.

He grunts and rocks back. I turn to apologize, but he's already straightened and is smoothing a hand over his hair.

Good. I need space. I don't need his mouth by my ear or his hand touching my arm or his chest pressing against my back.

He doesn't want me, remember?

I need Storm Grayson beside me, falling in love with my charming face and personality.

Devlin slips his hands into his pockets. "When you get paired up with Storm, just act natural. Smile. Be nice. I know it's hard for you, at least with me, but do your best."

I smirk. "How do you know I'm being paired with him?"

"Because I've already spoken to your aunt and made sure."

"My aunt? Where is she?"

Then I see her. Ovie's standing near the entrance of the garden, which is just like one of those fancy French ones with little pebbles on the footpaths and landscaped in tall hedges.

Ovie's wearing a sun visor and, for some reason, a tennis outfit complete with pleated skirt. She's also got a whistle around her neck. Someone's taking their job as events coordinator a bit too seriously.

She blows the whistle. Yes, blows, and from the back, Chatty Cathy snickers.

I want to punch her in the face.

"Welcome, y'all. Thank you for coming to our little event of magical spell ball. We're so glad that you could join us. There will be refreshments at the end, and I don't expect the game to take too long, but you know how games can go. Sometimes they take a little while."

She chuckles and no one joins.

That's when I see Nana's face peering out of the bushes a little ways off.

My stomach plummets to the ground.

Nana! Why can't you stay away?

I've got to cover her before anyone else sees.

Somehow I manage not to barrel roll myself over to the hedgerow. Instead I do a very quick walk that makes me look like I've either got ants in my pants or that I have to pee a river.

Trust me, it looks bad.

I reach Nana and she spots me, immediately breaking into a smile as if it's no big deal that she's a severed head sticking out of a bush.

I stop in front of her and block her view.

"What are you doing?" she whines. *Whines!* "I can't see anymore."

This is the part where I talk out of the side of my mouth like an amateur ventriloquist who really, really wants to be great at this but is really, really failing miserably.

"You don't need to see. You need to stay hidden because no one can find out about you." I think it comes out like that, but it might be a bit more like, *Zhou mede shtay hid, brrcuss no one cun fffind oout abooot zhou.*

She sniffs. The audacity! "I just wanted to see how things are going with you."

How things are going? I'm stuck living with my worst enemy, that's how things are going. But "Fine," is all I say. "Now get home. I'll talk to you later."

She sighs dramatically, as if it's all my fault that she can't stay and pretend to be alive. "All right. I'll leave, but keep me posted about Devlin. I mean, Storm."

I turn around and catch her fiendish smile before she sinks back into the hedges and disappears, hopefully forever, but no one can be certain. Least of all me.

This whole time Ovie's been talking, but I've drowned her out, so focused am I on keeping Nana's appearance a secret. Contrary to most Southern families, we don't showcase our crazy by putting them on the front porch with a fiddle and a spittoon. No, we hide our crazy away in the dark corners of our home.

Just like it should be.

"Ready, partner?"

His voice takes me by surprise. I glance up and do a double take. While I was deep in thoughts of *crazy*, Storm Grayson found his way over and is now standing beside me looking beautiful with his chiseled face and gray eyes. And that silvery-white hair! Is it natural? I love it!

"Good morning," I say brightly, remembering Devlin's suggestion to smile, which comes easy for me. He's the only person I don't smile at, and that's because I hate him with all the passion that is within me.

"You look lovely," he says, his gaze quickly flitting over my body, not at all in a suggestive way. He's not drinking me in like a jungle cat about to eat a meal. No, he's looking at me in a respectful manner as befits a billionaire.

"Thank you."

I'm about to tell him that he looks nice as well, but that's when Ovie blows her whistle like a frustrated junior high gym teacher who dreamed of coaching high school football but somehow got stuck with this gig.

"Y'all ready?" my aunt shouts. "Line up and good luck!"

I sneak a glance at Storm and think that I need all the luck that I can get.

athy shoots me a dirty look as she gets paired off with a werewolf who's shorter than she is. I make a point to wink at her as she walks by to grab a mallet and ball.

"Did you stay in Castleview last night?" I ask Storm as he picks a blue striped mallet.

I've still got the mallet in my hand from when Devlin helped me. I just need to retrieve my ball.

"I've rented a house, so yes, I'm staying here," Storm tells me.

"Rented a home?"

He shrugs. "I don't know how long I'll be staying." He gives me a look that practically has hearts in his eyes. "And I still have a company to run, so I thought a house would be best."

"Are you inventing while you're here?"

He smiles shyly, revealing a dimple in his left cheek. It's adorable. *So* adorable. "I'm always inventing because inspiration comes at the strangest times. I'm afraid it's been very hard on my previous relationships."

"I'm sorry to hear that."

"Don't be." He gives me a thousand-watt smile. "It's what

led me here." He scans the rack of mallets and frowns. "Where's your ball?"

"Oh. I left it on the grass. I was practicing earlier."

He grins. "Trying to get a head start?"

"No, trying to be good at magical spell ball. I'm not all that great."

He leans over conspiratorially. "Good thing you're with me, then. I'm a champion at this game. But then again, I'm great at everything I do."

Such confidence! It's a turn-on. My panties are practically soaked even though they aren't. "I'm glad we're paired together, then."

"Let me get your ball." He opens his hand, and the ball lifts from the ground and flies into his open palm. He hands it to me. "There you go. Now. Let's line up. I'm ready to win."

Okay, so Storm Grayson has magic, so he's definitely got wizard blood and a lot of it. I'll have to tell Chelsea, because I know she's dying to know what he is.

As I follow him across the lawn, I find myself absently scanning the garden. Not for anyone in particular. Nope. But when my gaze happens to land on Devlin, my eyes stop moving.

He's been matched up with a little redhead who's cute as a button. I don't know her, but I recognize her from last night's ball. She's smiling up at Devlin like he holds the whole damn world in his hands, and he's smiling at her, too.

Smiling.

What a pig. He's "helping me" with my game one minute and then hitting on some cute little redhead the next.

Whatever. It's not my problem. I don't care.

"Are you ready," Storm asks, sidling up, "to wipe the floor with the competition?"

I drag my gaze from Devlin and grit my teeth. "I sure am."

Storm was not exaggerating when he said that he's great at spell ball. He's amazing, actually. It only takes a few swings and we're in the lead. Like, by miles.

Cathy keeps shooting flaming arrows of death from her eyes at me, that's how I know that I'm winning at more than just the game.

And Storm is nice, too. He really is. You wouldn't think that a billionaire would be nice given that most of them seem to want to run our planet the way that they see fit. But he's not like that.

He comes across as a big nerd who just loves inventing things.

"And what about you?" he asks, genuinely interested in me and my likes. "Have you ever been interested in creating?"

"Yes. When I was in high school, I was really good at potions."

"Potions?" he snorts.

"Yes. There's so much that you can do with them. Potions can become spells that change the world. You can shift entire industries with the right potion. Beauty, for example. You could create a potion to replace glamours. You can create potions that attack certain diseases. People think of potions as something small, a charm. But they can be so much more."

Storm blinks. I must have impressed him. "I've never thought about it like that. When I created the instant warmer, it was a marriage of mechanics and spells, almost like a potion."

"The instant warmer," I murmur. "That's the one where if you're naked during the winter solstice, you immediately get hot, right?

"That's the one."

I frown. "Didn't Devlin create one of those, too?"

Storm stiffens. "He did, but *after* me. In fact..." He leans into my ear. His breath is soft, and it smells like peppermint. Perfect. "I hate to say this because Devlin is a great inventor, but just between us, I do believe that he stole not only the concept, but some of the mechanics from me."

My jaw drops. Devlin might be a lot of things, but he's not a thief. "What makes you say that?"

He straightens and shrugs, glancing at the other players in a bored stare. "It just seemed very coincidental that he would come up with the same idea at the same time as I did, is all." He smooths a hand over his hair as if he's also trying to smooth the words over my skin, so that the blow won't hurt when it lands. "I don't have proof, of course, but I got the patent first, if that tells you anything. Oh look, we're up. I'll go put us in a good position. If we play this right, we'll win the game."

He squeezes my hand, and the moment of affection takes me by surprise. I jolt, and my gaze darts from where his hand is on mine up to his eyes. Storm's smiling at me gently, and I can't help but give him a smile in return, albeit an uneasy one.

Then he strides off with those long, tree-trunk legs of his, leaving me to think about what he said. Devlin, a cheat? Not the old Devlin that I knew.

But let's be real, yesterday and today are the most time that I've spent with the man in years. *Years,* and honestly, there's no telling what someone will do to rise to the top of their field, scheming and cheating included. Being an inventor is a hard way to make it in life. There's tons of competition.

But it still seems strange that Devlin would steal someone else's idea and claim it for his own. My gaze tracks to where he stands, off to the side, still chatting up the redhead. She's looking at him as if he's a mountain and the sun just crested over his peak.

Yeah, I'm aware that's a terrible metaphor, but I'm still going to roll with it.

As they share a laugh, I can't help but feel a punch in the gut. Last night he opened up to me, and I felt something for him that I hadn't felt in years. My anger and resentment were replaced with compassion. And he seemed to feel it, too. I could have sworn that he did, that he felt just like me, that we'd shared a moment when he confessed things to me that he'd never explained in high school.

I felt sorrow for him, and I just wanted to hug him tight, give him a teddy bear and tell him that everything would be okay.

It seemed like such a real connection, like we were on the verge of kissing, even, or of at least moving forward an inch.

But now here he is, flirting it up with a redhead that he just met. Yeah, I know that I'm not one to talk, as I've been paired with Storm and have every intention of nabbing him. I do see the irony here, trust me. But that doesn't stop me from feeling just a teensy bit jealous, as if what Devlin said last night was only for show.

But isn't he all about show? He's flash and pizzazz, putting on a face for the world that's so different from what he was like last night. He gave me a glimpse of who he really is, and then this morning he snatched it away by walking around naked.

I don't even want to think about his body, but now I can't help but recall the taut abdomen and those sculpted shoulders.

And then there was his...nope. Not going there. I'm not going to even let my mind trail down past his belly button.

Oh, I just did.

Well, let me just say that all looked good down there. Very good. Exceptionally good.

Is it hot out here? I could use some lemonade.

My gaze shifts to Devlin again, and he's pointing something out to the redhead. From the looks of it, he appears to be explaining spell ball.

It's not at all how he explained it to me. Oh my gods, how his breath danced over my skin, and how he tucked my hair over my shoulder. My entire body felt that jolt.

His touch was fire. He woke up my body, made me feel alive, not only with his words but with his touch.

I've dated only a few guys over the years. As I've mentioned ad nauseum, once they figure out that I can bend them to my will like an evil sorceress, they tend to bolt, wondering how much I'd already influenced their behavior.

Answer: none.

But anyway, of course before they figured out my evil ways, we'd kissed. Lots. And done other things. My body always responded, but it wasn't like it is with Devlin.

Man, I hate to say that.

But it's true. There's something about the way his flesh feels on mine that's just sinfully...right.

Wrong. I'm supposed to say wrong. And I'm supposed to put all thoughts of him away and focus on my new Juke Box Hero, Storm Grayson, inventor extraordinaire.

"I think we're going to win, Blair!" It's Storm. He's smiling and about to hit the ball through the hoop, which he does. "You're up!" My turn. I grab my mallet and he gives me a thumbs-up. "We can put this one in the bag."

As I take position, I feel the eyes of not only my family but everyone else on me. They've been watching me with Storm, and the fact that he's being so familiar and comfortable with me earns an approving look from tennis pro Ovie. It also earns a scowl from Cathy and the minion club.

But what it does not earn is any attention from Devlin. He's still talking with the redhead, deep in conversation, I'd like to add.

What's the deal? He's supposed to be helping me, not

flirting with his next fling. How could he touch me so scandalously an hour ago (let's face it, his touch was one degree away from making me feel filthy) and then just ignore me?

It's maddening, is what it is. Just purely insanely maddening.

As I stand facing the ball and looking at the jiggling and jangling hoop that's wiggling and bouncing in what most people would probably consider koala-bear cute, all I want to do is yank that sucker out of the ground and stomp on it.

Deep breath, Blair. You've got this. You're heading in the direction that you want to go. Storm is interested in you. You are interested in him. Focus on that.

I pull the mallet back to hit the ball as a peel of laughter rings out from Devlin's side of the garden.

My head snaps in his direction, and the redhead has her chin up, and she's laughing. He's laughing, too.

And then his eyes go black.

Holy shit.

He's just used my power on her.

Hot rage shatters me, and I swing the mallet in fury. The crack of the ball is loud, like a shotgun exploding.

The next crack is not so deafening. It's bone crunching. But the scream that follows it is earsplitting.

My blood stops and I whip my head in the direction of the sound. I immediately spot my ball. It's on the ground, rolling aimlessly through the thick grass, away from Storm's feet.

My gaze tracks up to his face. Storm's cupping his nose with both hands. Blood's spewing through his fingers, and he's screaming, "My nose!"

The mallet falls from my hands, and all I can do is stare as the crowd rushes to help Storm, the man whose nose I just broke.

14

"*I* told you to be yourself, not break his nose," Devlin says, raking his fingers through his hair.

He's pacing back and forth in his living room. After I successfully cracked Storm's nose in two, the garden party disbanded. I tried to apologize, but Storm's bodyguards surrounded him and escorted him off while he howled in pain.

Pretty sure that for the rest of my life I'll be haunted with cries of, "My nose! It's broken! Why me?"

I added in the *why me*. He didn't really say that, but he might as well have.

I toss my purse onto Devlin's couch. "For your information, I wasn't trying to break his nose. I couldn't concentrate because *somebody* was using my power on a certain redhead."

He freezes. "What?"

I shoot him a look that says, *Yep.*

"Me?" He points both hands to his chest. "You're blaming this on me?"

Who else would I blame it on? "Yes, I'm blaming this on you. You were using my power on that woman. What were you doing to her?"

117

"This is unbelievable." He plows his fingers through his thick locks. "I try to help you get the man of your dreams, and you're blaming me for hitting him in the face with a spell ball."

"Yes, I am! If you hadn't been abusing my power with that hot little number, none of this would have happened. What did you influence her to do? Come over later and take off her panties?"

His jaw falls. He shoots me a blistering glare before dragging his gaze away. "For your information, I was not influencing Molly to do anything with me."

"Oh, Molly's her name, is it? A nice wholesome name, just ripe for the ravaging."

He drops his hands to his hips and taps his belt, obviously annoyed, and obviously trying to rein in his anger. "Why do you care?"

"Because you used my power," I explode.

"Okay, let's just calm down." He points to the couch. "Why don't you sit?"

"Because I don't feel like it."

"Of course not," he mumbles. He gazes around the room, shaking his head before saying, "First of all, I've known Molly for years. I dated her older sister. It was a long time ago," he adds quickly. "No time recently. And Molly was feeling insecure about a guy she likes."

"Oh?" He points to the couch again, and this time I sit. "That seems very coincidental."

"To whom? You?"

I scoff. "Yes, to me."

Devlin sits beside me and leans back on the couch. "She likes one of the men who was there, and needed a little courage to talk to him. So that's what I gave her—courage. You know, like I was telling you last night, a thing you can do with your power to make people feel good about themselves?"

He shoots me a scathing look, and I drop my gaze to my

fingers, which are currently fidgeting in my lap. Devlin continues with his tongue-lashing. "You jumped to conclusions about me—about what I was doing. Gods, Blair, how horrible do you think I am?"

"Do you really want that answer?"

"No. Never mind." He shakes his head and sighs. "Look, I would never use your power to do anything bad. I was only trying to help Molly. You can ask her yourself next time you see her."

"No thanks."

"So you don't believe me?"

Do I? Why would Devlin lie? I'm here, in his house. He wouldn't have someone over while I'm forced to stay here. Would he? No. We're sleeping in the same room, for goodness' sake.

So maybe he was telling the truth. "I'm sorry," I whisper.

He cups a hand to his ear. "What was that? I couldn't hear you."

I exhale a loud breath and roll my eyes. "I said that I'm sorry. I believe you."

He studies me for a moment too long and I look away. "Well? Don't you want to know if it worked?"

"If what worked?"

"Molly and the courage."

"I guess."

He grins. "It worked. She texted me a little while ago and said that they're going on a date."

Yay, them. Meanwhile I've probably destroyed my chances with Storm. I can't stand thinking about it. I need something to do. "Where are your rags?"

"Under the sink."

I leave him in the living room but hear him following me as I enter the kitchen, find the rags, get one hot and soapy and then start wiping down surfaces.

Cleaning calms me.

And I need some calming. I'll be lucky if Storm shows up to the next ball. Which is tonight.

Devlin talks while I wipe down his counter. "Besides, what do you care if I talk to Molly?"

"I don't," I snap.

"Doesn't sound like you don't."

I slap the rag against a table. "Just so we're clear, I don't care who you flirt with."

He growls and covers his eyes. "We just went through this. I wasn't flirting."

"Right. You were helping her find the man of her dreams. Just like you're helping me."

"Why does it bother you so much?"

"It doesn't," I snap, pausing to glare at him. "You were just very, very loud the whole time you were with her, and you laughed right when I was about to swing. That's what made me look up and see your eyes, that you were using the power."

"Not for anything bad."

"Yeah, I get it."

"You could do the same."

"No thanks."

He shakes his head as I move on to the appliances. I'm not one of those people who can't stand cleaning and who'll let dishes pile up in a sink. No, ma'am. My life must be in tidy order.

It's really too bad that Devlin also likes order, because there's literally nothing for me to organize in his house.

"If you want, I can toss some magazines on the floor," he jokes as if reading my mind.

I hate how well he knows me. Too well. It's like no time has passed since high school.

I shoot him a look full of flaming daggers. "This will do."

He sighs and sits in a bar chair that's pulled up to the

marble island. "The situation with Storm may still be salvageable."

"I doubt it. I broke his nose, Devlin. His *nose*. He's probably telling his security detail right now that if I ever get anywhere near him, I'm to be shot on sight."

Devlin makes a face that says, *Probably so.*

"See? Even you think it."

"However," he says calmly (how can he be calm when my life is imploding?), "there may still be a way to fix it."

"How's that?"

He rises. "Leave it to me."

"Last time I left something to you, I ended up becoming your kitchen wench."

He smirks. It's almost a smile, if the glimmer of mischief in his eyes is any indication. "And who do you have to blame for that? I didn't ask you to clean."

"It helps me feel better," I practically whimper like a sulking six-year-old who was just told that they have to put their Blow Pop away because the gum will wind up in someone's hair, either accidentally or accidentally-on-purpose.

"Give me five minutes and I'll smooth things over."

I narrow my eyes in skepticism. "What are you going to do?"

"Work magic."

He winks, which makes him look even more brutally handsome, and then he disappears from the room. I listen as he goes upstairs.

So of course I follow him.

I tiptoe down the hall, where I hear him talking from inside his bedroom. It sounds like he's on the phone.

He's left a teeny-tiny crack in his door, so I press my ear to the slit while pretending to clean the glass knob. See? I'm not eavesdropping, I'm *cleaning*.

"I'm sorry to hear that, man. But you're better now?" Pause.

Longer pause. "Tell you what—I've got something that you might be interested in learning about, a way to slow aging. Yes, it's real. No, it's not a glamour. All you have to do is show up tonight. She's very sorry about what happened."

Another pause where Storm (I assume that's who he's talking to) explains that he never wants to see me again and that I've ruined things between us for all eternity. Just imagining the conversation makes my heart shrivel to the size of a walnut.

"You don't have to do that. Just come and we'll talk."

My shriveled heart turns to dust as I realize exactly what Devlin's doing. He's willing to share an invention secret with his main competition if Storm will show up tonight.

Holy shit.

Devlin could make millions off an idea like that. Who am I kidding? Millions? More like billions. Every woman and their mother wants to look young as long as they look legal. In fact, I may be in my late twenties, but I've already got fine lines appearing on my forehead. What I wouldn't give to be rid of those suckers.

"No, no," Devlin says. *Why is he saying no? What has Storm asked him?* "I don't expect you to do anything. Just come. Great. See you then."

Conversation's over. I sprint away from the door and make it halfway down the stairs when I hear Devlin's rumbling voice.

"I know you were listening."

I wipe my rag over the last bit of banister, step onto the floor, and turn to see him standing at the top of the stairs, arms crossed. "I don't know what you're talking about. You have a lot of dust in this house. I'm finding myself very allergic. Ah-choo!"

"Good try." He smirks, and it's the most beautiful expression I've ever seen. Too bad it's on *his* face. "I guess you heard that Storm's coming to the dance."

"No clue what you're talking about, but that's great! Does he hate me? Tell the truth."

With his hand on the shiny banister, Devlin slowly slinks down the stairs, one step at a time. "The good news is that his nose is fixed."

"Uh-oh. I don't like where this is going. What's the bad news?"

He pinches his thumb and forefinger together. "He may be a tad mad at you."

"I knew it! He's never going to forgive me, and this is all your fault."

"My fault?" he scoffs. "I just spent time on the phone with a man that I dislike, convincing him to come to a dance for you. So that you can be with him. How is this my fault?"

"It's your fault because if it hadn't been for you, I wouldn't have broken his nose in the first place. Besides, you only called him so that you hold up your end of the bargain. If you don't get me together with Storm, then the deal's off."

"Right," he says, eyes downcast. "I've got to hold up my end of the bargain."

I'm not letting his little pouty face convince me that he called Storm for any other reason—not out of the goodness of his black heart, or even just because he wanted to be nice to me.

Devlin Ross called Storm because he needs me to have a stupid vision that I wish would hurry up and come so that I can leave this house—and him.

"Since I'm only doing this to hold up my end of the bargain," he says sarcastically, walking down the stairs and passing me, "don't bother thanking me."

"I won't."

"Great." He throws up his hands. "Because I don't want it."

AMY BOYLES

"Even better, because I'm not going to thank the person responsible for this entire mess anyway." Which has me thinking. "Do you really have an invention that will stop aging? And is that what you need me to help with?"

He stops, strong back flexing as if it's having its own conversation. *Should I tell her? Why should I tell her? All she does is annoy me. Maybe I won't tell her.*

He sighs. Sighs! As if I'm the problem here. "Yes, I do have something for aging, and no, that's not the invention I'm working on. What I'm doing is much more important than that."

I wipe a speck of dirt from a table beside the stairs and say as if I don't care (which I don't), "What is it, then? What are you working on? I mean, you told my parents that you need my help."

"I do need your help," he says quickly, too quickly.

I steer my gaze from the table to Devlin. There's an emotion in his eyes that I can't quite pinpoint. It looks like... longing? Regret?

Or maybe I got a little too sunbaked outside today when I smashed Storm's nose. Yep. I'm just imagining those feelings in him—and don't even think that I'm projecting my own, because I am not.

"Come and see what I'm doing."

"You sure? Aren't you afraid that I'm going to blab about your deepest, darkest secrets to your enemy?"

"No." He slides his hands into his pockets, watching me with eyes that skim my face, my body, making a knot inflate like a balloon in my throat. "I don't think you'll say anything. But if you do"—one side of his mouth tips up—"I'll have to kill you."

"If I do, then you can kill me away," I reply without thinking. "Just kidding. No killing."

"Darlin', I wouldn't dream of it."

Devlin stares at me for a beat too long, and flames lick up my throat, engulfing my face. I tuck my head and march toward him.

"Lead the way to this invention. I can't wait to see it."

Never mind that I'd also love to run for cover. But first thing's first.

15

"**W**hat *is* this?" I ask.

I'm staring at a glowing pink container that resembles an oversize capsule. It's pulsing, and it looks like there's some sort of liquid inside of it, but to be honest, I'm afraid to touch the thing because even though Devlin's not the type, there could be some mad scientist in him that I'm not aware of, and if that's the case, there's no telling if the capsule is actually safe. It could kill and eat me.

"This," he says with a mix of pride and frustration, "is a womb."

"What?"

He's got his massive arms folded, and his biceps are straining against his white shirt. Devlin's not looking at me, which is good, because I'm practically drooling at the sight of this brilliant man showing me his secrets. If he ripped his shirt off right here, I'd have no choice but to throw myself on him.

Stop it, Blair. You hate Devlin. It's very simple:

Devlin, bad.

Storm, good.

Me, ape woman.

I mean, I've got to get a grip.

He's looking at me, and I realize that I'm supposed to say something, so I clear my throat, which makes me sound like I'm trying to hock up a loogie, and manage, "A womb?"

"For babies born prematurely. I want to put the babies back in stasis and let them develop in this."

The wonder and magic of it hits me right in the solar plexus. I come up beside Devlin, ignoring his body heat as it swims around me.

Well, try to ignore it. Mostly it's impossible, but focusing on the magical womb helps curb the temptation to sink onto his arm and drink up his heat and scent.

"A magical womb," I murmur. "For premature babies. Because you had a sister…"

"Who was born premature and didn't make it," he whispers.

The weight of his words falls on me like a tidal wave. My throat shrinks to the size of an English pea. Here I assumed Devlin was coming up with some invention for his own good. Well, not assumed, just figured, I guess.

But that's not what he's been working on at all. He's working on something that will, like he said, change people's lives. This will *save lives.*

Tears prick my eyes. "This is so touching, Devlin," I say hoarsely. "It's beautiful, and amazing."

"But it doesn't work." He knocks on the table. "Not yet, at least. Hands and I have been doing everything to make it soar, but we're at a loss."

To emphasize this, Hands jumps on a table and bows his fingers over in a nod. I bite down a giggle. Even though the set of hands was at first terrifying, his presence is slowly growing on me.

"This is what I need you for," Devlin says quietly.

He turns and stares down at me. I step to the table and

drink in the sight of this pink glowing womb, this thing that could help keep babies alive. "So you want to put them back into stasis, so that they can come to term fully and then be born."

"Right."

"And where are you going wrong?"

"You name it. There's the umbilical cord issue, along with the placenta."

"So, feeding the child."

"Correct." He rests his hips on the table, facing me. "I can't figure that out, but I know there's a way, and not knowing is exhausting me. The answer has got to be in the vision."

I think about this for a moment. "And you're going to put nutrients in the womb."

He nods. "So that they can be absorbed by the growing child."

"And the placenta?"

"I'm going to use the mother's and still feed nutrients into it."

"And the umbilical cord?"

"If it doesn't get cut after birth we're okay, but if it gets cut..."

"Then you need to make one," I murmur, understanding. "And you've thought about a fake one?"

"I have, but I'm not sure how to make it." He eyes me suspiciously. "Do you have an idea?"

"You could use a potion to create such a thing."

He cocks a brow, interested. "Which one?"

"Maybe a transformation spell."

"And use the original umbilical cord."

"Right."

Devlin smiles. "That might work, but there's also the—"

"The problem of making sure the womb remains stable."

A twinkle shines in his eyes. "Exactly. All of that."

Wow. This is an amazing project. So much going on with spells plus the actual mechanical invention itself. Ideas are bouncing around in my head. I haven't had to problem solve spells or anything even remotely like this in years.

"Can I touch it?"

"Sure." He's staring at me. Do I have cheese on my face? Quickly, before I have time to ask, he sucks in a breath and moves out of the way so that I can get a better look. "But be careful. It's temperamental. There's a lot I haven't figured out."

I lightly graze my fingers along the smooth surface. The womb is pliable, and when I gently press on it, it resists slightly, like an overinflated balloon.

It's warm and looks cozy inside. Where I touch it, ripples form in the interior, and liquid sloshes.

I give it another gentle tap and it pulses.

"Get back," Devlin demands.

"What?"

The pulsing turns into a jiggling, and the whole womb wobbles like there's a tsunami inside trying to get out.

Hands jumps off the table frantically and runs under it.

"What's going on—oh!"

Devlin picks me up and rushes me back against the wall, covering me with his body. Just as I'm about to ask what's going on, the womb explodes behind him. It sounds like a million lightbulbs shattering at once, and the light that flashes is as blinding as a hundred suns collapsing in on themselves.

Okay, maybe it's not *that* bright—but it is bright.

The light hurts my eyes, so I clutch Devlin's shirt and bury my face in his chest. The explosion is over as quickly as it began, and I blink to find myself staring up at Devlin and him staring down at me.

His pupils are blown. Like, where did they go? He runs a thumb over my cheek, whispering, "Are you okay?"

"Me? Are you? It's right behind you."

There's that lopsided grin again. "I threw up a force field. I'm fine. I'm used to it."

"Exploding?"

"Yeah."

From the corner of my eye, I spot Hands crawling out from under the table and leaving the room.

"Is Hands okay?"

He shrugs. "He's just disappointed that the womb exploded. You'd think he would be used to it, it happens so much."

Our faces are close. Our lips are closer. He's a magnet, and I'm being pulled into him. He's cradling my face with such tenderness, and it doesn't help that his eyes have literally become liquid pools of want.

Just like my body.

My pelvis throbs; my palms break out into a sweat as he cradles my face, tipping it one way and then the other.

Before I can ask what he's doing, Devlin says, "I'm making sure you're not injured on your temple."

He brushes his lips over the spot, and my entire body reacts. I tighten my core as my spine convulses under his touch.

"No, you're not hurt there," he murmurs, his breath stealing over my face and wrapping around my neck like a vise. I can't move, and I don't want to, because his lips are cascading down my jaw.

"No hurts there, either," he murmurs.

All I can do is feel as my body reacts. My heart's pounding on my ribs like the Big Bad Wolf. *Little pig, little pig, let me in?* Or in this case, out.

Pinpricks of desire dance on my flesh as Devlin tips my head gently and brushes his lips up the opposite jawline.

"Looks good here."

And then something takes over me. It's aliens, obviously,

because I dare to point my finger at my cheek. "What about here?"

He kisses my cheek, and my entire body awakens like I'm Sleeping Beauty and I've been kept under a glass case for a hundred years, my body collecting dust while the world kept right on spinning.

But I'm no longer in stasis. I'm up, and my body's on fire. "What about here?" I point to my nose.

Devlin caresses the spot with his lips. "All good."

And then I do it. My heart's ping-ponging in my chest as I point to my lips. "What about here?"

What are you doing? My body screams at me. *Mayday! Mayday! All hands on deck while Blair gets her heart crushed.*

My mind might be yelling at me to think this through, to stop what I'm doing, but my body is pushing me closer and closer to the cliff that is Devlin Ross and I want to jump right on off it and kiss him.

My gosh, those soft lips and those strong hands as he holds me gently are just about enough to give me an orgasm right here and now.

His gaze darts to my lips, and for a moment I think he's going to back off, but instead he says, "Let me see."

And then his lips brush mine, slowly cascading over them like a feather before leaving them for greener pastures. But then they return, brushing against my mouth in the opposite direction.

A moan escapes me, and Devlin's hold becomes firmer. He presses his chest against mine and my body jolts.

I melt against him and grip his waist as his lips meet mine again. This time he kisses me slowly, gently, his tongue teasing my mouth apart, and I let him.

I let my entire self dissolve as his tongue sweeps into my mouth, exploring.

Devlin moans into me, and that sends a pulse of desire

straight down to my groin. I can't even remember why I'm letting him kiss me. Because it feels good?

It definitely feels good. It feels better than good.

I curl my fingers into his hips and tug him closer until he's completely pressed against me, until his entire body's heat has wrapped around me and I can't tell where he ends and I begin.

His kiss deepens, and I willingly oblige, giving back all the same passion that he's giving me.

His fingers scrape up the back of my neck as mine run up his chest and grip his lapels.

I remember what kissing him was like, how it was so easy to lose myself in Devlin Ross. It's why I lost my virginity to him. He was my first love, and if I'm being completely honest with myself, he's been my only love.

And right now, in this moment, I have him all to myself.

And I want everything that he's willing to give me.

He breaks the kiss and runs his mouth down my neck. I tip my head back and savor the feel of his lips against my flesh.

My entire body's on fire. I want to rip off his shirt and jump him right there.

"Should we go to the bedroom?" I whisper.

His lips stop moving, and Devlin's entire body stiffens. Wait. What'd I do? What'd I say?

He pulls back, taking his delicious body heat with him. Now I'm suddenly very cold (insert frowny-face emoji).

Devlin runs a hand through his thick hair. "I'm sorry, Blair. I didn't mean to mislead you."

Mislead me? Exactly how was he misleading me, because I thought that we were on the same page.

But then I get it. This is just horny old Devlin who can't stop being the player that he is. Why would I think that he'd care about anyone's feelings other than his own? Of course he doesn't. He can't. It's impossible for him to concern himself with others.

And I was just played.

"Mislead me into a mistake, you mean," I spit bitterly.

I push off the wall, and without looking back, I leave the lab, heading upstairs for my room and wishing that I'd packed my vibrator.

Of course I'm screwed on that end, too, because I didn't.

Well then, looks like I'll have to do things the old-fashioned way.

16

DEVLIN

*W*hat am I doing? What's wrong with me?

I only need Blair for the vision. I can't let her get under my skin.

Oh, I'd like for her skin to be under me, all right.

Stop. It.

I'm replaying what happened back there, trying to pinpoint the exact moment when I lost control. The womb was about to explode. I was afraid that she would die. Maybe not die but be injured.

So I picked her up and shielded her. When I wrapped my arms around Blair, I felt her heart fluttering, felt her body tense against me.

Feelings I suppose a psychiatrist would say that I'd locked inside of me were let go, and I felt.

A lot.

I experienced regret for betraying her, regret that I can't be with her, sadness that this isn't the way that I want things to go.

And then something snapped.

I didn't want to listen to that voice inside of me anymore,

the one who keeps telling me what I'm supposed to do. Instead I wanted to listen to a new voice, one that releases me.

So I did.

And when I pulled away, all these damned emotions that I've been bottling up, hiding inside of myself, just released like Old Faithful. When I looked at her, all I wanted to do was own her, take her, but I wanted to do it gently.

And I wanted to see if she wanted it, too. If she could begin to forgive me for lying to her, for making her believe in something that never even happened.

Well, guess I got that answer, didn't I?

Now I'm being tortured for acting on my desires. I can't stop thinking about how silky her skin was, or about how good her lips felt on mine.

I wonder how they'd feel wrapped around my—

A knock comes from my bedroom door. Please don't let it be Blair. My cock's hard as a rock, and I don't have a pillow to hide it behind because I'm not in my bed. I'm getting dressed for the ball.

"Come in."

The door opens and Hands enters. He shuts the door and then stops, facing me.

"Don't even start," I say.

You were kissing her.

"I told you not to start." I slip a link through the hole in my cuff and turn it. "It was an accident. It won't happen again."

Maybe it should happen again. I give Hands a hard stare. He pretends not to notice as he makes his way over to my bed and jumps on top of the mattress. *This hasn't seen any action in a while. The springs might be broken.*

"The springs aren't broken, and stop it."

But you were getting awfully cozy.

I sigh and turn to Hands. "Yes, we were getting cozy. If

you're not nice, I'll influence you to put on a hat and pretend to be the Hamburger Helper mascot."

Hands gives me the evil eye, though he doesn't have eyes, nor is he evil. *I'm only telling you what's obvious.*

I sigh in frustration. "What exactly is obvious?"

That you're in love with her.

"It doesn't matter what I feel. What matters is her safety."

Why don't you let her make that choice?

"No. End of discussion. I've made the decision."

Don't you think that's a bit toxic of you?

"Watch it," I snap.

You have a vision that she dies because of you, and you've never even told her. You've never given her the chance to decide what she wants.

I tug on my collar and smooth it flat. "And my parents weren't given a choice, either. But if they had been given one, if I'd known what I was doing and could have stopped them from getting on that plane, I would have. My life would have been different. I wouldn't have wound up with an uncle who did what he did. *Everything* would have been different, Hands. All of it. I don't need you telling me how to live my life and who needs to know what. This is for her own protection, and you'll do well to remember that. So please, I'm asking for you to drop it. Leave it alone. We can't be together, and that's the end of it. What I'm doing for Blair, I'm doing for her own safety."

My heart feels too big for my chest. Or my chest is squeezing my heart until it's about to explode. I don't know which, and I don't care.

This feeling is too much. I yank open my shirt collar, grab the end of the bed and breathe slowly, letting the air in and out, in and out.

Hands comes over. *I'm sorry if I upset you.*

"You didn't." I'd done it to myself. My own actions anger

me. Hurting people, it's not what I like to do, no matter what Blair would say. I drop my voice. "Hands, I know you mean well. I do. But let me take care of this.

"I'm not going through what I experienced with my parents ever again. If Blair and I get together, the future is clear—she doesn't have one. I will not stand by and watch her die, not for my own selfish needs. I would rather watch her marry another man than let that happen."

Hands sags, but he knows that I'm right. What I'm doing, what I've done since high school has been the only path. It's been the correct choice ever since the day I received the vision of Blair dying.

And she died because of me.

So no, thank you, I won't be the cause of it. Like I said, I care about her too much to let that happen.

I exhale a deep breath and push up off the footboard. "If there isn't anything else, there's a ball that I need to get to."

Hands signs, *By all means. Don't let me stop you.*

"I didn't think you would."

17

*W*hat *was* that? Like, seriously? Devlin kissed me and it was so HOT!

And speaking of—*why* did he kiss me? Why did I let him? Must be because I'm enduring the sex dry spell from hell. Otherwise I never would've let my guard down, and my girlie parts never would have tingled and done several cartwheels like they did when his lips were moving down my neck.

Oh gods, it felt so good.

Never mind. Must think about other things.

I've got to be concentrating on Storm and figuring out a way to make sure that he doesn't hate me after I broke his beautiful nose.

"What should I say to Storm?" I ask Devlin.

We're at the ball, just arrived—separately, I'd like to add, so that no one grows suspicious—but as soon as he entered, I scuttled over to him like a spider needing a fix, put my back to the wall. And started talking.

My gods, he looks good. His hair's smoothed back, and his jawline looks exceptionally sharp tonight.

Devlin takes two flutes of champagne from a waiter

walking by, and hands one to me. "I wouldn't say anything. Just ask him how he is."

"But you'll make sure that he's not mad at me."

He quirks a brow. "I will?"

"Of course you will!" I screech. People turn to look so I suddenly study the skirt of my green dress. Wow. It's very flouncy. When I feel the stares off me, I say, "I mean, won't you?"

"I got him to come," he replies, keeping his gaze on the crowd.

"But you promised that you'd get us tog—"

He holds up his hand to silence me. "I will. I'll make sure he dances with you tonight, and that you're well on your way to a blissful relationship."

Is that bitterness in his voice? "What's wrong with you? That's the agreement, remember? You help me, I help you, and you don't use your power to bed anyone."

He frowns, stares into the crowd, keeping his handsome face turned away from me. "What if I wanted to?"

My stomach drops. "What if you wanted to use the power to bed someone?"

"Not use the power," he sighs. He turns to look at me, and it feels like the world is slipping away. He's staring at me as if there's something important he needs, must have, desires above all else. "What if I wanted to bed someone?" he says in a husky voice that makes my insides shatter.

I lick my lips, ignoring how it feels like everyone in the ballroom's vanished and it's just the two of us. His eyes tear down my face to my mouth. Then they slowly drag back up to meet my gaze.

"What if you wanted someone?" I repeat dumbly like I've just learned how to talk.

"Yes. What if I do? And what if I don't want to use your power to have them?"

Pinpricks of desire dance down my spine as he shifts to face me. Everything about Devlin is massive and beautiful, and all I can think about are his lips grazing down my throat, and how my nipples are now hard as diamonds because I'm stupidly thinking about kissing the wrong man.

"Well, you can't bring anyone home, not while I'm in your house."

"What if I don't have—"

"Storm Grayson," the announcer booms.

I jump, startled at the interruption. My head swivels to the front of the room, and there stands Storm, looking beautiful and hot with his perfect face and even more perfect nose.

Thank goodness he was healed. I'm already in the doghouse enough. If he couldn't be put back together, my chances at a perfect match would have been finished.

"Oh, there's Storm. I'm going to say hello."

I start to walk off, but Devlin grabs my arm. "Hold on there, cowboy. Let me talk to him first."

"But I thought it would be okay to greet him."

Darkness flashes in Devlin's eyes. "Let me feel him out. You did break his nose."

"And I should apologize," I argue.

"Let me talk to him before you do." I lift a brow in defiance, and Devlin smirks. "You know I'm right."

Of course he's right. That's what's so annoying. Why does he have to always be right?

He glances down at my arm, seeming to realize for the first time that he's touching me, and drops me like a hot potato. Then he strides into the crowd, managing to make striding look swelteringly sexy.

"So have you hit that yet?" Chelsea says, sidling up with Dallas.

I scoff. "No, I haven't, and I'm not going to."

"Is that a hickey on your neck?" Dallas asks, squinting in my vicinity.

"What? Where? Quick. One of you give me a mirror."

My sisters stare at each other and burst into laughter. "Oh, I got you," Dallas says.

"You didn't get me." I fluff out my skirt in annoyance. "I knew there wasn't a hickey, because there's no reason for there to be one."

Chelsea clasps her hands behind her back. "Then why'd you look? Hm?"

"You surprised me," I mutter. "But anyway, Storm looks like he survived spell ball."

"Just barely," Dallas admits, clicking her tongue. "I heard he almost left because of it."

A pit opens in my stomach, and my body falls into it. This is a disaster.

Devlin's talking to him now. Storm looks all broody and delicious. Devlin's greeting him, saying something. Storm's gaze tracks the room until it lands on me.

Then he turns up his nose and looks away.

I become a puddle of sludge. I've ruined things between us. Completely. Irrevocably.

I can just see it now—Storm Grayson leaves, taking with him my last chance at marriage. I wind up manless, it being just me and my vibrator for the rest of my life. My family loses their magic and we're forced to sell the bookshop, because who needs a bookshop of magic when it doesn't have any magic?

My sisters all marry off, and I'm left at home, taking care of my parents and dead nana, who reminds me of all my past mistakes every day for the rest of my life. Then I die and am buried in an unmarked grave that no one tends, and it gets covered in weeds.

Wow. I've really got to get out and stop imagining terrible things.

But that doesn't stop the fact that Storm does not look happy to see me, and it amplifies the sinking feeling in my gut.

"Here comes Devlin," Chelsea tells me. "We'll leave you to it."

Before I can tell them that they don't have to leave, my sisters scurry off, nodding and smiling at Devlin as they pass him in the crowd.

I barely wait for him to arrive before pouncing. "Well? How'd things go?" I omit the fact that Storm shot torpedoes out of his eyes at me.

"Not well."

My chest seizes. "No?"

"No. Oh, he gladly took the information I had about the anti-aging treatment, but there's bad news."

His eyes flash on me in a way that says I don't want to hear what's coming. But of course I ask because I've got to know the truth. "What is it?"

His expression darkens and I recognize that look. It's disgust. Things must be really bad if Devlin's disgusted.

"Does he not want to see me? Does he hate me forever? What?"

"Come on."

He takes my arm, and I follow him over to the string quartet. They're between songs, and he whispers in the ear of the violinist, who nods and smiles.

Then Devlin drags me into the center of the room.

"What are you doing?" I hiss. "What's going on?"

He spins me into him, and I fall onto his chest. Devlin takes my hand and murmurs in my ear, "What's happening is that we're going to change Storm Grayson's mind about you."

"Why? How does he feel about me?"

"You don't want to know."

"Then how are you going to fix it? Influence him?"

He shakes his head, and a slow smile works itself across his face. "No. Better. We're going to tango."

"What?" I screech as the music starts up.

Before I'm given a chance to bolt, Devlin's got me in a tight embrace. The music kicks up, and he leads me with strong steps into the dance.

Now I've taken lots of dance lessons. Any good witch worth her salt can move and shake, but I've never done the tango. I've seen plenty of movies where there have been sexy tangoes, but watching and doing are different.

Aren't they?

"Make him want you," Devlin whispers in my ear.

"What?"

"Blair, you are three seconds away from losing the one shot you've got, and there's nothing I can say to Storm to change his mind. So unless you pull out the sexiest dance you can manage, he's going to walk out that door and never return."

My head snaps toward Storm. He's still here, but he's not paying attention to us.

"I could use your influence power," Devlin whispers in my ear, "but that's only a temporary fix, a bandage on a problem. You've got to convince him to stay, that you're worth it, that suffering from a broken nose was the price of being in your presence."

My skin shivers as his words float over my ear and trickle down my neck. Something happens in this moment. It's like a lightbulb's been snapped on, and I realize that I have two choices—let Storm leave or win him.

I decide to win.

So I throw myself into the tango.

The music is slow and sultry, and I take the opportunity to show off my dance skills. Devlin walks me back several paces, and I drop, extending my right leg between both of his while keeping my eyes pinned up at him.

A hush fills the room. Everyone's watching.

I rise and Devlin's hand splays over my lower back, across the curve of my rear end, and I suck air but keep my eyes latched onto him.

Heat is flaming like an inferno in his gaze, and that heat envelops me, spurring me on, pushing out the world as I follow his lead.

Our steps are quick, our legs entwine, tangle, separate. My torso's pressed against his as he pushes and pulls, dipping me down, his breath grazing against my bust before he dramatically whips me up and catches me in his embrace.

I'm breathless, intoxicated by this moment with him. There's only him. There's no one else in the world except Devlin, and I'm putty in his hands, water in his embrace.

He moves like a god, and the entire room knows it. I can feel all their eyes as I'm dipped, as I fall onto him and he catches me, as I tangle my leg in his like we're wrapped up in bedsheets, and as I unwind from him.

All he sees is me, and all I see is him. I haven't stared at Devlin this long in forever. This is more intimate than being with him, moving with him like this, it's like we've become one, and when I look at him, I can see all his vulnerabilities. He can't hide from me, and I can't escape him.

We've found our rhythm now, and we're fluid, dancing as one. I instinctively know what he's going to do before he does it, and I'm right there. There's no stumbling, no falling and no barriers between us.

The heat of his gaze (yes, there's heat, girl, an inferno of it!) sinks into my skin. He's all I see, all I know, all I want.

My breath comes quickly. I can't get enough air into my lungs because he's sucking it up as quickly as I inhale it. He dips me one last time and the music stops.

I lift my head and stare at him, and the connection I feel is like a rope's been tied between us, knotting us together so tightly that there's no space to breathe.

What in the world has happened?

Devlin slowly lifts me, both of us keeping our gazes locked on the other. I feel such a connection that I don't dare inhale or think or even blink because I'm afraid that this thing vibrating and humming between us will be lost.

"Devlin, I—"

And then the crowd explodes in applause and I'm snapped out of whatever I was going to say and I'm back in reality.

He slowly tears his gaze from me, and it feels like I've been cast out into the cold of outer space, facing away from the sun and life.

He flashes the crowd his mischievous grin and wraps an arm around my waist, pulling me to him. "Smile. I think that did what we wanted it to."

But what had *I* wanted it to do? Charm Storm? Now my brain's totally fogged up. I can't stop thinking about kissing Devlin and how he made my lips burn. Not like someone threw Tabasco on them, but more like burned with desire.

And then that dance. It was sooooooo hot! So hot that I need to add about a thousand *o*'s to the *s*. My hormones are doing all kinds of dancing in my pants, and Devlin looks yummy delicious.

Maybe my biological clock is ticking. That would explain why I've clearly suffered from brain damage and want to mate with someone as terrible as him. When hormones take charge, they win over all rational thought.

Me cavewoman. Me want to make baby. You man. You seem good enough.

Ugh. My brains must have spilled out of my head when Devlin was spinning me.

Before I get a chance to scour the floor for them, a shock wave hits me, sending a pulse zinging to my fingers and toes.

My mind opens and I'm suddenly tangled in bedsheets. I'm being kissed and I'm kissing back. A hand skates over my breast and doesn't stop until it dips between my legs.

It's dark in the room, so I can't see his face, but I feel his weight on top of me and how much I want him.

He breaks from the kiss and sits up. Moonlight slashes across his face, the face of—

The scene vanishes as quickly it appeared, and it takes a moment for me to realize that I'd just seen my first vision.

Wow. That was trippy.

And now I'm horny.

"Blair," a masculine voice says, "you were incredible."

I glance up at Storm, who's standing in front of me, clapping slowly, a small smile tugging up one corner of his mouth.

My gaze darts to Devlin, but he's not looking at me. "Um, yes. Thank you."

Storm does a little bow. It's very romantic. "Would you like to dance?"

Devlin's still not looking at me. He's talking to some guy I don't recognize. But he must be listening, because his arm slips out from around my waist and he turns to face the man fully, putting his back to me.

My heart gives a little shudder as I tip my chin up to Storm and smile. "Sure. I'd love to dance."

18

DEVLIN

I did what I came to do; so why do I feel so terrible, like I've just handed the keys of the kingdom to my worst enemy?

Because you have.

I need a drink.

Blair's dancing with Storm. He must be hilarious because she keeps tossing her head back and laughing. Either that, or he's tickling her.

I will kill him if he's doing that.

Got to get a grip.

My mind's a mess. I can't stop thinking about earlier, when I had her against the wall. The tango didn't do a thing to quell my desire, either. It made it worse. I can still taste her on my tongue, and when I curl my fingers, it feels like I'm digging them into her thighs.

Yes, I know that I mostly cradled her face. I can imagine, can't I?

But maybe Hands is right. Maybe I should tell her what I saw. Maybe I should go for it, let Blair decide her own future.

It's not my place to make her life choices for her. She should get a say.

It's just...when I think about what I saw, my heart shrivels into dust. I can't go through what happened with my parents all over again. I can't live with that sort of guilt. Experiencing it once was enough. Not again.

"Having a good time?"

I glance over and see Rebecca's face peeking out of the wall. Blair's nana really can't stay out of the limelight.

"I am," I answer. "And yourself?"

"Well it would be a lot more fun if I wasn't dead."

That makes me chuckle. "Yes, I suppose it would be. But shouldn't you be hiding? You know, it's bad luck for a family when their relatives return."

"I know. Believe me, I know." Her hand appears and she waves me away. "My Great-aunt Edith showed up when I was a girl, and my mother had a time getting her to disappear. She even tried to stop her up in the family well." She laughs at the memory. "But my aunt didn't leave until we were all married off, and I won't go away until I see Blair happily matched. But anyway"—she gives me a ghostly side-eye—"I just had to check up on you, and since Blair's angry with me, I'm not sure how honest she'll be about the way things are going."

I nod to the ballroom floor. "She's dancing now. Looks like they're having a good time."

I down the rest of my champagne and look for another glass. Hm. There's none to be seen, so I magic up another into my palm. I down it, too.

"Is she having a good time?" Rebecca asks in a voice that suggests her granddaughter is not.

"Looks like she is to me."

"Perhaps." The apparition turns her face to me. "You know, I always questioned why the two of you broke up. You were such a good match. And then, if I'm being honest, I worried about you when you started dating so many different women. You seem like a one-gal kind of guy to me, Devlin. Oh, you're pretty, yes, but you come from good stock, a grandmother that loves you very much. Not so much that uncle of yours."

She studies me for another moment before saying, "She told me about your parents. I'm so sorry."

Rebecca doesn't mean that they died in the crash. I know what she's implying. "Well, if my grandmother told you, then she must've known that you'd keep my secret."

"And I did, even when my own granddaughter's heart was shattered by you. It seemed to me that something more was going on there. Am I right?"

I grunt. It's the best answer that I can muster.

"I thought so. You know, in my experience, running from a problem never solves anything. No matter how much the truth hurts, no matter what we think might happen because of it, it's always best to face our fears. Pull out our swords and kill our proverbial dragons." She presses a hand to the side of her mouth. "Don't tell my son-in-law that. He loves dragons."

I can't help but smile. "So Blair has told me."

"And what's she telling you now?"

"Not quite what I need to know yet."

She lifts her brows. "Be sure that you get what you need before it's too late." She lets that sink in before adding, "Now, if you'll excuse me, I need to disappear before anyone recognizes me and word gets out that I've returned to ruin"—she adds with an eye roll—"my family."

I chuckle as Rebecca slips back into the wall and vanishes from sight. Then I sigh and slump my spine against said wall, staring out into the crowd.

Several women are eyeing me, but I make a big show of scowling and looking away to fend off any unwanted advances. The last thing I need tonight is a witch looking for a hookup or, worse, love.

There's only one woman who owns my heart, and she's dancing with another man.

I just want to die.

Or kill someone.

Maybe tonight's not the night for that.

Blair dances like she's made of wind, spinning and moving fluidly. Storm's a great lead, I'll give him that.

It's about the only thing I'll give him.

He doesn't hold her like she's something to cherish, though. He holds her like a possession. Of course, he doesn't know her. That *could* change.

Or it could not.

What would I feel if they married? Would I be all right with that? Wouldn't I have to be? Wouldn't there be no other choice?

There's always a choice.

I could make one tonight that will change my future, that will change everything. All I have to do is be honest with Blair, admit how I feel.

Tell her that I love her.

Whoa. Hold on there, cowboy. Maybe just tell her that I want to try again and explain what happened, why she thinks that I betrayed her. Explain that I was a teenage asshole who was afraid, but I'm not afraid anymore, and if she wants to walk away from me, she still can.

Once I get that vision.

The alternative is to watch her marry someone else, someone who will never love her like I do, will never love how she pulls her hair to one side of her shoulder, and how she plants one foot on top of the other when she's thinking, or how she loves puzzling out problems with magic.

The Blair that I remember and love.

Oh gods. I still love her. Why does it hurt to admit that? Why has it taken me this long to really admit it to myself?

Yes, I was halfway there when I decided to attend the ball. It was clearly because I didn't want Storm Grayson to have her, and I still don't.

There are things about Storm she should know.

But I don't want to seem like I'm pushing her away from him.

I glance up when I hear her laugh at something he said, and it feels like someone scooped my heart out with a spoon, let it slide onto the floor and then stomped it with their foot.

I love her. Still. Always have. Always will. I want her to be mine.

Is it worth it to have my heart crushed? Yes, it is.

After all, we haven't even talked about the kiss—more like we ran screaming from it like it was a building on fire. All I have to do is say I'm not sorry that it happened and that I want more, that I'm ready to be the man that she needs me to be. I'll explain why I purposefully sabotaged our relationship in high school.

The dance comes to an end, and Blair smiles up at Storm, looking like a star come down to earth, shining for all of us to admire.

She nods at something he said, and then he takes her hand and kisses the back of it like he's a duke or something. My chest tightens in anger, and I curl my hands into fists.

It's not until they part ways that my chest finally loosens, the knot unfurling inside my rib cage.

Blair sees me, smiles, and I suddenly feel a whole lot lighter, like the world's spinning just for me, just for us in this moment.

She makes her way over, grinning like a cat who just ate a mouse, and I slip my hands into my pockets, doing what I can to calm my nerves. This is it. I'll be honest. I'll be open. I'll say that I don't regret the kiss, that I want more, that I can't stand seeing her with other men.

I head over, grabbing two glasses of punch from a table. Hopefully these have lots and lots of alcohol. I have a feeling I'm gonna need it.

After taking a quick swig it is confirmed—no alcohol.

I hand one to Blair when she joins me, still grinning. My heart's so big it feels like it's going to explode. My palms are sweating. Is it hot in here?

No, not hot. I'm just about to put myself out there, let the woman I love know how I feel.

"How was the dance?" I ask, immediately regretting that I put another man into her head when what she needs to be thinking about is me, no one but me.

She takes the glass with a little nod and sips. "Thank you. I'm burning up. I should've rested after that tango—" Her gaze cuts away from me dramatically, and her cheeks turn bright red. Oh yeah, she felt it, too. "But then Storm asked me to dance and yada yada yada, here we are."

She slaps her forehead like either she forgot something or she's trying to fill up the space between us with as many words as possible because she's uncomfortable with the kiss and our public sex dance. For the record, I don't regret either of them.

"But you asked about Storm. It was good."

"Blair, listen…"

Her gaze cuts back to me, and she looks up, her big doe eyes shining with emotion. I think it's fear. I should make this fast before she bolts. Not that Blair would ever run away from a fight, but she might just run away from me.

"Oh, I saw my first vision."

I blink. "You did? When?"

"Right after we danced."

"Was it *the one?*"

She makes a funny face. "Um, no."

"What does that mean?"

"Never mind." She waves her hand in dismissal. "Anyway, what did you want to say?"

I lower my voice. "About what happened earlier…"

Her cheeks turn even more red. "About the dance? Oh, it was fine. I was worried of course that it would be too sexy and not get Storm's attention in the right way, but it did."

"No, I mean about the kiss."

Her eyes pop out of her head. "What? Oh, that. What about it?"

My gaze drops to the floor while I try to find the words to say this. "Listen, I know it was unexpected, but I don't reg—"

"Storm asked me out on a date," she blurts out.

The world stops spinning as my stomach crashes to the floor, where dancers smash it into pulp. "What?"

"Your plan worked. He's not mad anymore, and he asked me on a date for tomorrow. Of course, I'll need you to be there so that you can tell me what to say in a Cyrano de Bergerac sort of way." She stops, seems to notice that I've gone pale, that my life has ended. "If that's okay."

My brain catches up to the conversation. "You didn't need me with you when you danced with him."

"I know, but this is different. I need you there to make sure I do this right. Please, Devlin. Wow. Never thought I'd hear myself say those words." She laughs, but it quickly fades into a distant memory when her eyes darken. "Please. Help me win him. You said that you would. You promised."

It feels like my life is being strangled right out of me as I choke out the words, "Sure. I made a promise, and I plan to keep it." I lift my glass. "Here's to first dates."

She lifts her glass with me. "To first dates."

19

I do not want to talk about that kiss. No clue what Devlin was going to say—probably something like, *It was the worst kiss ever. I can't believe that I pressed my lips to yours.* Thanks but no thanks. I'm not interested in hearing that.

As far as I'm concerned, the kiss did not happen. It will go down in history as the Kiss That Never Was.

Exactly. It didn't happen.

And the look on his face when I started talking about Storm. I know that look. That's Devlin's angry look. His super angry look.

"Why don't you like Storm?" I ask when we're back at the house. I've changed into my pajamas, which tonight is a sleeping T-shirt that stops at my ankles and has a picture of a sparkling waffle on it. I think it's supposed to be magical or something. Oh well, nothing says sexy like a waffle. Sexy sleepwear at its finest.

If I'd let Nana pack my bag, she probably would've put in crotchless panties and a negligee.

Good thing I packed this bad boy myself.

Devlin throws a mountain of pillows onto the floor. I assume he's going to be bedding down in his equivalent of Mt. Everest, My Pillow style.

"Why do I hate Storm?" he repeats, hooking his hands behind his neck and pulling his T-shirt off to reveal rippling muscles that are screaming to be oiled down by me.

What?

No. Nope. I will not be doing any rubbing of oil on Devlin's body. But that doesn't mean that someone shouldn't. Seriously. His body is begging to be shiny and slick.

He drops his knees onto his pillows, and now I have to perch on the edge of the bed to see him better. So I scoot to the end as he lays on his mountain, arms tucked neatly behind his head, wavy dark blond hair smoothed away from his forehead.

"Why don't you ask me something else?"

"Because I asked you that."

He sighs, which of course means he doesn't want to tell me, and which also means that I must know. Now.

He leans over on his side and tucks a hand under his head, supporting it. "Do you like him?"

Do I? Do I think the sun sets with him? Does he give me butterflies in my stomach? No. But that could come in time.

"I might be heading that way." It's not exactly lying and not exactly telling the truth, either. "As long as he doesn't spread nasty rumors about me, then he'll be better than some people."

It's a low blow, I admit, but it'll keep Devlin from talking about that kiss. Bonus, it has the added effect of reminding us exactly what we are to one another—nothing. Just two people who need our powers back. Mine for the safety of all Castleview and Devlin's because, well, because he needs it to help humanity.

A noble cause, even I'll say that.

He frowns. "What do you mean, spreading nasty rumors?"

I roll my eyes and grab a billowy pillow, tucking it under my chest. "You know what I mean."

"No, I don't."

"Come on, Devlin."

Concern fills his hazel eyes, which look black in the low light. "No, I don't know what you're talking about. Please enlighten me. You're already making me sleep clothed; you can at least share your secret."

I fluff the pillow beneath me and settle back onto it. "Do I really have to remind you of what you did?"

"Yes, you really do."

This is the part that was the hardest to get over, and he doesn't even remember it. "I can't believe I have to tell you this," I mutter. "But all right. Since you can't remember." I put *can't remember* in air quotes, really layering on the sarcasm. I hope he can feel it like an anvil falling from a three-story window onto his head.

I take a deep breath and relax the muscles tightening in my chest. These are words that I've never spoken out loud. It's like holding on to a secret that is so humiliating you're terrified to say it because doing so will speak it into life.

"You really don't remember telling the entire school that I influenced you into dating me?"

There. I've said it. I've never confronted him with this, because it was the most painful aspect of what he did to me. Kissing Basheen was one thing. A big thing. A huge thing. But when I told him my secret, it wasn't even on the horizon that he'd use it against me.

He sits up quickly, his sandy hair falling in his eyes. "What?"

I groan and drop my head onto the pillow. "Don't make me say it again."

"Blair, I don't know what you're talking about. I never did that."

My head pops up. "What do you mean, you didn't do that? Of course you did. Everyone told me."

He rises onto his knees and plants himself directly in front of me, putting his abs at eye level. They should still be oiled, I randomly think, forgetting momentarily to be infuriated that he's lying.

I pull back and laugh. Maniacally. I sound kind of deranged, actually, so I stop. "Of course you did that. Everyone told me that they heard you say that I influenced you to like me, and that once you found out, you ended it. You were so mad that you kissed another girl."

He slowly shakes his head, regret filling his eyes. "Blair, I never would've told anyone that. I made you a promise that I wouldn't."

Why is my heart doing somersaults? "But they said—"

"They lied," he growls. *Growls.*

"But..."

"There are no buts. I didn't do it. I never spread a rumor about you."

He rests his hand on my arm and rubs it. I stare at it for a moment, not wanting to look into his eyes.

With his other hand, Devlin hooks his finger under my chin, which I really should've planted in my pillow better, and lifts my head until our gazes latch.

Then he says slowly, so that every word sinks in, "I never did that. I never would have betrayed you like that."

"Oh, you just betrayed me the other way," I spit out.

His eyes harden. "There are some things that have to be lost so that other things might be saved."

What does that mean?

He's looking at me as if there's some hidden message there, something he wants me to know. "Oh, I get it. You had to lose me in order to gain all the other women in your life, the revolving door of twinsets."

He sighs and drops his hand from my chin. "I know you won't believe this, but I've never really dated anyone since you."

My heart stops beating. He's right; I don't believe it. I laugh a little too loudly and hug the pillow tighter for protection. Whatever mean words he's going to say are not getting through this down or fabricated material and hit my heart. No way.

I roll my eyes dramatically. "Come on, Devlin. I've seen you with lots of girls over the years—usually two at a time. You're the envy of every man on earth."

His eyebrow curls. "Am I? Must be nice for them to think that I've slept with all those women."

Why am I even asking this? "You don't?"

"Would you believe it if I said that I'm not really a man whore?"

"No."

He laughs and pushes back before rising and sitting beside me. The bed dips dramatically, and it takes some serious core strength for me not to fall onto his hulking frame.

He rubs his thumb across his forehead. "I don't sleep with most of them, Blair. Those women are just for show."

Not only does my jaw drop, but my entire body becomes one big blob of putty. "What are you talking about? I've seen you with them."

"You've been staring into my windows at night?" he jokes.

"No, of course not." I whack him gently on the arm. "I'm not a peeping Tom. But—wait—I don't understand."

He turns and faces me, resting one hand on the bed. *My* bed. His bicep pops as it strains to hold him and all his muscles up.

It's times like these that I wish I had a cleaning cloth and a bottle of Pledge in my hands. There's nothing more distracting than cleaning when you're about to dive into a hard conversation.

"I only take those women out with me to events. I don't date them. I haven't seriously dated anyone since high school. I'll say it a third time if you need me to," he says with a twinkle in his eyes.

"But I don't understand." Wait. He said something earlier about there only being one woman that he ever wanted. Does he mean...? Nope. Not gonna even entertain the thought.

His lips tighten and he shakes his head. "I suppose that I'm just not good at dating. You ruined me for it."

I frown. "That's not true. If anything, *you* ruined *me*."

"Oh? You haven't dated much?"

"Devlin, no one here wants to date me because they all think that I'll influence them into loving me."

His expression falls as if he really, for once, feels pity for me. Well if we're being all in our feelings here, I feel pity for me, too. Not enough to throw a pity party, but some.

"I'm sorry, Blair," he whispers. "I never wanted that to happen to you."

"That rumor—"

"I didn't start it," he says harshly. "I don't know who did, but it wasn't me. I can promise you that."

I search his eyes, looking for any hint that he's lying, and I don't see it. I've been so hard on Devlin, so terribly hard. Well, not really. I thought that he'd told the school about my curse— I mean *gift*. But he hadn't, and looking at him now, with his big hazel eyes lined with those thick, dark lashes, all I want to do is kiss him again. I want to run my fingers through his silky hair and wind the strands around my fingers.

But I want more than that. I want him.

Wait. What? Where did that come from?

Do I need to remind myself that this man is dangerous? Yes, I do. He crushed my heart once. He'll do it again if given the chance. I know he will.

So I don't give him my heart, maybe. But that doesn't mean that we can't be friends.

Friends. The seven-letter word that all people hate when they're attracted to someone. No one wants to be just friends. But sometimes it's better to be friends than it is to be enemies. And I've spent a long time being hateful and angry with Devlin, and apparently blaming him for something that he didn't do.

Oh, he'd kissed another girl, all right. But that was back in high school, and people make stupid mistakes.

What I'd really blamed him for was humiliating me— something that he hadn't even done.

Maybe it's time that I bury the hatchet, and not in Devlin's back like I would've done a couple of days ago, but bury it in the ground and forget all about it.

"I believe that you didn't start the rumor," I tell him.

"You sure?" he asks, rubbing that delicious mouth of his. "I'd hate to think that I've been forgiven for something when I really haven't."

"You have been. Let's shake on it. To being friends."

I extend my hand, and he stares at it for a beat too long. Oh gods, I've completely misunderstood this whole thing. He doesn't want to be my friend. Maybe he'd rather go back to what we were—enemies with crackling sexual tension that will never, and I mean never, get resolved.

My cheeks are burning with humiliation. "If you don't want to be friends, I understand."

I start to draw my hand away, but he grabs it, surprising me and stealing my breath. My gaze cuts to his eyes, and Devlin's watching me intently. He does not have the look of a man who wants to be friends with me on his face. I can't pinpoint what the look means, but it doesn't signify friendship.

I swallow down a knot in my throat as he says, "Friends."

But why don't I believe him?

20

DEVLIN

*F*riends. Blair wants to be friends. I want to haul her over my shoulder, dump her on my bed and have my way with her, and she wants to be friends.

So I'm being a friend.

And what friends do is sit two rides away at a winter carnival in a magical town while listening in on their "friend's" date and telling them what to say next.

Three cheers for being friends.

A wizard dressed in tight leather pants and a short-sleeved shirt stops, opens his mouth and exhales a line of fire. Using his hands, he sculpts the tendrils into a bow and arrow. Then he slingshots the arrow into the air, where it explodes into fireworks. People who've been watching break out into applause. I do, too. Watching him has been the highlight of this whole night.

Right now Storm and Blair are sitting in the teacup ride while I'm hanging in the background like a secret service agent, incognito and looking like a creeper all by myself at a carnival filled with parents, children and couples.

Yes, several parents have already pulled their children away from me.

If Hands were here, he would be telling me to stop the date, tell Blair how I feel and get on with it.

To that I would reply that Blair has told me how *she* feels. She's been perfectly clear, in fact. She wants to be friends, so that's what I'm being.

Good old Devlin.

Before we left the house, I cast a spell that lets me communicate with her. I can hear their conversation and also tell her what to say next.

Yes, she insisted on that. Don't ask me why, because when she was dancing with Storm, she didn't need any help. But she swore that it's required now. I suppose all the pressure of marriage is getting to her.

It's also getting to me. I think that I'm coming down with a stomach ulcer.

The teacup ride ends, and Blair rises on shaky legs. She laughs and spills onto Storm, who catches her and chuckles. He takes her hand and guides her to a row of games.

"Oh, the squirt gun game. I love that one," she says.

"Want me to win a bear for you?" Storm jokes, clearly making fun of the fact that people do things like spend their money to win a giant bear.

But Blair doesn't catch his sarcasm. "Yes! Would you? That would be awesome."

He balks. "I was joking, but sure. If that's what you want. I'll win one so that you can put it on your bed and think of me whenever you look at it."

Do not say anything about taking her home. If something like that comes out of his mouth, I will walk over and punch him in the face.

Lucky for Grayson, he remains quiet.

Storm is the most arrogant man I've ever met, and that's

163

saying a lot coming from me. Because I know arrogance. Hell, I live and breathe it.

But he takes it to a whole new level.

"So," Storm asks, bending over in preparation to use the human squirt gun. You can't have everything be magical at a magical carnival. I suppose some things are better done the human way. "That was some dance you and Devlin did last night. You looked cozy."

"Cozy? Oh, we're not cozy," she says, her voice wobbly.

Is that hesitancy I sense?

Just to push her, I say, "Tell him the truth." I speak into my hand like any good Secret Service agent.

Blair glances over her shoulder at me, worry in her eyes. I nod encouragingly as a group of werewolf teens, fangs and claws out with patches of fur on their faces, dash across the grass, aiming for one of the rides.

A group of witch moms are following their kids, sipping drinks from Stanley cups. Probably not water in those, I'm figuring. More like alcohol to deal with the gaggle of children they're following. When one of the kids strays off, his mom uses magic to pull him back into the group.

Blair turns back to Storm. "I know Devlin from high school. We go back a long way. So that's all you were seeing in that dance—just two people who've known each other a long time."

"Did you ever date?" he asks, spraying water at the target. The water pushes the racing car disks up and up, but a kid sitting beside him has the lead.

"Don't make it sound like a big deal," I coax.

"Briefly."

She looks back at me. Oh, I may have forgotten to mention that I glamoured myself with some subtle but important changes. Gave myself darker and longer hair. I'm taller (why would I go shorter?), and I have a handlebar mustache.

Always wanted one of those but never wanted to keep it long term.

I nod, silently telling Blair that she's doing great.

When the kid beside them wins the water gun race, Storm looks agitated.

Blair places a hand on his shoulder. "It's okay. You don't have to win me the big bear."

"No, no," he says, pulling out his wallet. "I'm going to win it, even if I have to buy this whole carnival."

Have I mentioned that Storm's also one smug bastard?

The boy wins a small bear, but he wants to keep going. So does Storm.

When no one's looking, he uses a bit of magic on the boy's gun. It's so subtle that no one notices, and apparently the game doesn't have an anti-magic spell on it because the power is absorbed.

I smirk. If he can't win it the proper way, Storm will win the underhanded way.

When the bell sounds, the water starts spurting, but the boy's gun doesn't deliver quite as much punch as it did before. Surprise, surprise, Storm wins.

And no one is any wiser about what happened.

No one but me, that is.

Two rounds later and Storm's won Blair the big teddy bear of her dreams, and I want to punch a wall.

The kid walks off with his parents, his head hanging in disappointment. Before they pass me, I pull a teddy bear from the air with magic. "Hey, I won this but don't need it. Would you like it?"

The way the boy's face lights up makes my heart swell. "Thank you, sir."

His parents thank me, and they walk off happier. I do, too.

After that, Storm buys Blair some sort of deep-fried ice cream thing, and they sit on a bench while she eats.

"So you like your town?" he asks.

"Castleview? I love it, but it must be so boring compared to where you're from."

"Well, I own three houses, so I come from many places."

"Three? Wow. I still live with my parents."

"Why is that, exactly?"

A trio of familiar voices grabs my attention. Glancing over, I spot Cathy, Sadie and Cherie heading this way.

They're laughing and cackling about something. No clue that Storm Grayson's here. Good. Maybe it will stay that way.

Blair's voice grabs my attention. "Why do I live with my parents?"

"Yes?" he asks.

She flounders, and I take that as my cue to whisper, "You work with them, remember?"

She exhales and tells him the truth. "I haven't found a reason to move out. I love my town. I love Castleview, and I love my job helping put people into their favorite stories. So I don't need to move. Where would I go? Five feet away?"

She laughs. Storm smiles slightly.

"It's not that I'm not motivated," she explains, sounding like she's worried he'll think less of her. Any man who thinks less of her for that isn't fit to kiss the ground she walks on. "I'm highly motivated. A very motivated person."

"Breathe," I tell her. "Storm doesn't care if you're motivated or not. He's motivated enough for the two of you."

"Not that I'm crazy motivated," she adds, laughing slightly. "But I like having something to do."

"A family is something to do."

Oh, he's going there, is he? Just jumps right in trying to secure his legacy.

She blinks, clearly not expecting a man to mention children on the first date. "I love making potions," she tells him, talking quickly, obviously trying to figure out how to reply to his mention of family.

"Do you?" One side of his mouth ticks up into a smile. "You like playing around?"

"Well, it was more than playing around in high school. I won the state championship."

He quirks a brow, impressed. *Yeah, she's more than what you thought she was, isn't she?* "State champion?"

"Yeah, Devlin and I went. We were fierce competitors back then. That's probably why I pushed myself so hard—because I wanted to beat him. But anyway, I made it, beating him out. I loved potions."

"Why'd you stop?"

She pauses, and I'm hanging on the edge of my seat. I'd like to know this, too, and I'm hoping that I'm not the reason why she gave it up.

There was nothing cuter in high school than seeing Blair with a pair of goggles on, her hair bunched up on her head and her tongue sticking out while she thought about ingredients and how to weave them together.

If I don't stop thinking about her tongue, I'm going to need a cold shower.

Cathy's voice pulls my attention from the talents of Blair's tongue. "Is that Storm and Blair?"

"Oh my gosh." Cherie flicks hair over her shoulder. "It is."

"What do we do?" Sadie says.

"We make sure their date ends in disaster," Cathy says.

Absolutely not. As much as I'd love for it to wind up ruinous —for Storm, that is—I can't have anything happen to Blair.

I suspect that Cathy is the person who told everyone in high school that Blair had used her magic on me. It seems like something that she would have done.

She starts to stalk over to where Storm and Blair are sitting on the bench when I jump up. Cathy sees me. Stops.

"I'm sorry, but Storm Grayson is off-limits," I tell her.

She scoffs. "Who are you?"

"His bodyguard."

Cathy looks me up and down, her gaze lingering on my mustache, no doubt wondering if I'm lying or not. "I have something important to tell him about that woman he's with. Something that could save his life," she adds.

I rub my chin, pretending to think about it. "I'll be sure to tell his twin brother."

Her eyes pop wide. "Twin?"

"Oh yes. His name's *Stan*, and he's around here somewhere. Went to play mini golf, I think. But who knows? He's got so much money that it's impossible to keep track of him."

She frowns, folding her arms. "I've never heard of a *Stan Grayson*. If Storm had a twin, I would know it."

Cathy needs a push. I unleash Blair's magic, closing my eyes so that her friends don't see the change. "Stan Grayson is over by the Tilt-A-Whirl."

Cathy blinks and slowly turns her head. "Yes. Stan. Tilt-A-whirl."

She drifts off while Cherie and Sadie scramble to catch up. "What's going on, Cathy? Where are you going? I thought we were going to ruin Blair," they say, their words colliding and piling atop one another.

"No," she replies, her voice flat like she's been mesmerized. "We're going to find Stan."

Cherie and Sadie exchange a confused look but follow Cathy, because what else would they do?

Crisis averted.

I sit as Blair says, "I stopped working with potions when I started at the bookstore. It wasn't supposed to be my shop, but my older sister didn't have magic. So I was all set to inherit it. You can't be worried about potions when you've got a bookstore to run. So I threw myself into the family business." She tips her head, thinking. It's adorable how she scrunches up her nose as she figures out what to say next. "But then Addison's magic came in and now the bookshop's hers, so…"

"So?" he asks.

She shrugs, smiles. I know what that look means. She doesn't want to give him too much of herself. *Yet*. I consider it a win for me, even if we are friends.

Friends. I've officially entered the friend zone. I would've been happier staying in the enemies zone than being here. This is some sort of bullshit limbo, where I don't know which way to turn. I wish I'd just told her that I didn't regret that kiss. But then she told me that she did, so here we are—me in disguise and her on a date with a man I can't stand.

"So," she continues, "I guess that I just put potion making away." She tips up her face and smiles at him. "I haven't needed to think about it because I've been so busy with books."

Storm stretches out his legs and crosses one ankle over the other. "Well, having your little books is good, too."

Blair frowns, unsure if she should be insulted that he called the Bookshop of Magic a place of little books.

"I know what it is to be conflicted," he explains. "Sometimes an invention calls to me, and when I get into it, I realize that it's not the project that I'm supposed to be working on."

"Really?"

"Oh yes." He tosses his head back, flicking hair from his eyes. "I've been working on this anti-aging formula, and I'd set it aside because I wasn't getting anywhere with it and then suddenly, voila! The answer came."

Blair's gaze cuts to me because we both know how *voila* came to Storm.

"Is that so?" she asks, licking the ice cream off her spoon in big, long strokes of her tongue.

I think I might die.

"Yes." He crosses his arms, getting comfortable on the bench. "I was just daydreaming and bam! The answer came."

She frowns. He doesn't notice. "The answer just came to you?"

"Yes. That's how inspiration can be."

"Sure." She sounds very *unsure*. "I get it." She sticks her spoon into the rest of her ice cream and rises. "Ready to keep going?"

"Want to continue on?"

"Actually I'm getting tired."

He stands and slides his hands into his pockets. "I'll take you home, then."

They walk off and I don't follow. There's no need, because at this point I know that Blair isn't going to let him kiss her, not after he lied like that.

The best thing for me to do—the only thing, really—is to lean back on the bench, stretch my arms over the back of it and bask in this small victory.

That's one point for Devlin and negative points for Storm.

Maybe, just maybe I can turn this whole thing around.

I'm beginning to relax when a message comes over my phone. It's from Hands. He's probably asking when I'll be back. But when I open the message, my heart stops.

There's a picture of Hands beside a broken kitchen window. There's a long cut down his thumb, and blood is gushing from the wound. The words, SOMEONE TRIED TO BREAK IN, are printed below the picture.

Before I can even think, I magic myself away, praying that I reach my friend in time.

21

*A*s I was walking off with Storm, I glanced over my shoulder and saw Devlin look at his phone and then vanish. Instinctively I know something is wrong.

As soon as Storm drops me off at my house, I rush over to Devlin's, racing to his front door.

Have I fallen and hit my head? Why am I so worked up?

Because there is no reason why Devlin would have left in such a hurry unless something is wrong.

"Devlin," I call, entering the house.

"The kitchen," he answers.

Relief immediately floods my body like a shot of adrenaline. He's here. But that relief vanishes when I enter the room and see Hands. A bandage has been placed under his thumb and Hands is shaking—both of them.

Fear lodges itself in my throat, and it takes all my focus to arm wrestle it back down. "What happened? Are you okay?"

Devlin rises from a chair and moves to the sink. "Hands is okay. Someone broke in while we were on your date."

"What?" Hands starts moving furiously. "I think it's saying something," I tell Devlin.

He finishes drying his hands and glances over his shoulder, watching Hands before he looks at me. "Someone broke in. Hands fought them off. The would-be thief wore black, so he didn't get a look at them."

"But who? Why?"

He levels his golden-green eyes on me. "Don't know. I sent the video footage to my security team."

I scrunch my face in confusion. "First of all—you have a security team? And secondly, what about the police?"

He tips his head and shrugs. "In answer to your second question, the police have already been here. To your first question—my security keeps an eye on the house and travels with me when I need them to. The house has many wards on it, so I don't need them here most of the time. But whoever did this broke every single ward, which means they're experienced. It also means that from now on, at least while you're here, someone will watch the house." He wags a finger at me. "I'll give you three guesses as to who's behind this, and the first two don't count."

"It's not Storm," I reply, sounding doubtful even to myself.

"Who else has the most to gain from my inventions?" Devlin counters.

"Storm," I mutter. "But it could be that someone just wanted money—gold, loot, jewels. You're rich. You could have all of those stashed here somewhere."

I pause for a moment before dropping my purse onto the floor and sliding into a seat across from Hands. "Are you okay?" Hands does a little thing that's supposed to be a nod—I think. "Is there anything that I can do?"

He brushes one hand with the fingers of the other, and I get it—it wants a massage. So I give Hands a little semi-massage, making sure to rub between the fingers and knuckles. When I'm done, Hands is lying flat on the table, completely relaxed.

This whole time, Devlin's been watching from the sink, glowering. "Hands, if you're feeling better, why don't you get some rest?"

"I'll put him to bed."

"No," Devlin says sharply. "Hands is perfectly capable of putting himself to bed. Right?" It slowly lifts from the table and shuffles off, leaving the room. "I'll check on you in a bit," Devlin tells him.

As soon as Hands is gone and hopefully out of earshot, I turn on Devlin. "Why are you being so mean? He was just attacked."

"I'm not being mean," he spits. "You just don't need to be giving him hand massages."

I fold my arms with a huff across my chest. "And why not?"

"Because..." He drums his fingers on the counter impatiently. "Because you just don't need to, is all."

I study him. Devlin's jaw is clenching and unclenching, and he's barely looking at me. "Are you...are you jealous?"

He scoffs. "The last thing that I am is jealous. I just don't want him getting used to you, especially since you're throwing in your lot with a man who sends his cronies to break into my home and steal my inventions."

"It might not have been him."

He glares at me. "And who else would break in here?"

"I don't know." I toss up my hands. "Maybe one of your trysts who's gone psycho?"

"Would you quit it with the whole man whore thing? It's getting old."

"Would you quit it the whole Storm-is-horrible thing?"

"No, I won't. You know he lied to you tonight."

"Yes, I know," I screech. Why am I screeching? I exhale a calming breath and drop my face into my hands. "But you can't expect him to say that you bribed him into coming to the ball."

"Oh, I can't?"

I hear Devlin move toward me, so I sit up and there he is, standing beside me with a bottle of wine and two glasses. "Wine?"

"Yes, thank you."

He pours me a glass of red and sits across from me, lifting his ankle and propping it on the opposite knee as I take a swig of wine. It's good. It has alcohol. That is what I need.

The mood settles and I whisper, "I'm sorry about Hands. This is my fault, isn't it?"

"No." He scowls. "It's Storm's fault."

"You don't know that it's him." He shoots me a dark look, and I retreat to my wine, taking another gulp. "How did you meet Hands?" I ask when I sense that it's safe to speak.

Devlin drums his strong fingers on the table. They are so strong. I've always noticed it, but in this second I can't help but admire them. He also has nice forearms. I think most women are attracted to a man's chest, his shoulders, his physique in total, but I love a good strong forearm.

Don't ask me why, and Devlin has awesome ones—they're rock-solid, and the muscles flex when he moves.

He wipes a hand down his tired face and settles back into his chair. It's late, and he doesn't have all the lights on—only a few that are casting an amber glow in the kitchen, making the place feel intimate. It would be perfect if there was food, but earlier I ate a fried sushi roll that was stuffed with crab and cream cheese and slathered in smoky spicy sauce, and I'm so full. But honestly the meal was so good that if it was offered to me again, I'd eat it right now, full or not.

"I met Hands a long time ago, when he was a person."

My heart lurches in my chest. "What?"

He nods. "He helped me when I was just getting started in inventing. He was a good man, a great person, and he had the best advice. His real name is John, but after the accident he didn't want to be called by his name anymore."

"The accident?"

Devlin takes a long sip of his drink. "He was running an experiment on a traveling device. It exploded, taking his body with it, and leaving his hands."

My eyes flare in surprise. It's almost too much for me to even wrap my mind around. "So that was all that was left of him?"

"It was. He had a wife, but when she found out, she didn't want to have anything to do with him. So she abandoned him. I took him, and it was then that he told me not to call him John anymore. Hands was just fine."

My heart is breaking. This is the saddest story that I've ever heard, and Devlin looks broken too, even telling it to me now.

I cover his hand with mine and manage a smile. "I'm sorry."

"It's not me who's had to endure all the pain. It's Hands."

"Not about that. About earlier, when I yelled at you."

He smirks and it's glorious. "Is the great Blair Thornrose apologizing?"

I roll my eyes. "Don't get used to it."

We look at each other and laugh. His eyes hold so much warmth for me, so much that I can barely breathe. Maybe it's time for me to forgive Devlin. The amount of care that he showed Hands proves that he's not as selfish and awful as I've thought for so long. The man has a heart, even if he broke mine.

Maybe it's time that I gave him another chance—a chance to redeem himself. I'm not saying that I want to give myself to him. But maybe Devlin deserves some credit. He is trying to get me and Storm together, and he isn't using my power to frolic with a bunch of women—at least not in front of me.

"I'm sorry about the break-in," I admit.

His jaw flexes as he looks out the window. "I think you could do better."

"Better?"

"Than Storm."

I bark a laugh. "Better than a billionaire?"

"Better," he growls in a voice that makes the hairs on my neck soldier to attention.

Okay then. "Listen, if you find Mr. Better, let me know. Because right now my only option is Mr. Available, and that's Storm Grayson." Devlin's silent for a long moment, staring into his wine. Finally I ask, "Why do you dislike him so much?"

He rubs a hand down his face. "No reason."

"Liar."

I suppose Devlin's already been vulnerable enough with me for one night, telling me about Hands. If he's any more vulnerable, I may take a blow torch to the steel wall I've erected around my heart and start melting that sucker down for scrap metal.

He exhales and shifts in his seat. I sense a conversation turn. "Want to have some fun?"

"Does this involve giant teddy bears?"

"Where's yours, I might ask?"

"I left it on the doorstep of the house and messaged Chelsea about it. She has an affinity for giant stuffed things."

"Uh-huh," he says as if he doesn't believe me.

I poke his leg with my toe. "It's true."

Before I can pull my leg away, he grabs my foot, pulls off my boot, and starts massaging the tendons.

Oh gods. I'm sure my foot stinks. I have, like, loads of feet bacteria. I've met people whose feet don't smell. My sister Dallas is like that. She could wear sneakers without socks for an entire week, never once wash her feet, and somehow they'd wind up smelling like a field of lavender on a sunny day.

Not me.

But if Devlin gets a whiff of foul, he doesn't mention it, and I'm pretty much sure that foot massages are not in the friends department of our relationship.

But oh, oh wow, this feels so good. It feels Meg Ryan fake-orgasm good, except for the fake part.

I melt onto the chair and close my eyes. "What were you saying?"

"I was saying that I have a surprise for you."

"No, you weren't. You were asking if I want to have fun."

I hear the grin in his voice. "*Why* did you ask if you remember?"

I shrug. "This feels so good I can barely think."

"Maybe I should stop."

My eyes pop open. "No!"

He chuckles and drops my foot. Then he stands and extends his hand. "Come on."

I cock a brow. "What kind of fun are we talking about?"

"Not *that,* Miss Dirty Mind. Let's go."

He flexes his hand, willing me to take it. I do, and I shiver at the spark that flies down my arm when our flesh makes contact.

"You okay?"

I shake it off. "Yeah. Fine. Great."

Just trying not to be electrocuted by you, is all.

I drop off my other boot, and he leads me through the house and down the stairs to the basement, which is all high tech with steel walls and doors. I note the scents of cotton and linen as he flips on a light.

"Holy smokes," I whisper.

"Do you like it?"

"I love it."

The room that he's brought me to is filled with built-in

shelves that are lined with jars filled to the brim with potion ingredients.

And they're labeled alphabetically from A to Z. I could kiss him!

But I won't.

"I thought we could play around," he says, rolling up his sleeves, revealing more of those corded forearms. I almost wipe drool from my mouth. When did forearms become the sexiest part of the human body, ever?

My gaze flicks from his forearms (yes, I'm still staring) to the shelves and back to him. "You want to make potions?"

A slow smile curls on his face. "Yes. We can make potions."

Oh, this is too much fun. I haven't been in a room filled with this many ingredients since *never*, and I want to dive right in.

He gestures to a bookcase that's loaded with tomes that have broken, cracked and crumbling spines.

"You've got ancient texts," I squeal.

"I do," he says proudly, crossing over and pulling one off the shelf. "One of the perks of being rich. I can find and pay for one-of-a-kind potion books. If you don't know where you'd like to start, we can search until you find something that sounds good."

"No, I know exactly where I'd like to begin."

He quirks a brow. "I'm intrigued. And where, Miss Blair Thornrose, would you like to start?" I rub my hands together. When I tell him, Devlin laughs and agrees. "Then let's go."

WE DON'T STOP DEVELOPING potions until two in the morning, and that's only after Devlin tells me that I've got to get some rest, that we can't stay up all night. So I grudgingly stop.

But oh, the fun we had. We made potion after potion, and

even tweaked some recipes that were in the books with ingredients that I remembered from my high school days that would work better.

We made potions just for the sake of it—just to watch butterfly wings erupt from a vial, just to smell the ocean in a bottle.

And it was fun.

A lot of fun.

And we laughed. We laughed a lot. Devlin would hand off ingredients to me, and I would crush them with the mortar and pestle, instructing him on what to do next. I haven't felt so good and comfortable in my own skin in, well, years.

I yawn as I enter the bedroom.

"See? I knew you were tired," he chides.

"Yes, I'm tired. But that was great." I glance at him over my shoulder. "Can we do that again?"

"Anytime."

He chuckles as he unbuttons his shirt, and I avert my eyes. Oh my gosh, this man. All I saw was the tan valley between his pecs, and I need the fire department to come hose me down, cool me off.

I really need help.

I turn away and move to unzip the back of my sweater. Yes, I'm wearing a sweater with a zipper. But I can't grab the tab because it's just out of reach.

Suddenly Devlin's sweeping my hair over my shoulder, and his hot hands are on my neck. "Here, let me do that," he purrs in a voice that sounds like sex.

My stomach quivers as he keeps one hand on my neck and slowly unzips my sweater, taking his sweet time, I notice, until it's completely undone.

Speaking of undone, I feel about three seconds away from it.

Kidding. *Not* kidding.

I turn around and he's right there, standing inches away from me, his hazel eyes having gone inky black.

"Thank you."

"You're very welcome." His Southern drawl is pronounced tonight. Probably because he's tired. I'm tired, too. So very tired.

But the thing is—he's not moving away, and neither am I.

"Thank you," I say again, even though it feels like a rock's been shoved into my throat.

"Anytime."

"Not for the zipper. Well, yes, for the zipper. But for tonight, too. For helping me while I was on the date and for showing me your potion room."

He brushes a strand of hair off my cheek, and my knees nearly buckle. "Blair"—wow, the way my spine shudders when he says my name is a power no one else has—"you were meant to be a potion maker. You're a natural, and it's something that I wish you hadn't given up."

I nod and exhale, feeling like I'm releasing an entire atmosphere from my lungs. "I know, but my family needed me."

"I know they're important to you. But *you* need to be important to you, too."

I bite down on my bottom lip. He's right. I do need to be important to me. When did I stop being important?

I know when. When it became clear that I would have to take over the bookstore one day. But now that's not my destiny. Addison's in charge of it. She's the witch the shop is attached to. It's her magic that's making the place work. Not mine, and it will never be mine.

Besides, it's so clear that the customers don't want me anymore. They want her, and her ability to choose their perfect book to read. Who could blame them? If I was faced with deciding which one of us to connect with, I'd pick her over me, too.

But that doesn't mean I have to stay. It doesn't mean that at all.

"You're right," I admit to him. "I haven't considered what I wanted for a long time."

"Maybe it's time you start."

"Maybe so."

"You look nervous. Would you like a dust rag?"

I bark a laugh. "You keep your house so clean that it's hard to find anything worth dusting, but I'm okay. Just tired."

Then he reaches toward me and I can feel it coming—a kiss. Devlin's going to kiss me, even after I told him that I just want to be friends. How dare he?

But I would really, really like to kiss him.

What is wrong with me? We're just friends and barely that.

Oh, who am I kidding? He's becoming a friend, a really good one, and I remember what it's like to be around him, how easily we interact. I never have to think of something to say or work at conversation. It's just easy.

Not like with Storm.

Give yourself a break, Blair. You just met the man.

Yeah, but everything feels so forced.

Must give things time to progress. Storm's clearly interested in me. He has to leave town for a few days, but he promised that when he returned, we'd go out again.

He's checking all the boxes. Wants kids? Check. Good provider? Check. Handsome? Check.

And there will be more things checked off my list as we get to know one another. I can feel it.

But right now Devlin's closing in as he reaches toward me. When he pulls back, he's holding a hairbrush.

I exhale a breath that I didn't know I was holding.

"Brush?"

"Sure." I take it from him. "Thank y—"

Before I can get the word out, a flash flares in my mind, followed by a collage of images that flip like flash cards in my head, moving in sequential order. It all happens so fast that I'm barely able to register exactly what they all mean, and they're gone almost as quickly as they appear.

As the images fade, I'm able to sort it all out and put them together.

"Blair," he says slowly, watching me intently, "did you just have—"

"Yeah." I touch my stomach, stabilizing myself because I'm rocking back and forth. My gaze cuts up to his. "Yeah, I just saw your vision. I know how to fix the womb."

22

"*N*ana, I need you to stand still."

My grandmother hovers in front of me, a skeptical look smeared across her face. She knows I'm up to something; she just doesn't know what.

"Why?"

"I'm going to spray this potion on you, and it'll make you invisible."

She folds her arms. "Are you that ashamed of me?"

"Yes," I deadpan, but then quickly add, "No, of course I'm not ashamed of you; but you know what will happen if the town finds out about your existence."

My grandmother scrunches up her face and scowls. "What? They'll think that our family is cursed and that our daughters are horrible people? Does that sound about right?"

"Yes, it does," I say brightly. "Now. Are you ready?"

"I suppose."

"Stand still." I pull out the atomizer that Devlin had at his house. Who keeps an atomizer? An inventor, I guess. This was the potion that I most wanted to make—to make Nana invisible so that she could walk around freely without ruining my family.

I spritz her with the mist and she instantly vanishes.

"Did it work?" she asks.

"It sure did," Devlin says, coming up behind me. "Are we ready?"

I grin. "I think so. Nana, want to go for a ride?"

I can't see her, but I sure do hear her when she says, "I thought you'd never ask."

Normally we would travel by magic to get to a new location, but Devlin insisted on driving. I didn't complain because it's a perfect winter day for once—not blisteringly cold with a freezing wind chill. A warm front moved in last night, and it feels like early spring.

So he got out his convertible, we picked up Nana and we are heading into the countryside.

As we pass through Castleview, I get a good look at all the charming Tudor-style homes and the shops that line the center of town. Lots of humans are here today, visiting stores, buying clothes and jumping into books.

As my gaze scans the horizon, my phone buzzes. Storm's texting me. Yes, even though we're magical, we still use cell phones.

Had a great time last night.

I type back, *Yes. Thank you for the bear.*

When can I see you again?

My stomach clenches. When *can* he? After the break-in at Devlin's, I'm not sure when I want to see him, if I want to see him at all. *I'm working a lot the next few days. Let me check my schedule.*

Checking my schedule? That's the kiss of death in a relationship. I might as well tell him that I'm washing my hair, like women told guys they didn't like back in the olden days.

Plus, this is real. This is a serious decision I've made. This puts my entire family's magic in jeopardy to simply blow him off.

The weight of that is tremendous It crashes down on me, and I press a hand to my forehead in worry. But as much as I'd love to pursue things with Storm, it doesn't feel right. It just... doesn't. He's fine and all—I mean, on paper he's perfect, but just receiving this text made a sinking feeling open in my stomach.

I shouldn't ignore that. Should I?

But Storm just texts back, *I'll touch base with you when I'm back in town.*

It feels like I've been given a lifeline that I don't want.

"Everything okay over there?" Devlin asks.

"Oh yeah. It's fine." I tilt my head up and get an eyeful of sun that blinds me. "Just checking the sun. It's still there. Working overtime. Go, sun! I knew you could do it."

"Storm texted her," Nana tattles from the back.

Devlin doesn't say anything, and I glance over my shoulder at Nana and scowl at her. No clue if she saw me, but just doing it made me feel better.

We head out of town into the Tennessee country, and within minutes we're flanked on both sides by rolling meadows that were cut for hay in the summer. Large round bales sit on the empty fields.

Horses whip their tails and cows gaze lazily at us as we drive down the four-lane highway before turning off onto a smaller, two-lane road.

The area is simply breathtaking. The road is bordered with pines that stand tall. They remind me of an army of ants lining both sides of the long driveway.

When the trees recede, the view opens up to hundreds of gray grape vines.

My jaw drops. "Your grandmother owns a winery?"

"It's small," Devlin admits sheepishly. "But it pays the bills."

"How do I not know this?"

He winks. "Because my grandmother didn't get it until a few years ago. It was my present to her. She always wanted one, wanted to be like the French, so…"

"So you bought it for her," I muse, my heart warmed by his kindness.

We park and Devlin gets out to tell his grandmother that we're here.

"Try not to shed a tear, dear," Nana quips, ruining the moment. "Remember how much you hate him."

I crane my head around. "If you keep that up, I'll make sure that you stay invisible forever."

"Fine. I'm sorry. But you have to admit, it was nice of him to do."

"It was very nice," I say. "All right. Let's get out and I'll hit you with the antidote."

Five minutes later and Nana looks as good as new—if by new, you mean dead. And a ghost. Perhaps I should say, she looks perfectly Nana.

Devlin escorts his grandmother out of the charming stone home with vines crawling up the sides, to greet us.

"Blair," she says, opening her arms. "It's been so long."

Devlin's grandmother has her white hair pinned up, and she's wearing a long brown cardigan over a green dress. She pulls me into a hug, one that's so warm and soft I practically melt in her arms.

"Good to see you, Lilly."

She puts me at arm's length and studies me. "It's better to see you. I told Devlin he should've brought you by ages ago."

I admire the view of the country home. "You have a beautiful place here."

"It's all because of Devlin. He made my dreams come true." She gives me a wide smile and then turns her attention to Nana. "And Rebecca"—oops, there went her friendly tone. It's turned more chastising. "What do you think you're doing returning as a ghost? Trying to ruin your family?"

"Lilly, if you knew what we were up against, you'd thank me."

"I doubt *they* are," she replies, nodding to me.

Nana shrugs. "My family will come around."

Lilly tosses back her head and laughs. "Come in, all of you. I was just about to make cookies. Blair, you can help me while Devlin does what he needs to."

I shoot Devlin a look that silently asks if he wants me. He smiles warmly, telling me that he has enough to go on to do what we came here to.

"All right, then. Let's make some cookies."

"Have you ever made crinkle cookies?" Lilly asks.

"No. But I rarely ever bake at all."

She tsks. "Baking is one of the things that always made me happy. It would make Devlin happy, too, when he'd come home from school to a house that smelled like sugar."

"Hm. I'm going to have a look around while the two of you bake," Nana says.

Lilly waves her off. "Fine, fine. I'll catch up with you later. You can tell me what heaven's like." She lifts a gray brow dramatically. "Unless you went to the other place."

"Lilly Ross, you know as well as I do that my mortal soul was never in that sort of danger."

The old woman chuckles. "I just like to get your goat. Go on, I'll keep your granddaughter busy while you snoop around my house looking for my secrets."

Nana rubs her hands together like an evil genius. "Oh goodie. I get to pry. See y'all soon."

And without another word, she slips into a wall and vanishes.

For a moment I stare at the spot where she disappeared. "I would have bet that Nana wanted to talk to you before snooping."

"Oh no. Rebecca wants us to get to know one another," she says while pushing a cannister labeled SUGAR toward me. "We need one cup."

"It doesn't bother you that my grandmother has, you know, returned from the grave," I say, sounding all morose and Friday-night-horror-movie-ish with my voice.

"No, no," Lilly replies, smoothing her hands down her apron. "There are worse things in life than a dead relative returning to get her granddaughters married off."

She cocks a brow at me, and I bury myself in measuring the cup of sugar that she'd requested, letting the granules drop like a waterfall into the yellow Tupperware mixing bowl sitting in front of me.

"Now you'll need to sift two cups of flour," she tells me, and I'm relieved that we're no longer talking about my grandmother and marriage.

There's a steel contraption with a crank and mesh on top, and I assume that's the sifter. I go about my chore—I mean, *baking*.

"Aren't you going to ask why your grandmother wants us to get to know one another?" she says slyly, giving me a flirty look.

Well no, I wasn't going to ask, but since she said something… "Why does she?"

"I suppose it has to do with my grandson."

"Oh, of course. But we're not, you know, together."

She purses her mouth like she's trying to hold back a smile as she cracks eggs into her own yellow Tupperware bowl.

Wow. These mustard-yellow bowls must've been all the rage back in the day.

"Why not?" she says.

"Why not *what?*" This little crank thing is harder than it looks. I have to actually work to get the sucker to move.

"Why aren't you together?"

"We're just friends." Great answer because it does give her what she wants to know, but it's vague enough that I don't have to explain anything.

"Why's that?"

I dump another half a cup of flour into the sifter. "Why are we just friends?"

"Mm hmm." Lilly's still cracking eggs, not looking at me as if she's not paying attention, but I know from experience talking to women about relationships that she's probably hanging on every word.

"We're friends because…" Why is this so hard to answer? Why are we just friends? "Well, we dated in high school."

"I remember. Devlin has never been so happy in all his life."

I pause. "As in high school?"

"Yes. When you're done there, we're going to add our wet ingredients to our dry."

"Sure. I'm done."

She scoots her bowl over, and I do as she says, mixing until my hand is tired from working the spoon.

"Now dump it out, but first flour your surface." I do both and she instructs me on how to roll the dough into a ball. "Now wrap it up. We'll let it refrigerate for a few minutes while we drink tea in the sunroom. Then we'll put the dough through the crinkler."

All of that happens and ten minutes later we're sitting in a sunroom that's filled with so many potted plants that this space has instantly become my new happy place.

I'm ready to talk about anything—except Devlin—and

assume that conversation's over until she says, "But back to my grandson—like I said, he was the happiest I've ever known him when you were together. I don't know why you broke up, but he was never quite as cheerful after that. And to be honest, when I saw him happy back then, it was the first he had been so since the dark days with his uncle."

The what? "He never mentioned anything about that."

Lilly stirs honey into her herbal tea. She asks if I'd like some and I decline. She taps the spoon against the edge of her cup and sucks off the honey that's clinging to it. Then she looks around and takes a sip.

"Hm. Delicious. This would be even better with those cookies. But, soon enough. Anyway, what was I saying? Oh yes, about Devlin and his uncle. Did he ever tell you about that?"

"No."

Lilly nods. "Of course not. It was terrible. You see, after his parents died, Devlin blamed himself. He told me what happened, and he told his uncle, too. His uncle, instead of helping the boy through his grief, decided to use him to make money. He wanted Devlin to help him win the lottery. He expected the boy to perform like a trained monkey, and when he didn't, Devlin would be punished."

She shakes her head. "Devlin never told me all of it—but I know there were beatings; he was starved sometimes."

My heart explodes in sadness and anger. "His own uncle did that?"

"Yes," she replies, her tone heavy with sadness. "As soon as I found out, I took the boy away, but the damage was already done. Devlin saw his gift as a curse, and when his uncle got ahold of him, those feelings only intensified."

I could relate to that—kind of. On a very small level. I knew what it was to feel like the gift you'd been given was nothing more than an albatross around your neck. But I didn't know any of this about Devlin.

And it broke my heart.

"It's amazing how well he's turned out, considering," she says, pushing her rocking chair back and forth. "Oh, I know he's dated some women, won't get attached to them for fear of being used like his uncle did to him. But I will say this"—she tips her head to me, and her hazel eyes, Devlin's same combination of colors, are earnest—"he never brought any of those girls to meet me. You're the only one that I met, the absolute only one, and of course, I liked you best. Which I would have anyway, I'm sure, even if there had been others."

"But there have been," I argue. Why am I arguing?

"He's a man. Of course there have been women. But he never cared about any of them. Not like he does about you."

"But he doesn't—"

"He brought you here, didn't he?"

"Well yes, but that's just because…" My voice trails off because I don't know what I'm going to say. I have no idea how to finish this sentence.

She smiles kindly and pats my hand. "Come. The cookies should be chilled enough by now. Let's put them through the crinkler and bake them." She smacks her lips. "Our tea will taste so much better with a hot cookie."

It's impossible not to inwardly chuckle while this sweet old lady takes the reins and steers us back into the kitchen, where she pulls out what looks like a large Play-Doh shape maker that you push dough through a hole.

"Okay," she says, taking the dough from the fridge. She puts it down on the table and removes the plastic wrap. "Now we're going to make the crinkles. This is normally the shape of cheese straws, but I like the shape for a cookie."

She shows me how to load the "gun" and push out the dough. It's surprisingly fun to squeeze dough through the hole and then cut it. It's like being a kid, but much more fun because I actually get to eat the final product.

And while we work, I can't help but ponder on everything that she said. I'm the only woman that Devlin ever introduced to his grandmother? Wow. I don't even know how to unpack this information.

Not only that, but if I ever meet Devlin's uncle, I'm going to kick him in the kneecaps—and the balls. Who forces a child into seeing visions so that he can win money? And who punishes that child when they don't see the future? Devlin was already scarred enough from his parents' death. Then he was used for his gift. It makes me want to strangle something.

But it also makes me realize why Devlin never said one word to me about his power. Why would he have seen it as a gift when all it did was bring him sorrow?

Holy cow. We have more in common than I ever realized. We were both given powers that we saw as curses. So if anyone understood what was going on with me emotionally in high school, it was him.

Worse, it makes me realize that maybe my feelings are becoming more than friendly. Maybe I actually want—

"How's it going in here, ladies?"

Devlin's entrance is so abrupt that I jump out of my skin and drop the dough pusher thingy on the table with a clang. "Sorry! I didn't hear you come in."

"No worries. Hey, are those crinkle cookies?"

Lilly pats his shoulder. "They sure are."

Devlin kisses her soft cheek. "You know these are my favorite. Blair, have you tried the dough?"

"No."

"That's the best part."

Lilly swats at him. "Oh no you don't!"

But she doesn't try hard to stop him as Devlin pinches off a thumb-sized bite of dough, breaks it in half and hands it to me.

"Be warned, you're eating raw eggs," he lets me know.

"I'm warned," I reply with a giggle.

Lilly throws up her hands in mock frustration, but there's a spark of love in her eyes when she looks at Devlin. "You two. Get out of here if you're going to eat all my dough."

Devlin pops his into his mouth and grabs my hand. "You don't mind if I steal her, do you, Gigi?"

"I don't mind. She's been help enough. Come back in fifteen minutes for cookies. Maybe Rebecca will show her face and keep me company while you're gone."

Devlin leads me from the kitchen and glances over his shoulder, grinning. "I can't wait to show you what I discovered."

23

It's just like I saw in my vision. Devlin standing with a book, reading it, in the middle of his grandmother's library.

"It's right here." He points to a paragraph. "It says that stabilization of any sort of magic in flux must have a way to be anchored, and it goes on to say"—his voice fills with excitement—"that the way to anchor it is to create an opposite effect."

I fold my arms. "That's a mouthful. But what does it mean?"

"It means that it needs to be grounded to the earth. Tied to the mother. That's what. What I'm creating is a womb outside of the mother, so it must be tethered to her somehow."

I frown. "But it can't be physically tied to her. That defeats the purpose." He shakes his head, because he's already figured it out and is waiting for me to catch up. Then it hits me. "You mean it has to be tied to her mentally, psychically."

He snaps his fingers. "Yes! That's what we've been missing, and that's easy enough to do. You remember how to tether magic to a person, right?"

"Oh yeah, that's simple. You just create the connection. That can be done with a roping spell or even a potion."

He grins from ear to ear. "See? I knew you were meant to be a potion master. This is it, Blair! The breakthrough that I've been waiting for."

Devlin pulls me into a hug, and maybe it's because of what I've learned about him, maybe it's because it's genuinely a great moment. I am happy for him, so I hug him back tightly, and his arms constrict around me, too. Not in an anaconda I'm-going-to-smother-you sort of way. This is different.

It's full of feeling. It's like all the anger and all the longing that I've been stowing away for literally *years* unleashes. And I feel the same coming from him. His hug has got a thousand *I'm sorries* written all over it, and *if I could take things back, I would,* but I'm happy where we are now, and for some really stupid reason, tears prick my eyes.

I will them to vanish and they do. Stupid tears.

Ever so slowly we pull away, and when I say slow, I mean this happens in super slow motion.

My cheek drags against his sandpapery one. His skin scrapes against mine, and his fingers curl into my forearms as our noses meet.

The air shifts. The feeling in the room becomes heavy as our lips line up. There's this sudden change. It's not like the other night when we made out.

This is different in a way that I can't pinpoint.

We both pause when our lips are only an inch apart. My heart's drumming in my throat. Can he hear it? He can probably hear it. But I can't hear anything except the blood rushing in my ears, and the biggest surprise?

Our lips don't move. They hover exactly where they are as if we both know that we can either move in or we can move away, and neither of us is willing to make such a huge, profound choice.

His breath coils against my skin like home—warm and spicy. But this is wrong, right? I'm supposed to be with Storm. I shouldn't be thinking about Devlin.

Even though every cell in my body is on fire, yelling at me to pull away, I find myself unable to break from the force that is Devlin. He's like a whirlpool in an ocean, pulling ships down to the depths, and I'm a willing vessel, ready to head to my destruction.

Our lips touch. It's impossible to say who moves first. We actually may have moved at the same time. Yeah, that's it. I'm totally not culpable here.

We kiss, and his lips are soft and pliant. And sensual. I'm lightheaded from such a simple meeting of two mouths. I can't think straight because his lips are teasingly good, and everything about this kiss feels right. They're so perfect that they're practically begging for me to kiss them again.

But I don't. I pull away. "Sorry."

"Sorry," he repeats, taking a step back and scrubbing a hand up the back of his head.

We stare at each other for a long time, neither of us moving. I don't know what to say besides what I already have, and I don't want to move because to be honest, I don't want to stop looking at him. Devlin is absolutely, truly beautiful.

It's right here, in this moment, that I realize that I've forgiven him for what happened in high school. Yes, he broke my heart. But I've held on to that for long enough. I'm ready to let go of all that hurt and become someone new, someone who doesn't hate this man.

And craziest of all—I don't actually think he'd use my power for anything devious. Maybe he deserves more credit than I've been giving him.

But that doesn't change the fact that I've got to get married, and even though I may not be sure about Storm, at least he's talked about a future—wanting kids and all that.

Devlin hasn't been serious about anyone in a long time, he said that. He's not wanting to jump into a relationship. Which means that I can't entertain the idea of us, because we don't exist as a couple.

We're still staring at one another when his grandmother calls, "Cookies!"

I inhale sharply and step back as he also retreats. I wink. "Last one to the kitchen's a rotten egg."

And then I scamper off, not looking back to see if he's coming.

24

DEVLIN

*T*wice now we've kissed, and twice now we haven't talked about it. I'm not sure I like the way this is going. But for now, it is what it is.

Rebecca decided to stay with my grandmother. She said that she'd return to the house on her own. Blair questioned what would happen if she got lost, and her nana reminded her that she's a ghost and the Thornroses would love it if she *did* get lost.

Blair agreed. She also told her grandmother that she would give the invisibility potion to the family for their use.

Rebecca scowled at that.

All of that's to say it's only the two of us in the car as we head back to Castleview. Neither of us has said one word.

I've never been one to be intimidated by silence, but it's beginning to weigh on me. "Blair, I—"

"I don't want to talk about it, Devlin."

I give her a side glance. She's staring to the right, watching the sprawling meadows as we drive past them. All her body language screams, *Leave me alone.*

I'm not interested in that. "You don't even know what I was going to say."

"It sounded heavy, whatever it was."

"It wasn't heavy. Look, the more we're around each other—"

"I said that I don't want to talk about it." She glances over, her dark eyes burning with annoyance. The wind whips stray hairs from her braid, and she presses them down, only to have them fly around her head like a halo once she moves her hand. "You're not the man I need."

It feels like I've been punched, slapped and kicked in the balls all at once. Kids, do not try this at home.

I don't know which hurts more—the fact that she's right, or the fact that she said it.

But she is correct, and I'm not fit to be with anyone. I'm not. Never have been. Never will be. I'll die a sad, lonely man. I accepted that a long time ago.

"You're right," I murmur. "I'm not who you need."

She blinks. "You agree?"

"Why not? If we were meant to be together, we would be."

Her expression falls and she quickly turns her face away. "Exactly."

"Right."

"And now you have what you needed me for—the vision. So you can make your invention and move on with your life."

This conversation just went from bad to worse. I'd forgotten about that. But she's not wrong. I now have what I originally asked for, so there's nothing keeping us together.

"You're not worried that I'm going to attempt to impregnate half of Castleview so that I can spread my seed throughout the land?"

She snorts with laughter. Oh wow. I'd forgotten about the snorting. Just adorable. My heart tightens like someone's thrust their hand through my chest and is squeezing it dry.

"No, I'm not worried about that."

"Why the change of heart?"

She shrugs. "Don't know. I just don't think you're going to do it. But you do still have my power."

"I do."

"What does that mean?"

"Ask your nana. She's the one in charge of this, whether it's intentional or not. Now, I'm not saying that she used magic on us. But I'm not saying that she didn't."

Blair sighs and drops her arm on the top of the convertible's door. She lowers her head and rests it in her hand. "Nana will disavow any responsibility. She'll say that she doesn't know how to break this." She sits up quickly, an idea floating about in that brilliant brain of hers. "Maybe you have to influence someone, and then this curse'll be over."

"I've already influenced someone."

"Oh, right."

"What if it was something that would benefit humanity? Like maybe influencing the president to get rid of income tax?"

I tip my head back and laugh. "That sounds like more power than I've got."

She frowns. "You're probably right."

An uncomfortable silence falls inside the cabin. *What do you do now, Devlin?*

You let her go, is what.

This beauty. I can tell myself all day long and say that I don't have feelings for her, but it would be a lie. I should cut her off. Right here. Right now. Let the power fizzle out of me naturally.

But I don't want to. I want her near me day in and day out. I want to hear her snorting all the time. Her snorting is my favorite.

And I want her to help me build this invention that she's been instrumental in.

But is that what *she* wants? Pretty sure when she said that I'm not right for her, she meant it.

You're not right for me, Devlin. Thing is, I'll never be right for anyone *but* her, and I know that.

It's for the best that she feels this way. But that doesn't change the fact that my heart's been ripped out of my chest and is bleeding on the floorboard.

"I'll take you home," I manage without my voice breaking from sorrow. "I'll send over your things later. If you can wait a few minutes to get them, that is." When she doesn't reply, I prod her. "Blair?"

"Yeah," she murmurs. "I don't need all my stuff immediately."

"And you'll be fine with Storm. You don't need my help anymore."

"Yeah, I guess not. I held my own okay."

"You held your own more than okay. You'll be great from here on out. Just be yourself and he'll see that you're amazing. If he doesn't, then he's an idiot."

"Right," she says half-heartedly.

"Don't worry. You'll have that ring on your finger in no time. He's looking to get married. Otherwise he wouldn't be here. Don't lose heart."

"I'm not. I haven't," she adds quickly. She's quiet for a moment before adding, "You'll say goodbye to Hands for me."

"I'm sure Hands would love it if you visited now and then. He doesn't bond with a lot of people. You're one of the few."

I glance over and she's staring out at the countryside, her face turned away. The urge to grab her hand and press it to my chest is so strong it's like someone else has taken over my mind and all they want me to do is touch Blair. Hold her hand.

Run my fingers over her knuckles, kiss the underside of her jaw.

If I don't stop thinking this way, we'll never get back to Castleview.

Stop it, Devlin. Just stop it. She's made her intentions very clear. She does not want me. Period. End of story. It's time that I let her go, and the easiest way to do that is to drop her off at home and forget that any of this happened. Pretend it was a dream.

"Can I call you if I need help with Storm?"

"Sure," I choke out. Great. Now whenever my phone rings, I'll be hoping that it's Blair asking for advice. "Anytime."

Why did I say that? I'll never get over her if we keep in contact.

The truth is, I never got over her the first time. I'll never be over Blair Thornrose. I will want her until the day I die because she's not someone that I could or want to forget about. She's the very air that I breathe, and I want to bury myself in her.

So I'm going to let her go without looking back. It's the right thing to do.

We don't say much else as we drive home. I keep the car just above the speed limit as I don't want to arrive any sooner than I have to.

It's impossible to ignore the heaviness that's settled into both our moods, but I turn on the radio and do my best to ignore it.

By the time we reach Castleview, the mood is so weighted it's nearly smothering. I'm not sure if it's coming from me, her or both of us, but it can't be gone too soon.

Her phone rings as I pull up in front of her house, and she glances down at it, frowns and kills the call. I don't have to ask to know that it's Storm. At least she has the decency not to answer in front of me.

I stop the car, and she slowly gets out and turns around, tapping the top of the door and exhaling a loud puff of air.

"Well, I guess this is it."

"I guess so."

She frowns. "You sure that there aren't any other visions you need?"

"No. In the meantime, do yourself a favor and don't tell anyone about it. Trust me; otherwise, people will want to use you."

Her expression darkens as if she's remembering something, and then she says, "Okay. Right. Thanks."

She turns to go, but I can't release her just yet. "Blair?"

She whips back around fast as a bullet. "Yes?"

"Thank you for everything. Really. I couldn't have had this breakthrough without you."

"You're welcome." She turns around again, stops and faces me. "Devlin?"

Why is my heart thundering against my rib cage? It's beating so damn hard it feels like I might have a heart attack. "Yes?"

She twists her fingers together. "I was thinking. Will you need some help making the invention work?"

I break out into a smile. "Yes, I will. Hands can only do so much. Would you like to help me?"

"I would love—I mean, sure. That would be great."

I grin. "Swing by tomorrow morning and let's see how far we can get."

A wide smile breaks out across her face. "Great. See you then."

Then she enters the house and I drive off, feeling the best that I have in years.

25

For days we work on the womb, but without luck, and without kissing, if you can believe that. Finally I say to Devlin, "Tie the thing to me."

Hands, who's been standing on the counter mixing a potion, stops pouring and turns. He's still wearing the bandage, but the wound is mostly healed. I know because I made Hands show me, which the appendage reluctantly did. Devlin still doesn't have proof about who attempted the break-in. The security images haven't been helpful, and I'm pretty sure he still thinks that it was instigated by Storm.

Speaking of Storm—he's still out of town. He's texted a few times and I've replied—always. But my heart's not in it.

The only thing that my heart is into is making this artificial womb work.

Anyway, Hands is staring at me, stock-still, after I asked Devlin to tie the womb to me.

The handsome inventor has also stopped. He rakes his hair from his face and stares at me in disbelief.

"What?" I ask, not understanding why they look so concerned.

"Tie it to you?" Devlin folds his arms and frowns. "I don't think so."

"Why not?"

Hands makes all kinds of furious gestures that honestly look like he's cussing in sign language.

Devlin picks up a potion book and flips through it, his gaze dropping to the pages. "Hands is right."

"What did he say?"

"He said that it's dangerous."

I point to the pink womb and scoff. "If it's dangerous for me, then it'll be dangerous for a mother. Devlin, you've got to try it, otherwise you'll never know if it's viable. I mean, you can't wait until a baby is born prematurely before testing the contraption. That could be catastrophic."

Hands pivots toward Devlin and signs something. Devlin nods before letting the book fall with a thud onto the table. He shifts his weight from hip to hip, considering, and stares at the book, but speaks to me when he says, "You have a point, but I'm not willing to risk it."

"*I* am."

He drags his gaze from the table up to me. Clearly, this is his way of letting me know that the conversation is over. *Just stare her down and maybe she'll stop talking.* Well, it's not working.

I cross to him and slap my hand over the pages of the book so that he can't read it. "Just try. We can always disengage if it becomes too risky."

He brushes me away, and I wonder if the electrical pulse that throbbed in my fingers when we touched happened to him.

"No."

"Yes," I plead as he takes the thick, dusty tome back to the shelf and slides it between two books before picking out another one. "If you try it on me, I won't sue if things go bad."

He skims the books with his fingers and stops at one with a dark brown binding. He tugs the book out, raises his head and looks at me. "No."

I throw up my arms in frustration. "Hands? Will you please speak to him? He's being completely unreasonable."

"I'm not being unreasonable! I'm being safe."

"Well your safety could cost lives."

He opens his mouth. Closes it. Opens it again, and while looking at me he says, "Hands?" Then he drags his gaze away and studies the creature. "I understand that. But what about— oh, I see. So you've already come up with a plan in the two minutes that we've been talking about this."

I bite my bottom lip in excitement, because it's obvious (hopefully) where this is going.

"Uh-huh," Devlin replies while Hands signs frantically. "You think so? Is that right?" He slips the book back onto the shelf and sighs heavily, dropping his fingers to his hips and tapping them absently.

He's so sexy when he does that.

No, I'm not even going to try to filter that out with an, *I hate him. I can't stand him. Get him away from me. He's the devil.*

I'm past all that. I've seen who he really is—the smart, caring boy that I knew so long ago. Yes, there's been the kissing, but it's more than that. There's also been us spending time together and me seeing how he cares for his grandmother, and it's inspiring how much Devlin wants this womb to work, to *really* work.

Plus, just being in the lab fills me with complete and absolute joy. It also doesn't hurt that whenever I get a hankering to make a potion, he's right here, encouraging me.

"Okay," he says quietly.

My heart explodes with happiness. "Okay?"

"Okay. But"—he points a finger at me—"if anything starts

to go wrong, I'm pulling the plug, and I expect not to hear any whining from you."

I raise my hands in surrender. "You won't. I swear that I will fully comply with everything you say."

He smirks and rubs his chin, a mischievous twinkle in his eyes. "Everything?"

I grab a rag off the table and toss it at him. He catches it against his heart. "Stop it," I say with an eye roll the size of Kansas. "You know what I meant."

"I do." He drops the rag in my hands as he walks past me. "Let's get started."

"Hands, I want you to keep an eye on Blair. If she shows any signs of stress, you tell me immediately. I'll be monitoring the vitals of the womb, making sure it's stable."

Devlin walks around the medical table that I'm lying on and looks down at me. "You're sure about this?"

I bat at his arm playfully, like we're friends or something. "You act like something's going to go wrong." He winces. Why is he wincing? "You'll be here and so will Hands. Everything's going to be fine, okay?"

He touches my shoulder gently. "Anything feels off, you say something immediately, okay?"

"Okay." Everything's going to be fine. Why is he making such a big deal about this? "I'm ready. Now stop being so worried and let's do it."

"You're sure?"

I kick my feet against the table. "Yes! How many times do I have to say it?"

"All right." He gives my shoulder one last squeeze before striding off and letting his hand follow him, taking his warmth and comfort with him. "Hands! Get ready."

Devlin waves his arms over the womb and out from it reaches one long tentacle. With magic he guides the elongating limb to my head, where the soft point of it touches my temple.

A jolt rushes through my body as I merge with the magical machine. I can feel it, sense the fluid sloshing through it, experience its warmth.

"How're you doing over there?" Devlin calls out.

"A okay!" I give him a thumbs-up to prove it. "Just fine."

"You sure?"

"I'm sure."

He monitors the systems of the womb on a holographic screen he's got pulled up in front of him. I can see all sorts of numbers running on it.

He drags his gaze from the screen back to me. "Can you tell me what you're feeling?"

"Connected. I feel like I'm part of the womb. If there was a baby inside of it, I would know, I'm sure."

He tears his gaze from me to where Hands is playing Igor to his Dr. Frankenstein. "Okay, Hands, are you ready to see if it's stable?"

"What? It's not?" I ask.

"We've been holding it together with magic. I'm about to release my own hold on it and see if the womb will remain intact. If it passes that test, then I'll pull the tentacle away and see if it still holds contact with you. If it does, then we've achieved success."

I exhale a breath. My nerves are ratcheted up, because this is it. If the project fails again, I don't think Devlin will continue tinkering with it. He'll give it up, and it will feel like he's given up on a dream. My heart will break for him, because there's nothing worse than giving up something you love.

He catches me staring at him, which I didn't even realize

that I was doing, and my gaze darts away faster than a cheetah on steroids.

"We're about to sever the tie," he tells me.

"Ready over here."

"And...done!"

There's a brief moment where my connection to the womb wobbles like Jell-O, but after a moment of indecision, the connection strengthens.

"How're you doing over there?"

"Great! I still feel everything."

"That's good. Let's give it a moment to stabilize...Hands! How're things looking for you?" Hands gives two thumbs-up. He's carefully watching the womb for any signs of instability. "Are we ready to move on to the last phase?"

"I am," I tell him, tapping my fingers impatiently on the cushioned medical bed. Am I impatient or nervous? Nervous. I want this to work out for Devlin so badly. I want this for him in a way that I never thought that I would, and just being part of it has filled me with a feeling that I haven't experienced in forever—a freeing sort of joy.

Don't get me wrong—I love my job. I really do. It's been wonderful to help customers find the book that they adore and jump into the story. But for the past few months it's been sure drudgery. No one wants my help. I haven't been needed or wanted.

But now, here with Devlin, I've gotten to experience both. He's both needed and wanted my help in a way that I didn't think was possible.

And Devlin, for one, hasn't judged me in all the time that we've been together. We don't even talk about my power. It's like it doesn't exist. Every other guy I've dated, it's felt like I've been like walking on eggshells. *When do I tell him what I can do? How do I explain it without it seeming like I've conned him into liking me?*

But with Devlin things are just…effortless.

"Okay, I'm about to sever your connection," he announces, dragging me from my reverie back to the present.

"I'm here for it!"

He smiles over the holographic screen. "So am I."

My heart flutters. It more than flutters. It does a little hokeypokey and it turns itself around. That's what it's all about!

"And cutting," he says, lifting a hand.

The tether falls away, and for a second my heart races as the connection breaks. It feels like I've been cut off from the source of life itself and I'm falling into a bottomless pit.

But then I bounce back up, and the womb is there. I feel it breathing. I hear the sloshing of fluid inside. If there was a life floating within the fluid, I would feel it, sense it, be connected to it.

"How are you?"

Devlin's standing beside me now. My lids flutter as I breathe through the new connection that's formed with the old one being cast away.

"Blair?" His pitch goes up. "You okay?"

I grin from ear to ear. "You did it. It worked."

He drops his arms onto the table and bends down, placing his chin between the valley of his forearms. "What do you feel?"

"All of it." I wiggle my fingers and toes, just to make sure that it's all real. "I'm completely connected to the womb. I sense all of it."

He smiles and it makes my heart heat up with cozy fire-like warmth. "That's fantastic!" Devlin turns his head, giving me a full view of his beautifully corded neck and profile. "Hands? How's it looking from where you are?"

We get another thumbs-up!

Devlin rises and slaps his hands on the table. "You did it!

We did it! But before we celebrate," he adds, cooling his jets, "I want to make sure it's stable. Let's watch you for at least an hour. Then we'll break the connection."

I quirk a brow. "And after that?"

He winks. "After that, we'll celebrate."

*a*n hour later, Devlin cut the connection.

The invention was a success! At least temporarily. There would have to be more testing, but this was heading in the right direction.

He was elated. So was I.

He claps his hands. "What are we doing to celebrate?"

My phone dings and a reminder pops up. I groan. "Oh. I can't."

His entire body drops, and I feel awful for forgetting about this. "What?"

I scroll down my phone. "I have plans. Feylin and Addison are throwing a dinner party."

"Oh." He slumps against the wall in his living room. He's surrounded by all his inventions. It's very impressive. Makes me feel like I haven't been doing anything with my life. Like maybe I should be inventing a pocket cauldron or something. Oh wait, Devlin already did that.

But he looks so sad, like a lost puppy dog. Can't have that, not on such an important day. "Why don't you come with me?"

He stretches his arms over his head, touching the top of the doorframe. His shirt rides up, revealing a trail of dark golden hair that disappears down into his pants. "You sure?"

I rip my gaze away. "Yeah. I don't think they'd mind, and it'll be fun. You like Feylin and Addison, right?"

"Very much."

"Then come with me. Be at the house at five. That's when we're leaving."

He gives me a questioning look. "You're sure? You're inviting me to do something with your family. You realize that."

I smirk. "Of course I realize that. So come. They'd love to see you. And I"—butterflies flutter in my stomach, so I look down—"I'd like for you to be there."

My cheeks are burning when I lift my head and see him studying me. He blinks, breaking his gaze, and flashes his lopsided smile. "All right. Pick you up at five."

I roll my eyes. "You won't be picking me up. We'll all be going together."

He grins, showing off the dimple in his right cheek. "Then I'll be there."

"YOU DID *NOT* INVITE DEVLIN," Chelsea says, plopping onto my bed and grabbing Mr. Mittens, my stuffed kitten, from on top of my pillow and hugging it to her chest. "Why'd you invite him and not Storm?"

I wrap a strand of hair around the curling iron. Yes, some things you do the old-fashioned way instead of using magic.

"Well, because we made a big breakthrough in his invention today, that's why. Plus, Storm is out of town."

"Sounds like somebody's in love," she says in a singsong voice.

"Stop it." She rolls onto her back and tosses Mr. Mittens into the air. "Be careful with that. He's old."

"Don't worry, I'm not going to harm your stuffie. But what about Storm?"

I shrug. "I don't know. He's great and all, but I don't know…"

He's not Devlin. It's as simple as that. Devlin may not be the man I need, but he's the man I want. The past few days— hell, the past few hours have proved that to me.

Chelsea sits up and stares. "Wait. Are you and Devlin… together?"

"No. No we are not. We are definitely not together. Not in even the closest sense of the word. But we have become… friends, maybe?"

"Friends. I see. Friends who kiss?"

"Quit." I pull Mr. Mittens from her hands and toss it at her. She catches it two-handed. "We're just friends and I only invited him tonight because I promised to celebrate this breakthrough he had with his invention."

"Whose invention?" Dallas asks from the doorway, a tooth-brush in her mouth.

"Blair has the hots for Devlin," Chelsea tells her. "They're smooching."

"No, we're not! We are not doing that, and if you say one word to him tonight, I'll hide all your nail polish."

Her jaw drops. "You wouldn't."

"I would. I'd even hide Cajun Shrimp."

She gasps. "But that's the best color."

"I know."

Dallas laughs. "You can have all my nail polish."

Dallas is the tomboy in the family. Very little interest in makeup, doing her hair—all of it.

"Anyway," I say, finishing up my curls. "Isn't it almost time?"

Chelsea jumps up. "Yep! Let's find you something to wear."

"Why can't I go in this?" I joke, flashing my bathrobe.

"Because it's going to rain," Dallas says, walking away. "I gotta go spit."

Chelsea drops Mr. Mittens onto my bed and heads to my closet. "Let's see. What should you wear?" She grabs a yellow sundress from the rack and spreads it over her chest. "It might be winter here, but it's summer in Feylin's garden. So, this. You should definitely wear this. It shows a lot of shoulder, and your boobs look great in it."

I laugh. "My boobs look great in it?"

"Yes, they do," she confirms.

"Fine. Now get out of my room so that I can finish getting ready."

Fifteen minutes later I'm downstairs with the rest of my family, including Nana, who keeps shooting me funny looks. It feels like she wants to ask me something but doesn't have the nerve to do it.

Surprising, I know. Since when does social etiquette stop my grandmother from anything?

My mother's wearing a blue wrap dress that cinches at the waist, and my dad's in a blue shirt with a sports coat over it.

Mama steps up. "Are we ready?" Oh, I hadn't noticed her strappy heels until now. They're adorable. Almost as cute as mine.

Just kidding. They're cuter.

"Wait." I clear my throat. "We're waiting on one more."

"Who?"

The doorbell rings and Dad walks to it. "I guess this is our mystery guest?" He opens the door and pauses. "Devlin. What a surprise to see you."

Every head turns to me. Even Chelsea and Dallas, who already knew about this, of course. "I invited Devlin. Addison told me that I could bring someone."

"But I thought you'd be bringing Storm," Nana whispers in my ear.

I'd elbow her if I could—old or not.

Mama approaches Devlin with a wide smile on her face. "Devlin, good to see you. Everyone, say hello."

All five of my sisters give a round of *hellos,* and Devlin greets them in return.

Mama clasps her hands in front of her. "Are we ready then?"

Devlin threads his way through my sisters to stand by my side. "You look pretty," he whispers.

"So do you," I say with a wink.

He grins and little bluebirds flutter in my stomach.

He's showered since I last saw him. His hair's brushed back and his shirt collar lies open, revealing just enough tanned skin to make me want to see more.

Before I'm allowed to think too much about Devlin's naked flesh, my mother says, "Then it's time to leave."

She claps her hands, and a halo of magic drops on me. I'm sucked from my spot in the middle of my living room.

Next stop, the castle on the hill.

27

"Blair, it's so good to see you." Addison kisses my cheek as we hug. "You look beautiful." Her gaze swishes from me to Devlin and she beams. "And you brought my favorite wizard."

Devlin grins and hugs her. "Good to see you, Addison. These are for you."

He produces a dozen yellow roses and she gushes. "Thank you. That's very thoughtful. Come in. Come in, everyone. Feylin's outside with Ryals. I think they're playing hide-and-seek."

We head through the castle that's all vaulted ceilings and tall windows, out to the garden, which is lush with blooming magnolia trees, fragrant gardenias and colorful crepe myrtles, not to mention the many rosebushes and hedges that make the space absolutely delightful.

Feylin picks up his little cousin, Ryals, and places him on his shoulders. Then he makes his way over to us, beaming. "I'm just getting the barbecue started. Who wants steak?"

There are many *yes, pleases* to that, and Feylin puts Ryals down so that he can properly greet us. When he gets to

Devlin, he invites him and my father to help him with the barbecue.

"Someone said trucks keep dropping onto Main Street, just appearing with magic instead of driving in," Dad murmurs to Mama before walking away. "Sounds dangerous. Reminds me of how dragons act."

"Yes, dear," she says, patting him on the shoulder. "Go do some manly cooking."

"I'm serious, Clara," he insists. "I heard about it happening just this week."

"Well I haven't," Mama counters.

Dad shrugs and wanders off. Devlin smiles at me before meandering to help.

I find Addison fidgeting with the table settings. "Feylin's barbecuing?"

She laughs. "He's very hands-on for a king."

"And for a fae."

My sister grins. "I can't say you're wrong. Here. Help me inside. I've got some salads to put together. We wanted to do this ourselves, so we gave the servants the night off."

She takes my hand and pulls me into the kitchen. Everyone else stays outside, enjoying the warm air. It is a nice change from the cold. My sisters seem to be especially enjoying it as they fight over the hammocks while my mother spends time with Ryals, who's become her adopted grandson. It's very sweet.

Addison shows me a bowl of tomatoes and asks me to cut them in half while she slices a roll of mozzarella.

"So, Devlin," she remarks, brow curled.

"Oh, as if you have any room to comment. You're the one who made me take him the books that Nana ordered. And just so you know, I'm not happy that you knew about her existence and didn't tell us."

She flashes me a sweet smile. Addison is a good, kind person, the sort of person that it's impossible not to love.

"Nana made me promise not to tell."

I grab a celery stick and chew it loudly. "So you say."

"But Devlin?"

I finish eating the celery and pick up a tomato. "I don't know what the big deal is. So I brought him. I've been helping him with an invention."

"You have?"

"Why do you sound so happy?"

She scoffs and layers cut circles of cheese in a glass platter. "Because you love working with magic. You used to be so great at potions before you..." She wrinkles her nose. "What did happen, there?"

"She went to work for your mother, and she didn't have time to do it anymore," Nana tells her.

Where did she come from? The wall. She literally slipped through the wall to interrupt this private conversation with my sister.

Addison frowns. She's so pretty, even when she frowns. She's got auburn hair, brown eyes, skin that will fry if it even sees a peek of sunshine, and she's got just the sweetest personality. Before Feylin met her, he was a big old grump. I'd never spent any time with him, but all you had to do was look at the man to know that he was grouchy inside and out.

But now he's a big old teddy bear. Her teddy bear.

"But you don't have to be at the bookstore as much as you used to. I'm there now. In fact, you could pursue potions or something else if you wanted." She sighs. "I know that for a long time you were obligated to work at the shop, to make it your life. But it doesn't have to be that way anymore."

"Yes, Blair," Nana adds, eying the mozzarella like she's about to steal one, "the world's your oyster. What used to be true isn't, and what isn't true, is."

"What does that mean?"

She scowls at me and I wink. "I get it. You're talking about Devlin."

My grandmother lifts her transparent hands. "Now why would I ever be talking about him?"

"Would you quit? You've been trying to get us together ever since you came back."

She smooths a hand over her hair. "I have no idea what you're talking about."

Addison takes a handful of the tomatoes and layers them on top of the cheese. "You do make a handsome couple."

"We are not a couple. I only brought him because I helped him make a huge breakthrough in an invention. He wanted to celebrate, but you'd invited us to this, so I invited him to come. End of story. Would everyone stop acting like it's such a big deal," I announce, thwacking the knife on the cutting board.

"Touchy, touchy," Nana whispers.

Addison nods toward the kitchen window. "They do look comfortable, don't the three of them?"

Outside, Devlin's with Feylin and my dad. The three are holding sweating beers and standing by the grill. It's about as suburban a picture as you can get for magicals.

And as much as I hate to admit it, Addison's right. They do look very, very comfortable.

"Come on," my sister says, pulling my attention from the window. "Help me make a green salad. And Nana, if you're not in here to help, go outside and make yourself busy."

"I know when I'm not wanted," my grandmother mutters as she slinks through the wall.

Addison just rolls her eyes, and we share a laugh.

AFTER HELPING Addison in the kitchen, I head outside, where Devlin sees me. He strides over, slips his hand down mine, which makes fireworks explode on my skin, and whispers in my ear, "Why don't we explore the grounds?"

"But dinner's about to be served."

"We won't go far," he promises, dragging me off.

It's impossible not to giggle as we walk through the hedges. He asks me what I've been doing these past ten years besides working, and I don't have an answer for him. He tells me what *he's* been doing, which is impressive enough to make me want to hide under a rock, but he also admits that his life has been lonely.

"But I do have my grandmother," he says.

Her words about his uncle bounce around in my head, and my heart aches for him. Since he hasn't said anything about what happened, it doesn't feel right for me tell him that I know. So I stay silent.

While we walk, he holds my hand, entwining his fingers through mine. It's a rush, this jittery feeling that's inside me, and I don't know what any of it means.

But I also don't pull my hand away, because even though my chest is exploding with butterflies, dragonflies and small birds, this feels right.

Okay, so I *do* know what it means, but I don't know what *we* mean. I've told him already that kissing him was a mistake (and it was, right?) but I'm letting him hold my hand and relishing his warmth, this feeling of bliss. It could all be fake. It could all be temporary, but right now I'm soaking it up.

"It's a beautiful evening," he says.

"It is. So beautiful. And a great view."

He stares at me, and I feel a blush creep across my cheeks. "It is beautiful." Somehow I don't think he's talking about Feylin's garden. He points to a tall hedge. "What's that?"

"A maze. Do you want to do it?"

"Yeah. I'd love to get lost in a maze with you. No telling what kind of trouble we could get up to."

"Devlin—"

"What?" He turns to me and stops. "What? What is so bad about going into a maze with me?"

My heart squeezes so hard that my entire chest cavity hurts. That's when the fear hits me. Fear that the past will repeat itself, fear that none of this is real. But it is, isn't it?

I'm simply not ready to take the leap to find out. "It's just... we've been here before, and you..."

He nods. "I get it. You're right. Maybe it's for the best if we remain friends."

"Friends who hold hands?"

"You caught me." He stares at me a moment, his eyes searching mine for something. "Listen, Blair, there's something you need to know." His gaze drops to my hand, and he runs his thumb over my knuckles.

"So serious," I joke. "What is it?"

"There's a reason why we broke up."

Why is he dragging this up from the pits of hell? Immediately my heart jackhammers against my chest. I don't want to talk about this. We've come so far.

"Devlin, all that was a long time ago."

"Yes and no." With his free hand he tucks a strand of hair behind my ear. "Blair, look. I feel like you're wishy-washy because of me, and I'll be honest, for a long time I've run away from feeling anything for anyone."

Oh my gods. He's pouring his heart out. Right here. In Feylin's garden. This is not what I planned on. I'm not expecting this. But what do I want to do about it? Make him stop?

No. Devlin broke my heart. I loved him. *Loved him.* Like first love kind of love. The love you never get over. The love you never forget. The love that settles into your bones and deposits there like minerals that fuel every single blood cell that makes up your body. He was my very essence for existing, my happiness.

And all that was snatched away.

And here I've been given a second chance with him. Yes, I hated him. Or thought I did. Really it was just my wounded heart that was still licking its wounds ten years later.

We've been given this time, and clearly there's still something between us. But at every opportunity I've told him to bug off. I've said that he's not right for me.

What if I've been wrong? Maybe it's time to hear him out.

"Why have you run away?" I ask.

"Because I never got over you."

It feels like an anvil just dropped on my head. "You what?"

"I've always cared about you, Blair." Emotion flashes in his eyes, and the way he's looking at me makes me glance down. It's so intense. This moment. This isn't what I expected would happen tonight. "I've never been able to let you go." He leans back and laughs bitterly. "No matter how hard I tried."

"I don't understand." Now I'm just angry. He's telling me he's always cared about me, but he cheated on me. What in the world? "Why'd you kiss Basheen? Why'd you do that?"

He grazes his fingers up my arm and lifts the strap that's fallen, slipping it back over my shoulder. "That wasn't what you—"

"Dinner's ready!" Addison calls. "Come on, y'all!"

My emotions are a knotted ball of twine with a kitten tangled up in it. "We'll talk after dinner."

"Okay." He nods, but his mood has shifted. He looks disappointed, like he's waiting for his own anvil to drop.

We all sit outside at the table that Addison's decorated. It's lovely. Cut hydrangeas are stuffed into mason jars. They make a line down the center, with food sprinkled between them. And what a spread it is—chicken and steak, with potatoes and fresh vegetables, and of course the mozzarella and tomatoes.

Devlin sits beside me, and I don't know what to think. I'm so confused. Why did he dump me if he's always cared about me? Why did he decide to tell me *right now*, in this moment? When we're not even alone and can talk about it?

Yes, I'm irritated, but I'm also heartbroken. We've wasted so much time. There are so many years we missed. I don't understand any of it.

But I try to arm wrestle all of that out of my mind and just focus on the food, which now I have little appetite for.

Devlin sits beside me, talking to my dad and keeping his knee pressed to mine. Even though I'm irritated, I don't move. I like the way he feels against me. I like touching him. It feels natural. It feels right.

The sound of silverware ringing against a glass steals my attention.

Feylin and Addie rise. "There's a reason why we asked you here," Feylin says, wiping his mouth with his napkin and glancing at Addie.

She's beaming at him, and the love in both of their eyes nearly brings tears to mine. *This.* This is what I've always wanted. I've always wanted to find my other half, and when I do, I don't want to let him go.

I envy them, but I don't harbor envy *against* them. Addison and Feylin are perfect for each other, and I'm honestly elated that they're together.

Feylin looks at her and she beams. "We have an announcement."

Mama shoots Dad a look and he just shrugs. No one was expecting this.

Then in unison, our hosts say, "We're pregnant!"

The entire table erupts in applause and shouts of joy. I hoot and holler along with everyone, so happy for them. Addison, a mom! *Me,* an aunt! I can't wait.

We all rise and give hugs and congratulations. When it's my turn, I wrap up my sister tightly and whisper, "I'm so happy for you. I can't wait to spoil him or her."

She pulls back, dragging her hands down my arms. She gives me a huge grin. "I can't wait for you to spoil my baby, either."

As the congratulations go on, I step off to the side and head back to my chair. I'm almost there when an explosion rocks my head.

A bright light flares like a supernova, and when it recedes, I see Devlin. We're talking about something. We're happy. I'm happy.

It's nighttime. The ground is wet. The air smells like rain. My arms are sticky from the humidity.

I walk away from him, out into the street, but turn around to give him a smile. Then a bright light's shining on me, and when I turn to look, lights are bearing down, a horn's blaring, and then everything goes black.

The vision disappears, winking out like a light. I am not okay. I grab hold of the table, sucking in air and clutching my trembling hands to my chest to ease the tremors that are racking my body.

I suddenly understand why everything happened the way it did with Devlin. All of it makes sense now.

My heart is beating frantically. I search him out, and when we lock gazes, his eyes flare with worry. He knows I've seen it. He knows I've seen his secret, and nothing will ever be the same.

28

"*L*et's go to the maze," I tell Devlin after dinner's cleaned up.

I've been silent for the past hour, replaying the vision in my head. Devlin's attention has been stolen by my dad, who wanted to talk about inventions and dragons. I don't know how those two work together, but in my dad's mind they must.

Outside, the air's thick. It's going to rain. When we arrived, the sun hadn't fully set, but now the sky's inky, and not a star nor the moon can be seen.

"Blair—" he murmurs.

"The maze," I say. "I thought you wanted to go."

"I do." His eyes cut to my face, and he must see the hard set of my mouth because he says, "Okay. Let's do it."

The maze hedges are tall, at least nine feet, and they're so thick that you wouldn't want to try pushing your way through them to reach the other side.

The walkway's glowing with footlights, and the inside is bright, yet it's intimate, like even though my family's only a few yards away, it feels like Devlin and I are in our own universe.

He exhales a slow breath as soon as we step on the pebbled path. "You *know*."

I fold my arms. "Know what?"

He rolls his eyes. "*The* vision. The one with you in it."

"You mean the one where I get hit by the truck?"

He winces. "That's the one."

He's not looking at me, and I want him to. I desperately need him to look at me. I want to be wrong on this more than I've ever wanted anything, but there's no way that I am.

"When did you first see it?"

He's staring straight ahead. "When do you think?"

"I wouldn't know, Devlin. Just answer."

"The day before you saw me with Basheen."

I'm furious. I'm just so mad that I can't even speak to him right now, so I keep walking. He keeps walking. We do this in silence until we're well inside the maze.

"If we stay to the right, we'll eventually get out," he tells me.

He veers right and I follow, but if we leave too soon, we won't have this conversation, and I need to have this conversation.

So I stop and he stops. He turns around.

"Is that why you did it? Why you kissed her?"

He looks away, giving me that beautiful profile. "Blair, I was going to tell you all of this earlier, before we got interrupted, but now you're pissed off, and you're not going to listen to me. Maybe we should talk about this in a couple of days after you've had time to cool off."

How dare he assume how I'm feeling right now! Even if he is right about me being pissed off. "I don't want to talk about this in a couple of days! I want to talk about it now. I want to know it now! Tell me everything. I deserve it. You don't get to tell me that you've always cared me, and then not give me all of it, Devlin—all of you. That's not fair."

He bobs his head and slowly drags his gaze from the hedge back to me. "Okay. All of it?"

"All of it."

Thunder rumbles overhead. It sounds far away. He looks up, studies the sky and says while he's still staring up, "The vision came the day before you saw us together. I woke up and saw it, and it scared the shit out of me. It scared every molecule in my body. Shit, Blair. I didn't know what to do. All I could think about was the vision that I lost my parents to, and how I could have stopped that from ever happening."

"You were too young to know that," I attempt to soothe him. No idea why, because I'm royally pissed right now.

"But I wasn't a kid when I saw yours, and I wasn't going to let anything like that happen to you. And you saw the vision, so you know that we're together in it—really together. So I asked Basheen to meet me and paid her to make it look like we were kissing."

My jaw drops. "You *weren't* kissing her?"

"Gods, Blair." He tips his head up and shakes it back and forth like he's damning the gods above for handing him a horrible lot in life. "Do you think that you're so easy to give up on? To forget about? You owned me. You still own me. I've just spent ten years trying to deny it."

Fat raindrops splatter on my arm. A few at a time, then the sky opens like it's been slogging through a repressed memory and it's finally made the breakthrough in therapy that it's been working toward.

I completely understand the feeling.

"Yes, I did think that I was so forgettable," I tell him. "I believed it, because the next thing I knew, everyone was whispering how I'd influenced you into caring about me."

His hair's wet. His shirt's soaked. He takes a step forward

as water drips off him. "Do you think that I ever needed magic to fall in love with you?"

And right there, my heart cracks open. It feels like a rocket just blew it up. My lower lip trembles, and I have to choke down a sob. "Why? Why did you keep this from me? Not the part about the rumor. You've already explained that. But all the rest of it?"

Oh, I'm soaked now. My skin's slick and it's pouring. No longer are there just a few raindrops. We're in the middle of a torrential downpour, which the South is known for. These sorts of storms are epic for causing flash flooding.

Rain splatters the grass. It pelts my skin. My feet are soaked in my shoes, and my hair's plastered to my face and neck like leeches.

"I didn't want you to be hurt," he yells over the sound of the rain. Water falls from his hair like he's in the shower. "The vision I had was clear—if we stay together, you die. End of story. I'd"—he looks away, chokes on his words, looks back and drops his voice—"I'd already lost two people that I loved. I refused to let another person die. I couldn't go through it again. Not like that. My heart couldn't take it."

He looks at me, emotion swirling in his eyes. I feel the same way. My heart can't take much more of this, either. For so long I'd wanted him—for ten years. So much time. Okay, yes, I'd hated him. But I'd only hated him because I wanted him so much. Because I cared for him so deeply.

"All my life," I shout, and then choke on the words. The rain is seriously hammering us, but neither of us is moving. I'm sure the earthworms are trying not to drown, but not Devlin and me. We're holding our ground in this standoff.

"All my life," I begin again, "the way was decided for me. When Addison's magic didn't come in, I became the next in line to take over the bookshop. There's was never a question about what *I* wanted. My life was planned out. And then this whole thing with the balls—it's the same. Get married, Blair! It's your turn! Maybe you'll be lucky and Storm Grayson will want you. It's not about what I want. It's never about what *I* want. Even with you"—my words come out strangled in my throat as tears push against my eyes—"you made this decision without me. You decided what was best for me without asking, and that's not fair. For once, I want a choice in what happens. I want to be the one deciding."

He plows his fingers through his hair. "You don't get to decide if you die. Not when I can save you!"

This man! Doesn't he understand what I'm telling him? Furious, I march over, my feet splashing in pools of drowning pebblestones.

"No, you don't get to decide for me, Devlin. You denied both of us happiness for the past ten years. You took that away from me. You took it away from *us!* What gives you the right?"

"Your life," he roars. "That's what gives me the right."

I shake my head. "I'd rather have one day of happiness, one day of knowing that I'm loved and in love, than a lifetime without it."

He blinks, raindrops dripping from his thick lashes, and looks away. "Blair…"

"No, Devlin. No." I grab his face and turn it until he's forced to look at me. "I understand why. I do. But ever since I lost you, my heart's had a hole in it the size of Kansas, and I've never even *been* to that state."

He laughs and then goes very still. His eyes search mine, and they fill with so much worry and regret that it makes my heart knock against my ribs.

"I never wanted to let you go," he admits.

"Then don't. Don't let me go, Devlin. You did it once. Don't do it again."

I'm begging him. I really am. I'm pleading with every cell in my body. Every part of me wants him. I've always wanted him, and I've always been so jealous of every woman he dated after me.

His gaze drops to my mouth, and when his eyes flicker back up, there's heat in them. I grab his soaked lapels and tug him forward, my mouth tipped toward his.

"Don't let me go, Devlin. I can't go through that again."

He lifts his hands and cups my face; then he drops his mouth to mine and kisses me.

29

$\mathcal{W}$e don't bother searching our way out of the maze. Devlin magics us back to his house, directly into his bathroom. It's dark, but there's enough light breaking through the window that I can make out his silhouette.

We're kissing. We haven't broken apart in minutes, and I don't want to stop—ever. His tongue sweeps into my mouth, and a little moan whimpers out of me.

He smiles against my lips and curls his fingers under the spaghetti straps of my dress. His fingers are soaked. My dress is soaked. Water trickles down my legs and back. Rain falls from his hair and splashes gently onto my cheeks.

This is the hottest moment ever.

He tugs the straps down, and his mouth drops from mine to caress my neck before he brushes kisses on my shoulder.

"I've loved you since the first day we had potions together," he murmurs against my skin, making goose bumps ripple across my flesh.

I smile so wide it hurts. "For that long?" I say breathlessly as his hands slide up my sides and his fingers lazily graze over my breasts, sweeping across my nipples. Even through the fabric they're pebbled and sensitive, aching for him. In fact, all of me is aching for him. My panties are soaked, and not from rain, as pressure builds between my legs.

"Mm, for that long," he confirms.

It's almost impossible to concentrate, but I recall when I first felt something for him. "I fell for you when we were lab partners and you suggested that we make the leapfrog potion."

"Because we had extra time," he says huskily before nibbling my shoulder.

I moan and drop my head back as my skin lights on fire. "And then you gave the potion to Cathy," I recall with a laugh.

"She was hopping for an hour," he replies, chuckling into my flesh.

"We were lucky Mr. Spencer believed that it was all an accident."

"You were such a teacher's pet," he murmurs.

"We were so bad back then."

He pauses, pulls his lips from my shoulder and looks at me. "I want to be even badder now."

A deluge of moisture liquifies my panties.

He kisses me and when we part, I grab his bottom lip between my teeth. I sink my fingers into his waist. He sucks air in surprise and grabs my face, plunging his tongue into me, which makes my insides somersault.

He kisses me deeply, and I entwine my fingers in his hair. He wraps his arms around my waist and pulls me to him, marrying me to every hard surface that is Devlin, including his cock, which presses against my stomach like a lion in my pocket and baby he's ready to roar, to quote the great artist formerly known as Prince.

My mind's swimming and everything's fuzzy. All I can think about is that I'm kissing Devlin and I don't hate him anymore. He's always loved me. *Always loved me!* Why have we waited so long?

It's been so stupid. We've been so stupid, and I'm tired of playing games and pretending like I hate him when he's who I want.

I push his jacket off his shoulders and unbutton his shirt. He helps, and something feverish takes over both of us, as if we'll never get this moment again if we don't make the most of it now.

He sheds his shirt, and it drops with a plop onto the floor. I undo his belt and unbutton his pants. The whole time our mouths stay feverishly connected. It feels like if we break apart, this moment will dissolve and we'll never get it back.

His pants drop and he kicks them away. My fingers skate down his chest. His stomach flexes as I rake my fingers down to his boxers and push them off. His cock springs forward, and I take it in my hand.

Devlin hisses as I wind my fingers down the silky flesh.

He lets me touch him for a breath before stepping back. "You keep doing that, and I won't last two seconds."

I wait to see what he'll do next, and I don't have to wait long. He rakes his hand up my cheek into my hair and kisses me. He stops, presses his forehead to mine. Then he tugs down the straps of my dress and pulls it down.

Cold air splashes over my nipples, which somehow manage to grow even harder once they're naked. Devlin takes his time teasing off my clothes, and when he tastes my nipples, I just about explode right then and there. But I bite down the ecstasy and moan as his hands wind their way down my body, feeling every inch of me as he goes.

"You are so beautiful," he whispers at my feet. "A woman to be worshipped."

It's the most amazing thing that anyone's ever said to me.

He takes my hand, and I step out of the dress. And then here we are—naked in front of each other.

And I want him.

There's a split second where I know this can go one of two ways—slow and easy, or passionate, where I release all the pent-up sexual frustration that I've been housing for this man for the past ten years.

Let's just say I go with the latter.

So I throw myself on Devlin, crushing my mouth against his. Lucky for me, he does not seem unhappy about this development. He grabs my thighs and hooks them around his waist.

"I cannot wait a moment longer for you to be inside me," I say into his mouth.

He groans as his kisses become more feverish. He pushes me against the tile wall. My fingers rake across his back, doing everything they can to get him closer. I cannot have too much of him. I've waited so long for this. My breasts are aching. My sex is swollen. I want all of him and I want him now.

"You sure?" he says.

"I'm sure."

He pulls back and stares at me. Moonlight slides across his face at an angle. I can only see one of his eyes, his nose and chin.

"I haven't been with anyone in a year," he tells me.

I understand what he's saying. "I have protection."

Then I kiss him. Can we please just get on with it? I'm dying here.

He presses my back into the wall, hooks his fingers into my ass and then slides his cock into me.

I gasp for air as he stretches me. Oh. My. Gods.

Devlin was my first love. The man I lost my virginity to. But when we did this in high school, it was not like this. That was two young kids trying to figure everything out.

Now Devlin's a man, and his cock feels like it's about a

thousand times bigger than it was back then as he slowly plunges into me.

"I want you to come," he whispers, sliding in and out. I think I'm going to die. "Touch yourself."

I pause as my brain clicks into gear. He said words. Did he say what I think he said?

"Touch yourself," he repeats.

My brain has sex fog clouding it, but I manage to think— *how the holy hell am I supposed to do that?* I can't even formulate a sentence.

"Blair," he growls when I don't move. "I've got you. You're not going to fall."

I pull my hand from his back and rub my clit as he slowly eases in and out of me.

"That's my girl," he whispers.

This is the sexiest thing I've ever done. I suck air and my entire body quivers.

"Come for me, darlin'. Come for me and let me hear you."

One part of me wonders about Hands, but I figure he probably has a soundproof room given that I wouldn't be surprised if Devlin's other lovers have done quite a bit of screaming over the years.

For once the thought of them doesn't bother me.

"I want to hear you."

It's his husky voice, our slick bodies, his giant cock, and the fact that I'm touching myself in front of him—it's all of it that makes me cry his name as I'm shattered apart in his arms.

"So beautiful," he murmurs as he kisses me back to life.

"Come for me, Devlin," I say between kisses.

"I want to come only for you." It sounds like a sacred confession, like he's admitting his deepest feelings, and when he does come, when he plunges into me so hard and fast that I can barely breathe, it feels like we're beyond this world and touching the source of all life.

He finishes and collapses on me, dropping his face to my shoulder. I hug him close, and he holds me pinned to the wall for a few seconds before straightening and walking me to the bed, where he gently lowers me onto the mattress.

Without a word he grabs a towel and cleans me up, taking his time on all my sensitive parts. Then he pulls back the covers and we get under. He snuggles close, pulling my back against his chest and kissing the spot behind my ear.

"Next time"—he nips my neck—"I'm going to taste every part of you."

"I'll let you," I confess.

We fall asleep. When we wake up it's a few hours later. Even though it's still dark outside, Devlin keeps his promise, feasting on me until I'm ripped apart all over again.

And I return the favor.

30

The next morning Devlin makes pancakes and we eat them in bed.

"I didn't know you could cook," I marvel as he enters the room, boxers low on his hips, hair messy, which fills my brain with lusty thoughts.

He grins, his teeth and eyes flashing. "You can't be a bachelor for too long and not know how to cook. Hands can't be expected to do everything around here."

It's impossible not to laugh as he settles a tray over my hips and hand feeds me strawberries dipped in whipped cream. It's delicious.

The whole morning is lazy. My mom calls to make sure that I'm okay. You know, since we left without telling anyone, and I assure her that I am with Devlin, safe.

And I am.

We're in no rush to leave each other. It feels like I've been starved of him and now I've been served a Devlin buffet, and all I want to do is feast.

It's after breakfast that he broaches all the subjects.

"What about Mr. Grayson?" he asks, studying my hand before rubbing his own over it.

I sit back against the pillows. I'm wearing one of his button-down shirts; it's big and comfortable. It also smells like him. I will never take it off.

"What about him?" I tease.

He rolls his eyes. "Are you making me have *this conversation* twelve hours after I first brought you home?"

A smile plays on my lips. "You're the one who brought it up."

He rolls onto his side and drops his head onto his hand. "Okay, then I'm bringing it up. Please tell Mr. Grayson that you are taken and that he will have to move on to greener pastures."

"Aye, aye, captain." I push him with my toe. "See? Was that so hard?"

"That was the easiest of what we've got to talk about."

"Stop. Just stop. If you're going to bring up that vision—"

I lightly jab his chest, and he takes my hand and kisses it. He looks at me earnestly, because this is real. It's happening. It's not going away, and it must be faced. "This is what we'll have to live with—knowing that it's coming."

I look him dead in the eyes and say with certainty, "I've made my choice." My stomach tightens, because this is terrifying, but I'm willing to face the future. I'll be with Devlin. His strength will help me. We will help each other through this. And in my opinion, this is spilled milk, and there's no point in focusing on it. "I hope my family's magic..."

"What?"

I shake my head.

"Hey now." He gets up on his knees and touches my cheeks. "Look at me."

My gaze drifts up to meet his. "Listen, I am all in with this

—you and me. And I will do everything in my power to make sure that your family keeps their magic. *Everything.*"

Does that mean what I think it does? I scrunch up my nose and give him a curious look.

"And before you start asking me what I *mean*—Blair Thornrose, now that I've got you, I'm never letting you go. I have always loved you and I always will."

My heart swells with more joy than I thought possible, and my lips tremble as I release the words that have been locked inside my heart for years. "I love you, too."

"And here I thought that I was unlovable."

I throw my arms around him. "Only sometimes."

He laughs as I slip back onto the pillows.

This is it, I realize. I've got Devlin; he's pledged that we have a future. It's everything that I want.

Except for the dying, of course.

But I'm not going to think about that. Right now I just want to focus on him, on us, on giving myself what I've been deprived of.

"When do you think our powers will switch back?" I ask.

He pulls me onto him, and I rest my face on his chest. If I never move, I'll be happy.

He kisses my head. He smells like a fresh river stream, and he's warm like the best heating pad in the world.

"I don't know. Maybe they'll never switch back."

I lightly pinch him and he laughs. "Now, now. Violence is never the answer. But I suppose that the spell will break soon. I imagine, soon as we tell your grandmother about us. She'll be elated that you've stopped insulting me on a minute-by-minute basis."

I nudge him. "You wounded me. I was scarred for ten years."

"And I loved how much you *pretended* to hate me."

I sit up. "You loved that?"

"Such a good actress." He brushes hair from my eyes. "Those were my favorite days. Sometimes I'd go into the bookshop just so you could verbally assault me."

I laugh. "You're joking."

He stills. "Blair, even a moment of your pretend hate is better than a lifetime without you."

I kiss his chest and smooth the hairs that sit over his pecs. "I hated you for so long."

"No, you didn't. That wasn't hate, like I said. It was pretend hate. You loved me the whole time."

"No, I didn't."

He launches up, grabs me around my waist. I squeal, and he flips me onto my back. Devlin entwines his fingers in mine and stares down at me. Butterflies clog up my throat as I look at this man. He's so beautiful. He's not perfect. He's damaged like me, but he's so perfectly everything.

"I will tickle you if you don't admit that you loved me."

I smile. "Of course I loved you."

"That's better."

He drops his mouth to my neck and nuzzles me. He stops and his head pops up. There's sadness in his eyes. "There's something I want you to know about my power."

I curl a tendril of his hair around my finger. "What is it?"

"After my parents died, I went to live with my uncle. I told him about the power, but instead of helping me understand this gift, he used it against me. He tried to get me to see the future of sporting events so that he could bet on them, make money."

Devlin sits back and I rise, pulling the comforter to my chest. "He used you."

He nods and bends his knee, dropping his arm to rest on it. "When I couldn't see visions, he beat me, locked me in closets." He shakes his head. "I still can't have a door on a closet." He nods to his own, which is an open doorframe that leads into a room lined with shelves with racks and racks of clothes.

I touch his knee. "Your grandmother told me some of it, and I'm so sorry that it happened to you."

"She told you?"

"I hope you're not mad."

He takes my hand and kisses it. "Now how could I be mad at you? You've just given me the best sex of my life."

I swat him. "Is that all I'm good for?"

He shoots me a stern look. "You know that I'm joking."

"Wait. It's not the best sex of your life?"

"Oh, it's the best sex. But you mean more to me than that."

I kiss the back of his hand and let both of them fall onto the bed. I sigh. "Your power...you've let it control you for so long, too long."

"There's the pot calling the kettle black," he jokes.

"You can see another person's future. You could help people, Devlin. Like, a lot of people."

He sinks back on the bed, dragging me on top of him. I'm not complaining. Lying with him has become my new favorite thing. "How do you figure?"

"What if there were things in a person's future that they should know? What if you could help other wizards or scientists find cures for things—diseases, ways to improve society. What if you could do that?"

He shakes his head. "And what if all I found were people who wanted to lock me up and extract my power?"

"You're rich. You'd have a security detail."

"You've got a point." He kisses the top of my head. "But enough about me."

I sit up and stare down into his beautiful eyes. "You're not taking this seriously."

"It's not that I'm not taking it seriously." He rubs a thumb over his forehead. "It's that you *don't know* what you're asking of me."

"I know what I'm asking. I'm suggesting that you take control back. Your uncle stole it. You've reclaimed it, and you can turn around and help others. You've already done so much, but you can do more."

He slaps my thigh. "I'll think about it."

"Will you?"

His mouth ticks up in a lopsided grin. "Only if you consider not thinking of your talent as a curse."

I scoff. "That's not fair."

"Isn't it?" He sits up and kisses me. I melt as he slides his fingers up the back of my head and I toss one leg over his hips, straddling him. He breaks off the kiss, leaving me breathless and wanting more. "Isn't it fair? You're the same as me. You need to stop thinking that people will judge you for it. Your friends won't. I *don't*. I never did. And if someone does judge you, then they're the asshole. Not you."

"It's not that simple," I argue.

"How is it not?" He brushes strands of hair from my eyes. "You are more than just the sum of this power. You've lived a long time hiding from it. Maybe it's time you embraced it."

"Big words coming from you."

He laughs. "Guess who I learned them from?"

I kiss Devlin to shut him up, because I know what he's saying—that the suggestion came from me.

I *have* lived a long time hiding from my magic, being ashamed of it, allowing it to rule my life. I shouldn't let that happen anymore. I need to embrace it, and if people don't accept me because of it, then it's their fault.

Of course that's easier said than done. But with Devlin beside me, I feel strong, like I can do anything.

"Do you know what I want to do?" he asks.

"What's that?"

"Take a shower." He splays a hand over my belly. "Soap you up and make love to you."

I toss my head back and laugh. "I might let you. On one condition."

"Anything. You own me, Blair Thornrose."

"I own you, huh?" I joke.

"Oh, you do." He nuzzles his lips down my neck and unbuttons the shirt, revealing my breasts. He sucks one nipple into his mouth and my spine shudders. He swirls his tongue over the pebbled surface and lets it fall from his lips. "How about I take you into the shower and prove how much you own me?"

Before I can answer, he sits up, cups his arms under me and pulls me to his chest, dragging me out of bed, squealing. Next thing I know, my back is against the shower wall, Devlin's sucking on my clit and slipping two fingers inside me. He's worshipping my body like I own him.

Even though all of this feels right, a little flutter of insecurity in the back of my mind pushes through, making me wonder how long this will last, because my future is dim. So dim that there isn't a future at all.

31

DEVLIN

I'm buying a ring.

When you've loved someone for as long as I've loved Blair, you don't waste time. Besides, we don't have time to waste.

And when you don't know when death will take the person you love, you want to spend every waking moment with them —and doing it making them happy. This will make her happy.

It will also make me happy.

It may have been foolish to buy the ring so soon. We've had a lot of catching up to do these past days, but she's still the girl I fell in love with all those years ago, and I think she sees that I'm still the same boy from high school.

"Here you are, sir," the gemstone dealer says. I'm at the jewelry store in town. It's a magical shop, where the gemstones sing high-pitched songs when you walk by them, trying to get your attention, willing you to purchase them instead of looking at any of the other rings or bracelets tucked under the glass cases. The stones remind me of a songbird holding a note on a spring morning.

The dealer looks like what you'd expect of someone who

buys and sells gemstones—hawkish nose, thin fingers, thick glasses. He opens the velvet box and reveals a bloodred gemstone surrounded by diamonds set in platinum. The gemstone is clear, brilliant, and the diamonds sparkle.

"The painite that you requested," he says.

I take out the ring and lift it to the light. "Rarest gemstone known to man. Only found in Myanmar."

"You have excellent taste, Mr. Ross."

"Thank you. It's perfect." I tuck it back into the box. "She'll love it."

"I do think so."

"Please wrap it and I'll pay."

I'm back outside when my phone dings. I pull it from my jacket pocket and smile because it's Blair. *Are we still on for tonight?*

I stop to reply. *Absolutely. There's this new restaurant in Nashville I want to try. Pick you up at six?*

Yep. I get off work at five. See you then.

Hands is sitting in the car when I sink into my seat. He did not want to come inside, afraid that his appearance would draw too much attention. When people see a pair of disembodied hands, they tend to be disturbed.

We know. We've been through this rodeo.

Well?

I pull the box from the bag and show him. "What do you think?"

He makes the sign for whistling. *She's going to think you've lost your mind.*

"I have lost my mind—for her. I'm going to propose in a couple of nights. There's another ball. The last one for a while. I'm doing it then, in front of everyone."

Hands signs, *You want to claim her publicly.*

I grit my teeth. "I want the people in that room who looked down on Blair to know that she's better than them. That's what I want. She deserves it. It's the least that I can do after what happened in high school, when she was humiliated."

Will Storm be there?

"How would I know?"

Because he's walking into the bookshop.

I look up and do a double take. "Well, son of a gun."

Sure enough, Storm Grayson, wearing a black coat and with his hair coiffed like he spent an hour styling it, is currently striding into Castleview Books, where Blair is right now.

he Bookshop of Magic is in absolute chaos—or at least as close to chaos as I've ever seen it.

There's a line of angry customers winding through the store, around bookcases and the counter, snaking all the way to the front door.

Every person has an appointment to jump into a book, but we're unable to get them inside.

A man raises his fist. "What's going on?"

"I paid to be inside a story right now," a bookish woman says meekly but with bite.

"What kind of magical bookshop is this? You can't even get us into a book," a short, squat woman snaps.

"We came from out of town," a father with his two daughters says, exasperated.

Mama stands in front of them, patting the air. "Please be patient. I'll get this straightened out in a moment. Just give us time."

A woman jabs an open copy of *The Odyssey* that sits on a lectern. "My sister went into that book two hours ago and still hasn't come out! Is she okay? I need to know if she's all right."

My heart races like a horse speeding around a track. Never in my life have I seen anything like this. Books are scattered everywhere—on the floor, on the tops of shelves. Mama asked Chelsea and me to clean up, so that's what I'm doing.

I'm picking up books and shoving them back where they belong. But as soon as I push one onto a shelf, it shoots itself right back out and lands with a thud on the floor.

"We need answers," a man shouts.

A book flies from a case and uses its cover as wings to careen around the room like a bird. It dive-bombs a woman, and she shrieks before throwing up her hands and running for the exit.

"Please, everyone," my mother says. "Give us just a minute to try to get things solved."

"I'm not waiting one more minute," the squat woman says. "I'm taking my business somewhere else."

"Where else will she go?" Chelsea whispers, approaching me with a handful of books. "There aren't any other magical bookshops that I know of."

"Let me get your sister out of this book," Mama tells the woman who's nibbling her fingernails, worried sick about her sibling.

My mom places her hands on the book and concentrates. Her face is pinched, and she looks anxious. I've never seen her anxious.

Hell, I'm anxious.

The sound of books falling off the shelves and hitting the floor with thud after thud fills the shop. The only way to explain what's going on is that the magic isn't just dying, it's broken like a spring has shifted out of place. Simply put, the bookshop has gone haywire.

There are so many more books on the floor than there are put away that I'm just about to give up this job. Then the door opens.

Who the heck would be coming in here now? Doesn't everyone know that the magic is broken?

And don't think that I don't feel the pressure to get this all fixed. When Addison married, the magic was better for a while, but now it's clearly cracked its head open and is letting its brains spill out all over the floor.

And enter Storm Grayson.

My stomach falls. What is he doing here?

As if Storm has his own gravitational pull, every head in the room turns to gawk at him. I get it. He's rich. He's famous. He's handsome.

Chelsea presses her shoulder to mine and whispers, "I thought you ended things with him."

"I did."

"Then what's he doing here?"

"How should I know?"

"Why isn't she coming out?" the woman snaps at Mama.

"I'm trying. I could use more magic." Her gaze lands on Chelsea. "Chels, can you help me over here?"

With a huff, my sister drops the books she's holding on a table. "You've got to be kidding me. And miss this?" She shoots me a look. "I want all the details. Don't leave anything out."

I scoff. "He might not be here to see me."

"Oh, he's here to see you," she says before going to help Mama.

Storm looks around, taking in the madness of a dying empire—I mean, bookshop—and my heart sinks. Good thing I'm not still dating him. He'd probably dump me after seeing this mess.

"Hey," I say to him. "If you're here to jump into a book, now's not a good time."

He punches his hands into his pockets. "Actually I'm here to see you."

A book launches off a shelf, flapping its cover as it heads

straight for me and Storm. I grab the inventor by the cuff and pull him away just before the book smashes into a case and falls limply to the floor.

"Like I said, now's not a good time."

I walk away in a vain attempt to retrieve more books from the floor, but he jumps in front of me. "Look, I was wondering if you'd give me another chance. As you can imagine, I'm not someone who's used to hearing the word 'no.'" He chuckles. "I realize that my being out of town contributed to why our relationship fizzled out, but I'm willing to stay here, in Castleview, for a while."

Storm appears genuinely sincere, and it hurts my heart to say this, but it has to be done. "Storm, I was being honest when I told you that things weren't working. You being gone had nothing to do with it."

No, I didn't tell him that I'm with Devlin. There was no point in hurting him any more than I had to. Why twist the knife after you've plunged it in?

And speaking of Devlin, I'm so glad he's not seeing this. If he witnessed this insanity, I know what he'd do—he'd want to save me, and the only way to save me would be to save my family. But I don't want that. I want Devlin to marry me because he wants to, not because my family's magic is broken.

"Blair, I could use you over here," Mama says, still trying to pull the stuck woman from the book.

"Sorry, Storm, I've got to go."

I move to pass him, but he grabs the sleeve of my shirt. "I promise things will be different this time."

I exhale a loud breath. I hate hurting people's feelings. I'd rather hide under a rock than face someone to break up with them. But here we are. "I'm sorry, Storm. We're better off as friends. I don't think that we're a good match."

He frowns. "Not a good match? We want a lot of the same things."

Flustered, I reply, "Yes, I know, but there needs to be more." He's still holding my sleeve. "Please, let me go."

"What more does there need to be?" he snaps.

"Chemistry? Love? You name it. I don't think we've got it."

"But we could."

Mama looks pained, and I'm beginning to worry. My heart's fluttering in my throat. I've got to help her. Things must be bad with the woman trapped in *The Odyssey*.

I try to pull away, but he's still holding my sleeve. "We're just not meant to be."

"Blair!" Mama's voice has turned all high-pitched. She's panicking. "I need you now, please!"

I tug the arm that he's holding tight. "Let me go."

Storm scowls. "I'll let you go when you agree to see me again."

What? Is he joking? Now I'm just pissed off. He might be rich, but he can't buy me. "No, I'm not going to see you again."

"Blair!"

"Just one more time," he begs.

"No."

"Blair," Mama shouts.

Books are flying, Mama needs me, Storm won't let go, and he's still muttering about how he never begs, but won't I just go out with him one more time, and it's all too much, and then a flying book smacks me in the chest.

I yank my arm away and shout, "No, Storm! I won't go out with you ever again. I'm with Devlin now. There. That's it. Now, leave me alone!"

The room goes silent. Even the books are quiet.

Storm's face is red. His eyes are bulging, and the sincere look he had only a few moments ago has vanished, all traces of it erased. A vein is pulsing in his temple, and his throat is tight, all the corded muscles expanding like his head's about to pop off.

I inhale sharply. "I've got to help my mother pull someone out of a book. If you'll excuse me."

I move to pass him, but he grabs my arm one more time. I whirl around, ready for a fight.

But he releases me and drops his face close to mine, sneering like he's made of nothing except sheer evil. "No one humiliates me. No one. You will regret this, Blair Thornrose."

And then he vanishes in a spiral of smoke, and my hands are shaking. I curl them into fists to stop them. No big deal. Everything's fine. My ex-whatever didn't just threaten to destroy me like an evil villain in a cartoon.

I exhale and shrug off the threat, making my way over to my mother and sister.

As soon as I add my magic, the woman pops out of the book and lands with a smile. "That was great! Let's do it again."

At least someone's happy.

"I'm afraid that I must ask everyone to leave," Mama tells the crowd. "You must go now. We'll issue any refunds to those of you who've already paid."

"What was that all about with Storm?" Chelsea murmurs when we have a moment to ourselves.

"Nothing," I whisper. "It was nothing."

But I know it wasn't nothing. You don't cross a man as powerful as Storm Grayson and not pay for it.

The question is—how much will I have to pay?

33

"*A*re you ready?" I ask Devlin as we stand outside the entrance to the ball.

He's wearing a black tux with a silky white tie. His hair is combed back, and his eyes sparkle with love, as I imagine mine do.

I didn't bother telling him what happened with Storm. It would have only angered Devlin, and I didn't see a reason to do that. Why tarnish happiness with a vague threat?

He offers his arm, and I release my hold on the skirt of the midnight-blue gown that I'm wearing. It's got sheer shoulder straps that are thick, and they reach down to a bodice that has a low V. The full skirt is covered in rhinestones that are meant to represent stars. It's the most beautiful gown I've ever worn, and when the town tailor, Daisy, had it delivered to the house today, I was shocked and also elated. So elated that I called her immediately and thanked her for the lovely surprise.

She told me that Devlin had ordered it. Of course he had. He has great taste. Don't worry, I've already thanked him.

"Are *you* ready?" Devlin asks.

"I asked you first."

He pretends to think about it. "Maybe we should go back to my place, pop in a movie, cuddle up with Hands between us."

I toss back my head and laugh. "Hands does seem like a good cuddler."

"You have no idea."

I laugh again as he squeezes my wrist and wraps my arm under his. "Come on. Let's make the entrance of the year."

My face hurts I'm grinning so hard as the doors open and we're announced. We timed our entrance to make sure that most of the guests have already arrived.

"Mr. Devlin Ross and Miss Blair Thornrose."

Every set of eyes focuses on us. There's surprise on many people's faces. Some envy—of course you're going to get that when Devlin's involved. Most of the town has assumed, and rightly so, that he would never settle down.

Not that he *is* settling down, but you know what I mean.

This is the first time I've stepped into a ball with a man, and the feeling is powerful. Being with him makes a strong statement to the supernatural community—Blair Thornrose is officially taken.

He escorts me into the room, and I feel like a lightbulb, like I've been turned on, my wattage at one hundred thousand. It's an amazing feeling, and one that I won't soon forget.

I smile at the guests, ignoring the jealousy popping in their eyes. There is some surprise and even a little happiness for me, though that comes from my own family.

Devlin walks me to the center of the room as the music flares to life. I feel heat smear my cheeks.

"Now what's got you blushing?"

I shrug. "Nothing. Everything. I don't know. All of it."

He grins, dimple shining. "Drink it up, Blair. This is your moment. All of this is yours. No one can take it away from you." He pauses and looks around. "This is what you've wanted, isn't it? Your whole family proud, society marveling at you, not looking at you as if you're different from them, but that you're one of them." He pulls me closer and presses his lips to the top of my head. "You are one of them. You're more than one of the people looking for a pound of flesh."

As he sweeps me into a dance, I realize that he's right. I am more than the gossipmongers and haters. I've survived them, outlasted them, and now here I am. I've arrived.

Devlin has claimed me publicly, and it's not something that he would do carelessly. He knows the stakes.

We dance for so long that my feet begin to hurt. But I don't want to stop. I want to keep on moving, continue being held by this man that I love. I want to drink up this moment as long as I can, being as happy as I can.

When the music finally stops, the dance floor begins to thin out, and I move to leave.

"Hold on a second, Blair."

I turn to see that Devlin has dropped to one knee.

Oh, oh, oh.

My heart flutters. My pulse is pounding in my ears. I gaze over at my dad, who's smiling. Oh, that weasel! They're in on this.

A hush moves over the crowd like a lazy wave, and Devlin pulls a red velvet box from his pocket. He opens it and inside sits a ring.

Devlin's staring up at me like I'm his north star, the one point in the sky that he knows will always be there for him.

"Blair Thornrose, I have spent a good part of my life denying how much I love you, but not anymore. I don't want to waste another moment without you by my side." He pauses, inhales deeply. "Will you marry me?"

My eyes are blurry because tears are spilling down my cheeks. I'm overcome with joy and love. My chest feels like it's going to explode. "Yes. Yes. Yes. Yes."

He slips a gorgeous ring on my finger. At least, I *think* it's gorgeous. Not sure because I can't see it properly through the tears blurring my vision. Devlin rises. He takes me by the waist and kisses me. We hug and the room erupts in applause.

I wipe tears from my eyes as he murmurs into my hair, "I love you so much, Bee."

"I love *you*."

He hands me a glass of champagne from a waiter, and we both drink in celebration as people clap.

As the applause begins to quiet, one very loud person clapping fills the ballroom. "Bravo! Bravo! A grand performance."

The crowd parts for Storm Grayson, who slowly applauds as he swaggers toward us. "Bravo, Devlin. I see that you've stolen from me again, but this time it wasn't an invention. This time it was a person."

Devlin tenses. He stares at Storm for a beat before saying in a voice shining with all pleasantries imaginable, "And here I thought you were congratulating us."

The crowd laughs nervously.

Storm's eyes harden. "Not at all."

Devlin's smile vanishes and his voice drips with warning. "You'd do best to turn around and walk out that door, Grayson. You do not know the can of worms you're about to open."

"Oh, don't I?" The crowds' gaze is latched on to Storm as he opens his arms and declares loudly, "Don't I know? First you steal the Spell Book of Unlimited Pages from me."

My mouth falls. What is he talking about? Devlin would never steal from anyone. He's honest. He may have been a player in the past, but he is honest.

Devlin spits out, "Stop talking and leave."

"Why should I?" It's the invitation of someone who's either too stupid to know who they're dealing with, or they're overconfident in their own talents.

Storm takes an intimidating step forward. "Years ago, you had that creepy set of hands sneak into my home and take the plans. Oh yes, he did. For all of you who don't know," he plays to the crowd's open astonishment, "Devlin Ross is a thief. But I just happen to be smarter than him, and I got the book out first."

"That is a lie."

"The truth," Storm shouts, spinning around with his hands in the air so that his audience can worship him before he comes to a stop facing us.

These are serious allegations, and Storm is obviously jealous and humiliated that I chose Devlin over him. But even so, to accuse Devlin of stealing—this threatens my brand-new fiancé's freedom.

Devlin's jaw flexes. "Take it back."

"No. It's all true. I did release the book first."

"Not that. What you said about Hands."

Storm tosses his head back and laughs. "About the creepy little creature you keep? Never." He steps closer and drops his voice. "Tell me, Devlin—is it true what they say the creature does *to* you at night?"

Devlin drops his empty glass of champagne, and it shatters to the floor. Storm smirks, and Devlin looks like he wants to kill him.

"Devlin, it's not worth it." I tug his sleeve. "Everyone knows that you would never do anything like that."

My fiancé's voice is ground rocks. "Take. It. Back."

"No," Storm says flatly. "I won't take any of it back. You think that you're better than me. Well, you're not. You even think that throwing me a bone here and there is something that I'll take. Well it isn't. It's about time the world knew the truth—that Devlin Ross is a thief and a liar." He cocks his head at me. "But that wasn't enough for you, was it? You had to steal Blair from me too, didn't you?"

"I was never yours to steal," I spit.

He leans forward sloppily, and the heavy scent of whiskey wafts up my nose. Storm's drunk. That explains this.

"Weren't you mine? Or was that a game? Do you play with all men's hearts? Tell them that you like them, seem to have the same goals, and then jump into bed with another man?"

People gasp in shock. Murmurs scatter across the room. People are staring at me accusingly. *It wasn't like that,* I want to say. *Devlin needed me for his invention.*

Devlin speaks through clenched teeth. "Leave now, Storm, before you say anything else that you'll regret."

He scoffs. "You think that I want to be with a woman who works in a bookstore and has no ambition? Do you actually think I'd care if I won her or not? There are millions of women who want to be with me. *Millions.* Losing someone as pathetic as her isn't worth one thought. But between us, I just regret that I didn't screw her *first.*"

There's a split second where this could go in any direction, and then Devlin punches Storm right in the face.

He stumbles back and covers his nose. The crowd takes a step back. Blood drips through Storm's fingers, splashing onto the marble floor. He pulls his hand away and wipes his sleeve across his face, smearing blood onto his cheek.

"Not broken this time," he says victoriously about his nose. "But you are, Devlin. You're done for. I'm bringing formal charges of assault against you. I'm also charging you with stealing the Spell Book of Unlimited Pages."

He starts to walk off, but Devlin says, "Wait just a second."

"Go to hell."

Inky black power floods Devlin's eyes for the briefest of seconds before vanishing. I suck in a breath. Why is he using my magic? How will this make anything better?

Storm stops dead in his tracks. He takes a labored step, his foot scraping against the marble. Stops again, like he's having to will himself to walk. He moves forward, and his foot lifts like a hinge, spinning him to face us.

As he plants that foot firmly on the floor, his body lunges forward, stopping just before he collapses on the marble. Then he straightens like a marionette being pulled to life by a puppet master.

A moan erupts from his mouth as it slowly yawns opens. He's fighting it. It's obvious to me. Everyone else may think that he's suffering from some sort of episode—bloody nose, stuttered movements, but I know the truth.

He's in Devlin's hold just like Chatty Cathy was in mine all those years ago. My heart rams against my chest. This will not end well. It can't.

"Do you have something to say?" Devlin calmly asks him.

"M-m-m-m I-I-I'm s-s-sorry, B-Blair."

He's *definitely* fighting it. I've never seen anything like this. It's almost admirable, really, how much of a fight Storm is putting up.

"What else?" Devlin coaxes.

My eyes flare in disbelief. That's not all? It's bad enough that Devlin's using my power to nudge Storm into saying things against his will. What else is there?

A lifetime of hatred brews in Storm's silvery eyes as he glares flaming arrows at Devlin. He knows that Devlin's controlling this and he's pissed.

"I"—his mouth opens slowly like someone's prying it with a crowbar. "I s-stole the Sp-Spell Book fr-from Devlin. He had the i-i-idea first."

Storm's face is crimson, steering toward plum. Veins are popping on both temples and in his neck. I'll hand it to him, he's really trying hard, here. But the power of the nudge is too great.

"D-Devlin w-was easy to steal from. All I h-had to do was p-pay off one of his employees and they gave me the information th-that I was looking for, and what a b-b-brilliant idea it was."

"Devlin," I murmur. "Stop. They'll know it's you doing this."

"Not until he's done," he says grimly.

But my stomach's a knot of nerves. These people, they're going to know that Devlin's using magic, and they're going to hate him just like they've always hated me.

Storm continues, the words coming faster. "D-Devlin knew what I'd d-done, and he didn't t-t-turn me in. He didn't file a lawsuit. He just let it g-g-go."

"And what about Hands?" Devlin coaches.

"Hands?" Storm's face contorts as if he's in pain. He probably *is* because sometimes telling the truth hurts. "There's n-n-nothing going on b-between the two of you. I t-t-tried to convert the creature. W-wanted it on my side, but it wouldn't come."

I squeeze Devlin's hand, willing him to stop this. Hoping that this is the end.

But it's not.

"And a few weeks ago?" he prods Storm.

Storm lifts his chin. Blood is dripping down his mouth and making a small puddle on the floor, but he's forgotten all about that. The only thing he can focus on is the nudge.

"I-I-I had someone try to br-break into Devlin's house to steal his most recent invention—something that's supposed to change the w-w-world. But Hands got in the w-way."

People are appalled by this, and they're shrinking away from Storm as if he's carrying the plague.

"Anything else?" Devlin asks.

Storm shakes his head, but his nostrils are flared and he's breathing in and out hard. He's furious. When this wears off, it won't be good.

"So you won't be suing me?" Devlin says in his smooth, velvet voice.

"N-no."

"No, what?"

"I-I w-w-won't sue."

"That's what I thought."

"Devlin," I whisper.

"I'm done."

Storm turns around and makes his way toward the door. I suspect that Devlin's forcing him out, but Storm moves quickly. Even so, a couple of men follow, I assume to make sure that he doesn't come back.

"Well, that was exciting," Devlin says to the guests. "Time to forget about that nastiness and celebrate. Let's all raise a glass to our engagement."

I'm about to exhale in relief when Cathy steps into the center of the room.

"Stop!" She's wearing a pink gown with skintight sleeves and a mermaid skirt. She marches over and points to me. "She did this! Blair Thornrose made Storm say all those lies. She influenced him into it. That woman made him do something against his will, and she should be punished!"

34

*I*t's funny how one moment you can be riding high, and how in another, you can sink so far down you're not sure if there's any place left for you to go.

That's what's happening now.

Cathy points to me and shouts, "Get her!"

But no one's moving. People are glancing at one another in confusion. *The bad guy just admitted that he's bad. What's the problem?*

Cathy stalks the room, moving in a circle and staring down the crowd as she walks. "What? Is no one going to get Blair?" She points into the crowd. "Cherie! Sadie! Don't just stand there. Do something. Grab her!"

She yanks her friends, or whatever you call them (because let's face it, Cathy doesn't have real friends) from the crowd and pushes them toward me, but they barely move.

My dad steps forward, standing tall and looking regal in his black tux. "Let's all take a breath and calm down. We've had enough trouble for one night, Cathy."

Cathy smirks. "I'm only doing what's right. She's a menace to all witching society."

"It wasn't Blair."

Devlin takes my hand and squeezes it, giving me a warm smile before he steps forward. The crowds' eyes are playing ping-pong, volleying from Cathy to him. They're entranced. This is probably the most drama they've seen in weeks, months maybe.

He continues. "It was me. And what crime have I committed, Cathy? Tell me. Is it the crime of having Storm reveal the truth? Where's the wrongdoing in that? I didn't ask him to lie."

"You took control of him," she snaps. "You used magic on him against his will. That's a crime, and stop lying for her. Everyone knows that Blair Thornrose has the power to influence. She did the same thing to you. Made you fall in love with her."

"No, she didn't," he bites out, "and I would appreciate it if you didn't talk badly about my fiancée."

The crowd breaks apart into little clusters of whispers. Cathy glares at them angrily. "Stop lying for her, Devlin. We all know what happened back in high school, just like we all know what happened here. She made Storm lie. She made you love her. Those are crimes. Using magic on someone against their will is wrong." She waves her arms at the crowd. "Why is everyone staring with your mouths open? Are y'all trying to catch flies? Do something. What if she used her powers on all of us? Made us do something stupid like jump off a bridge? What if she hurts someone? She's not fit to walk around freely."

Cathy points at me. "We've tolerated Blair up until now, but how many of you really trust her? She can destroy us with her power! Don't you see it?" When no one answers, she throws back her head and screams, "Don't you want her gone?"

The crowd is silent. So silent, and my mind is spinning. I haven't done anything to deserve this.

This is why I hate my power. Because in my town I'm always one step away from being an outcast, from being punished for using this curse in a manner that could hurt someone. It's one thing to influence someone to bring me cake. It's another to force a person to admit a deep, dark truth. Because the reality is—how much of what they say is the truth, and how much of it is the nudge?

Except in this case. I know that Storm stole the idea for the Spell Book, and that he had someone attempt to break into Devlin's house. But Devlin would never use the power to do more than simply ferret out right from wrong.

But I'm probably the only person who realizes that.

Cathy's still waiting for someone to step up. When they don't, she slaps her thighs in exasperation. "Fine. I'll demand that it be done. Someone lock Blair Thornrose up and throw away the key."

Devlin tugs me behind him in a protective stance. "You will do no such thing. Every single one of you has been affected by this family, and not in a bad way."

Cherie drops her gaze to the floor before quietly saying, "Blair's always helped me when I wanted to jump into a book."

"Yeah," someone else says. "She's patient and kind."

A girl from high school with long dark curls says, "Blair never once rushed me at the store or wanted me to hurry, and I never felt her use power on me. She's not like what you're saying, Cathy. She's not a bad person."

Other people agree, murmuring that I'm not bad. People who I never expected to, they take up for me. People who rarely speak to me in public, who barely say two words to me. They are all disagreeing with Cathy, telling her that I'm not a terrible person, that I'm good, kind.

Good and kind?

I've lived my whole life in Castleview thinking of myself as an outcast, as someone unworthy of this sort of praise. But here is my town all rallying behind me, telling Cathy that even though I have this terrible power, this intimidating magic, it doesn't make me a bad person. That I'm good, in spite of it.

"Maybe you're the bad one here, Cathy," Sadie accuses.

Cathy's jaw drops. "It's not me. It's her. It's Blair. Don't any of you see?"

Her minion shakes her head. "All I see is you trying to hurt someone."

Devlin's hand tightens on mine as the entire crowd agrees in a chorus of "yes" and "yeah" and "leave Blair alone."

Tears spring to my eyes as folks turn on Cathy. "Maybe you should go," Cherie says.

And Cathy—red-faced and collarbone flushing with embarrassment—takes a long look at the crowd. "Will no one stand up for me?"

When no one replies, realization washes over her face. Nobody in the room believes her. She's all alone, her bullying having gotten her absolutely nothing.

She nods slowly. "All right. But don't say I told you so when *she*"—Cathy jabs a finger at me—"does something that ruins one of you here."

She stalks out of the room, just a few minutes after Storm.

Would anyone else like to step up and spar with me and Devlin?

Ha. Just kidding.

There is a collective sigh as the crowd looks at me and I realize something. For my entire life I've believed that my power made me different in a bad way, so different that these people didn't like me, that I was *less than*.

As I stare into the ballroom, the chandeliers bright with light, the room smelling of gardenias and the hems of silk ball-gowns swishing along the floor, all I see are faces smiling at me.

Perhaps it wasn't the town who believed that I was bad;

maybe it was me. Maybe it wasn't that none of the guys wanted to date me because they were afraid. Maybe this whole time—for years—I've been giving off the signal that I didn't *want* to be dated. I thought, *No man is going to like me anyway,* so that's what I expected. And it's been my own limiting belief that's pushed dates away (it turned out good in the end, hence Devlin, don't get me wrong). I made myself unapproachable, turning into someone so chilly that not even the warmest fire could thaw my heart.

Maybe, just maybe, I've been the problem. I felt too sorry for myself to see the truth.

Poor little old me, with all this intimidating power; no one wants to be my friend.

The power *is* intimidating, but everyone here realizes that I don't use it willy-nilly. I've had an entire town full of friends this whole time. But that fact has never dawned on me before, because I was so convinced of one truth that I never bothered to look for a different one.

Seek and ye shall find.

This whole time I've been seeking the wrong thing, and of course that's what I found.

Devlin presses his mouth to my ear and kisses me. I drag my gaze from the crowd to him and realize that for as awful as this night has been, it's also been absolutely perfect.

He smiles. For a long time I thought that smile was smug. It was, I think. But there's always been warmth in it as well. A lot of warmth. More than warmth, actually. Every time Devlin smiled at me, he was saying something else this whole time, a secret language that I only just now realized.

I love you, his eyes have been telling me. *I've loved you for so long.*

I squeeze his hand. And I've loved him, too, and I'm ready to jump into the next phase of our life together, even though I've been scared. I've been scared to let my heart be hurt again, to let myself fall as hard as I did for Devlin before, afraid that if I was hurt, that my heart wouldn't recover because it would be shredded. The pieces would be too jagged to be stitched back together, and I'd wind up without a heart at all.

But I would rather live a thousand lives of heartache than one life without love. Or Devlin. Period.

He leans over. "Do you want to leave?"

I grin. "No. I want to dance with my fiancé."

He beams and starts to lead me to the dance floor when Nana's voice booms over the crowd, "What's all the commotion?"

The crowd turns to see my nana and her ghostly form sweeping into the room, all eyes on her.

And that's when the screaming begins.

35

DEVLIN

*Y*ou can certainly say that Blair's nana knows how to make an entrance. As soon as she showed her face, that was the tipping point of the night. Not when I used Blair's power on Storm, and not when Cathy demanded that everyone join her in the ninth circle of hell.

No, those reactions were mild compared to how the crowd responded when Rebecca slid through the wall and started talking.

People screamed. They whispered. I think someone even cried. Don't ask me why.

Either Rebecca had gotten her hands on the invisibility antidote, or no one had bothered to give it to her in the first place.

Which is too bad because supernaturals take their ghostly wives' tales seriously. It was only a matter of seconds before people were vanishing in whirls of smoke, making excuses for why they had to leave so quickly.

We knew the truth—they ran off to blab that Rebecca had returned as a ghost, which meant that the Thornroses were in deep shit as a family.

Old wives' tales, like I said. They die hard in Castleview, and with witches.

The Thornroses were pretty upset with their nana. Clara looked like she could've killed her mother if she wasn't already dead. There was a lot of arguing, which ended in Rebecca shrugging and telling everyone that it would all blow over soon enough.

She's probably right about that.

Blair had already dealt with enough, so I asked if she'd like me to walk her around to the main house.

"I'd rather go home with you," she says.

My brows lift. This is unexpected but at the same time not. "You sure?"

She drops her head to my shoulder and nods. "Oh, I am more than sure."

"Why am I even arguing with you?"

"Yeah." She lightly pokes my shoulder. "Why are you, fiancé?"

Her parents are talking, and I don't think they'll mind if I slip off with their daughter. At this point they know my intentions, and I have to say that Phillip wasn't too surprised when I requested his blessing to marry her.

"Do you like your ring?" I ask once we're outside. It's cool tonight, so I take off my jacket and slip it over her thin shoulders.

She holds out her left hand, inspecting it. "It's gorgeous. Is that a ruby?"

"Painite. Rarest gemstone on earth, just like you're rare to me."

She clutches her left hand in fright. "This must've cost a fortune."

"*You* are worth every penny and then some. Besides"—I curl my arm around her shoulders—"it gave me an excuse to buy the rarest gemstone on earth."

She covers her face in embarrassment. "Stop it."

"No." I tug her hands away from her face. "You are a gem—*my* gem."

She kisses me lightly and then pulls back, sucking air. "Oh my gods, could you believe Storm?"

"Whew. From the way you gasped, I thought you were going to say something terrible instead of talking about Storm. But"—I brush hair from her eyes—"nope. Not surprised at all. He got what was coming to him."

"Yeah, he did. And then Cathy!" Blair admires her ring again and then clutches it to her chest like she's afraid it'll fall off. "I thought for sure the crowd was going to turn on you. Devlin, I was so scared. The whole time that you were influencing Storm, I thought it was going to turn around and bite you in the ass."

I chuckle. "I knew the crowd was with me. After he insulted you, there was no redeeming himself."

"Yeah." Her face falls.

I stop. "Wait. Wait. Wait." I tip her chin until she's looking at me. "You don't believe any of what he said about you, do you?"

"No. I mean, of course not."

I study her. She nibbles her bottom lip. I pin her shoulders between my hands. "Darlin', nothing that he said is true. You don't lack ambition. The bookshop is amazing. People come from all over the world to see it. He was just being jealous and petty. Put it out of your mind."

She nods lamely.

"Blair," I warn.

"Fine. Yes." She snaps her fingers. "It's gone. Just like that."

"That's better." We start walking again, and I slip my left hand into her right one and kiss it.

She strokes the hill of my hand gently with her thumb. "I'm sorry for what he did to you."

"Don't be. Storm's a bad guy. I've known that about him a long time."

She rears back. "And you let me go *out* with him?"

"Are you serious? You *wanted* to date him. If I recall, you were happy to have me help you go out with him."

"That was because I hated you."

"Because you *loved* me."

"That, too," she admits with a smile.

We lock gazes and laugh. She throws her arms around my waist. "I love you, Devlin Ross. I'm never letting you go."

"I don't want you to."

She stops walking again. "What is it?" I ask.

She straightens and pulls the jacket tight as a breeze blows past. "Shouldn't our powers have switched back by now? I mean, you got your invention. I've learned my lesson about the influence. I don't resent it anymore." She points from her to me. "We've gotten engaged." She folds her arms and pouts. "Speaking of which, when are we getting married?"

I pat the air to suggest she settle down. "Now, hold on. Let's take this one at a time. To answer your first question, I have no idea when they'll switch back, and to answer your second—whenever you want to."

She looks right and left as if waiting for the other shoe to drop. "Seriously?"

"As seriously as a heart attack. We will walk down the aisle next week if you want."

"That's too soon." She nibbles her finger. "How about next month?"

I laugh. "Next month it is."

"And maybe everyone will have forgotten about Nana by then."

"Doubtful, but it will probably all be smoothed over." She shoots me a look and I shrug. "It's true."

And as I tug her into a hug, inhaling the peach scent of her shampoo, it hits me that I love her with all my being.

I love her—this I've known. I've never stopped. But it's the depth of this feeling that bowls me over. That's why the thought of her marrying someone else made me angry, why the idea of her with Storm made me want to punch him in the face, why I've never truly been able to let her go.

And I don't want to.

I want to keep her, protect her, love her with all I've got for as long as I've got her.

Her fingers curl into the lapels of my shirt. It's a nice night, perfect for a walk. Winter solstice lights that haven't been taken down flare along the street. It rained earlier, filling the air with the scents of ozone and earth.

"What are you thinking?" she asks as I hold her.

"About the Roman Empire," I joke, referencing a pop culture phenomenon. I kiss her forehead. "I'm not thinking about anything other than you. What are you thinking?"

"I'm thinking that I love you, that I can't wait to be your wife"—my heart nearly explodes—"and that Nana just ruined a great moment." She presses her nose into my shirt and sighs. "Way to go, Nana."

I chuckle and tighten my arms around her. "Why Blair Thornrose, are you saying that your nana planned this? That she let you have all the glory so that she could come in and steal it?"

"No, I think death gave Nana brain damage, is what I'm saying. Pretty sure that she's out of her mind to show herself like that."

"I think Rebecca knows what she's doing."

She tips her face up. "What makes you say that?"

"Oh, I don't know." I shrug. "The woman's had plenty of time to reveal herself up until now. The fact that she took this one moment, this one second to do it says that there's some other plan."

Blair rolls her eyes. "Or she's out of her gourd."

"Or that."

We laugh and her eyes crinkle as she grins up at me. My heart's so big I don't think it can hold one more drop of emotion.

She turns and we continue on our stroll. "What are you going to do about Storm? Are you going to call the police? Tell them that he admitted to the break-in?"

"Yes. He will be punished." My body coils in anger at what he said about Blair. But I got revenge for her. It's over; that's what I should focus on. "You know he cheated at the carnival?"

She pulls away and shoots me a look of surprise. "What?"

"The night when y'all went to the carnival, he used his power to sabotage the boy who was firing the water gun beside him."

She gasps. "He did not."

"He sure did. I watched the whole thing."

Blair lightly slaps my arm. "Why didn't you tell me?"

"Why should I have? Would you have believed me?"

"Well, I don't…"

"No, you wouldn't have. You would have thought that I was lying, trying to get you into bed." I wink at her and she turns to me. "To be fair, I would've definitely been trying to get you into my bed."

She giggles and nudges me with her shoulder. "You are so bad."

"Badly in love with you. I've never stopped wanting or loving you."

She shakes her head. "Me neither. You're the first and only person who's ever seen me. Who understands what I feel. I have a house filled with sisters, and they get me, but you get me *more*. And when I was cut off from you"—she looks away, exhales, looks back at me—"it felt like I was cut off from myself."

Now there are tears in *my* eyes. "Come here."

She slips into my arms, and I cradle the back of her head. "I will work for the rest of my life to never let you down again. I won't make the same mistake twice and lose you."

"You won't," she says, muffled in my shoulder. "You won't lose me."

There it sits, the one thing that we know isn't true. I *will* lose her, and when it happens, it will destroy me. But for now I'm going to live every moment with Blair to the fullest and not take a second for granted.

Because a life without her is no life at all. I know that now. I knew it then, too. That's why I spent the last ten years immersing myself in work and never seriously dating, because no one could compare to her.

They never have and they never will.

Like I said, we've wasted so much time. I don't want to waste another moment.

The air shifts. A breeze picks up, and cherry blossoms appear out of nowhere, circling us in a tornado of light pink petals.

"What is this?" she asks.

"Magic," I whisper. "Or Rebecca."

She laughs and pulls back, smiling at me from ear to ear, her brown eyes shining. "Devlin?"

"Yes?"

She tugs on my shirt flirtatiously. "Take me to bed, or lose me forever."

It's a line from *Top Gun*, a movie I know well.

I kiss her. "With pleasure."

She walks off and for a moment I watch her, admiring this beautiful woman. A second later a tingle works its way up my spine, crawling to the top of my head. My fingers pulse with energy.

Oh shit.

"Blair—"

She's taken a couple of steps into the street and when she turns around, our gazes lock. There's a split second of recognition. The heavy smell of ozone, the way the light's pooling around her, the feeling that we've been here before.

Because we have.

I reach out my hand. One burst of magic and she'll be out of the way, safe.

But before I'm able to release my power, something slams into my head. Light explodes in my eyes, and I'm knocked to the ground.

I can only watch in horror as headlights appear out of nowhere, a truck barreling down the road, and the next thing I know, she's gone.

36

I'm trapped in darkness. It's a thick sludge that won't release its hold on me.

My mind races to put pieces together. I was with Devlin after the ball. We were outside, walking back to his house. He'd just proposed. It was the best and worst night of my life, what with Storm making a scene and Nana revealing herself.

I had just walked in front of Devlin, into the road, and turned around when he said my name.

It felt like déjà vu. The halo of light around him, the expression on his face—his lips parted, his eyes brimming with concern—it was all familiar.

Then it hit me. I was in the vision, standing right in the middle of a future that we had both seen, and I think we realized it at the same time. There was a split second of recognition on his face, a frantic worry, and then he reached for me.

And here I am, trapped in darkness. Unable to get out.

Where am I? Is this heaven? Worse, is this hell?

I better not be in hell.

"Any changes?" It's Mama.

Mama! Mama!

"No." It's Devlin! His deep voice is rumbling in that sexy velvety way it has. But he sounds raspy, tired. A pressure releases from my hand, and I realize that he's been holding it. "Nothing has changed."

What are they talking about? Why don't they hear me? Why can't *I* hear me?

Now that I think about it, I can hear more than just their voices. I hear beeps, and I feel something inflating on my arm —a blood pressure cuff. Wow. That thing's really tight, like cut-off-your-circulation tight. Someone should adjust that.

I'm in a hospital—a human hospital. Things must be bad if they've brought me here instead of having a healer take a look at me. Then again, maybe a healer *did* look at me, doing what they could before sending me to this hospital.

"You need to go home, Devlin, get some rest," Mama says, her voice full of concern.

I'm here, I try to say, but it's impossible to break through. My mouth doesn't open; the sound isn't being created in my throat.

Oh my gods, I'm in a coma. I've read about this—people in comas can hear what's being said, but they can't respond. They're trapped, just like me.

My heart falls. I can't reach them. *Impossible.* I love Devlin. I haven't waited ten years to be with him only to have this ripped away. I've got to try.

"I can't leave," Devlin tells her. He sounds so, so tired.

"You've been here for a week straight. You've got to go home, even if only for an hour."

"Yes, son." My dad, now.

I hear a chair's feet scraping across the floor. "Please sit, Clara," Devlin says.

"I'm okay. Has there been any progress?"

"No. And the doctors..." He chokes up. Why is he choking up? What about the doctors?

Mama sniffles. Dad exhales. Devlin swallows down a sob.

I'm here, I scream. *I'm right here.*

There's a pause for several minutes as if no one wants to broach whatever topic follows *the doctors.*

Mama stops sniffling, lightly blows her nose and says, "How's your head?"

Devlin sighs, I imagine he's plowing his fingers through his hair. "It's fine. Storm didn't do much damage to me, and he'll be in jail for a while once the judge hears everything." His voice comes out shaky now. "If he hadn't hit me, I could have stopped this. I could have saved her."

His voice cracks and my heart is breaking.

So Storm attacked Devlin when we were outside. That's the only thing he can mean by saying that he could have saved me. That jerk Storm was hanging around, waiting to get back at Devlin for influencing him.

This could have been avoided. The future could have been changed if it wasn't for Storm. But then again, he was probably in this future all along.

I'm glad that he's in jail. It's the only good thing about this situation.

"Have you eaten?" Mama asks.

"I'm not hungry," he says.

There's a pause before Mama sighs. "I need to check in with Chelsea and see how things are going at the bookshop."

"Better than last week, I hope," Dad says.

"I don't think so." She sighs. "The only thing keeping us going right now is that people actually want to see books flying around on their own."

Devlin's voice is filled with concern. "What's happening?"

There's a swish of clothing—Mama sitting in the chair. "Our magic is so broken I don't know how to fix it, even temporarily. We went through this before Addison married."

"I didn't act fast enough," Devlin murmurs.

What?

"It's not your fault, son," Dad says. "Luckily they caught the truck driver and are putting up a magical barrier to stop any other vehicles from appearing in the middle of the road."

Why did Devlin say that he hadn't acted fast enough? He didn't propose to me just to save the bookshop, did he?

No way. No. Certainly not. Devlin would never do anything like that. He proposed because he loves me and I love him. It has nothing to do with the fact that my family's magic is obviously cracked wide open and Devlin would do anything to make me happy including marrying me before he was ready.

Right?

"The magic," Devlin says. "How bad is it?"

I can just picture Mama rubbing her head with worry. "It's unbelievable."

"Why didn't Blair tell me?"

"Because she wouldn't want you to worry."

"You need your rest." It sounds like Dad claps Devlin on the shoulder. "Even if it's just for a few hours. We'll watch over her and let you know if anything changes."

No, no, I don't want Devlin to go. Maybe I can communicate with them, flutter my eyelids or move a finger—my ring finger, and show my mom that sparkling gem.

Oh wow. I must be really drugged up if I'm thinking about gemstones and not trying to wake up.

I focus on trying to move my pinkie. *Is anything happening? Hello? Does anyone see my pinkie moving?*

"About the bookshop"—it's Devlin again—"maybe there's a way that I can help."

I can practically hear my mom shrug. "How can you do that?"

I can just see him smiling tiredly. "I'm an inventor, aren't I?"

He gets up from the chair. Devlin touches my hand, and his skin feels so good, like I've been starved of human contact for my entire life until just now. I try so hard to reach for him, but I'm locked down tight—every single muscle. They're not obeying.

I've got to break through this wall.

"What are you going to do?" Dad asks.

Devlin's voice rumbles, sounding fatigued. "Give me a few hours and I'll figure something out to help the bookshop, and I'll go home to do it."

"You need a break," Dad says with sympathy.

A knock sounds from the door. "Oh good, I'm glad everyone's here."

It's a very masculine voice.

"Dr. Jones," Mama says. "Any change to my daughter's prognosis?"

"Maybe we should talk outside," he replies.

That can't be good.

I hear them shuffle out, and the door softly closes. Their muffled voices float in from the hallway. The doctor's saying something, but I can't hear clearly enough to know what.

And then Devlin explodes. "No! We are not doing that! You will not stop feeding her!"

My heart stops.

Oh my gods, they want to stop feeding me. That's what my family was saying earlier about the doctors. That's why they were all crying.

If I can't come out of this, break through the wall that I'm trapped behind, the doctors will let me die.

I'll lose everything, *everything*, and worst of all, Devlin.

And our life together has only just begun.

I'm here, I try to scream. *Don't go. Devlin, please! You've got to hear me. Please help me. Somebody help me!*

37

DEVLIN

"They've given up on Blair," I tell Hands when I get home.

He signs, *What?*

I slump into a kitchen chair and fold over, resting my elbows on my knees. "The doctors want to stop feeding her. No way in hell am I going to let that happen. I'll bring her here if I have to—set up a bed, have nurses around the clock—whatever it takes."

Hands's finger deflate over the hill of his body. *I'm so sorry.*

Tears fall from my eyes and drip down my chin. "They're trying to convince us that she's already gone, that she won't ever come back because there's no brain activity. But Hands, I will not—"

My voice breaks and so do I. I sob like I haven't done since my parents died. My entire body shakes and convulses.

How dare they. Wanting to let her die. Blair's inside her mind. I know it. She has to be. I just can't reach her.

When the tears stop, I sit up and press the heels of my hands into my eyes for a moment. I exhale hard, pushing out all the oxygen in my lungs. "The bookshop."

What about it?

Hands plucks several tissues from a box and offers them. I take the fingerful and blot my face. I wad up the tissues, gulp down several breaths and fall back on the chair.

Thinking about something besides Blair helps, and if I talk fast, maybe I won't break down again. "The magic is broken, and the place is a mess. I told Clara that I'd try to help. I think there may be a way to stabilize it. It won't work long term, but it could last a few days. It's the least that I can do."

And then sadness overwhelms me again. It comes in waves, ebbing and flowing. At the hospital it's easier to keep it in check, to be strong for Blair's family. But when it's just me and Hands, I can't hold up pretenses any longer.

"Hands, this is my fau—"

He grabs my fingers and shakes them. When I look up, he signs, *Stop. This is not your fault. You can't blame yourself. Blair knew this would happen, and she wanted to be with you. You wanted to be with her. You've got to stop guilting yourself.*

That's easier said than done. But Hands is right. Blaming myself isn't going to help anything. I have to stop. Got to focus on something else, at least for a few hours, give myself a task. If I can't save Blair, then maybe I can save her family.

"You're absolutely right. Now, the bookshop."

Hands waits a moment before replying, studying to make sure that I'm okay.

I roll my eyes. "I'm fine. Not fine, heartbroken. Destroyed. But the bookshop needs stable magic, something to bring it together and focus it."

There's a long pause because Hands knows what I'm suggesting and he doesn't like it. But right now I don't care. I want to be reckless. I want Blair back.

Yes, it's an absolute miracle that she lived at all. The truck hit her, but it didn't run over her. That's the only thing that saved her life. She broke so many bones—pelvis, leg, arms, cracked ribs.

And then there's the brain damage.

Devlin, Hands warns.

"Don't *Devlin* me. It's the only way that I know to lock down the magic enough so that maybe it can repair itself. Magic is alive, you know that, and if it's fed what it needs, maybe it can mend itself—at least for a little while, until one of the daughters can..."

The thought of marriage hits me hard and I'm overtaken again. It's a few minutes before I can speak.

I exhale. "This might not even work. But it's worth a try." I rise from the chair, entwine my fingers and rest my hands on the back of my neck. "And you can't stop me. Even if you attempt it, I'm still going to do this, so you either help me or you stay out of my way."

He scratches the fingers of the opposite hand. *I don't like it.*

"I'm doing it for Blair."

You'll have to be careful.

Not interested in that, but sure. "I will be."

How much power do you want to draw out?

"As much as I can lose without dying."

No surprise there, he signs. *I'll monitor you.*

Downstairs in the basement, I find the holding vessels that I've tucked away, locked in a cabinet. They're ancient oil lamps, the kind that genies are supposed to be locked inside. They're empty now, all genies having vacated the property, and they're perfect for what I need.

How many are you going to use? Hands signs.

"Three." He flexes his fingers frantically. "Yes, three," I growl. "If you don't like it, you can leave."

He jumps onto the table and drags himself over to the first lamp. Point taken.

I place both hands on the cold metal and close my eyes. I

feel magic inside me, trapped, waiting to be released, so I let it go, allowing it to flow out of me and inside the vessel.

I open my eyes to make sure this is working. Power drips from me, falling in a stream. It's a beautiful thing to witness, golden energy filling the lamp, the lamp drinking up as much as I want to give—and more than that, even. So much more.

Each second that I give of myself, the effect is instantaneous. I was already tired, but fatigue hits me like a wall. I stagger forward and catch myself before I collapse on the table.

Hands flicks his fingers up at me frantically.

"I'm fine."

I'm not fine, but I'm going to keep on.

When magic begins to spill out from the top of the first lamp, I stop. Hands caps it and reluctantly grabs the second lamp, opening the lid.

His disdain for what I'm doing is obvious. I don't care. If Hands was in the same situation, he would do this. He would help the family of the woman he loves.

By the time we fill the third lamp, I'm so drained that I can barely stand. "Thank you," I say weakly before heading upstairs and falling onto the couch.

My eyes close and I sleep. It's the first sleep I've had in days. Every time I've shut my eyes before then has been plagued with worry, fear for Blair, guilt. But today, I sleep.

It doesn't last long, maybe an hour. When I wake up, I'm still exhausted, but at least I can walk.

I shrug on a jacket, call the lamps to me. They don't come. Apparently I used too much of my magic. I walk down the stairs on shaky legs and retrieve them.

Upstairs I catch a glimpse of myself in the mirror. Haven't shaved in days, and a patchy beard's beginning to grow in. My eyes are sunken; so are what I can see of my cheeks. Can't remember the last time I ate.

I wipe a hand down my face and head out without saying goodbye to Hands.

The bookshop looks closed. The lights are dim as if they're trying to keep people away. When I enter, I understand why.

Soon as I step over the threshold, a book flies at me. I duck in time. It just misses me and hits the wall behind me with a splat.

If I had energy, I would react to that. But I'm just barely hanging in there. I stagger in and see Chelsea.

"Devlin!" Her eyes widen in concern. "Are you okay? No, obviously you're not okay. None of us are okay. What are you doing here? Wait. Let me get you a chair."

She finds a chair, and my legs nearly give out before I sit on it. The store is a wreck. Books lie everywhere. Some are trying to lift from the floor, limply flapping in an attempt to get airborne. Another flies in circles.

"I just talked to Mama. I can't believe what they want to do."

Tears swell in her eyes, and she plucks a tissue from her pocket, blows into it and shakes out her hair, pulling herself together.

"As you can see, the place isn't suitable for customers. I'm trying to clean up, but the books are fighting me more than they are helping."

I hand her the box that I'm holding. My words come out shaky. It's hard to talk. If Hands saw this, he would strangle me. I went too far, he would say.

Hands would be right.

My hands tremble as I point inside. "These lamps hold my power. This isn't permanent, but the theory is that when magic is broken, sometimes it needs a battery, if you will, and the extra charge will help it right itself."

Her eyes light up with understanding. "You're trying to fix this."

I nod.

"With your own magic?

I nod again.

"Devlin, you shouldn't have done this."

"Just try it," I whisper. "Open one and see."

Her brow wrinkles and I can tell she's trying to figure out a way to not take the gift. She even starts to push the box back into my hands, but I push it back. "No. Do it. Try."

She sighs. "Okay. Tell me how."

"Just open one up and the power will release. It'll mingle with the magic here." I point weakly to the ceiling. "If it works, the bookshop will suck up the magic"—my breathing is labored—"and it will right itself. At least temporarily."

Her fingers tighten on the box, and I can tell she wants to —no, *needs* to try this.

"Do it, Chelsea."

With a slow nod she steps behind the front counter and opens the box, dipping her hand inside.

"Ouch! It shocked me!" She yanks her hand out and sucks on her fingers.

"Secondary effect," I tell her. "They're charged."

"Wish I'd been warned," she mutters. She grabs a cleaning rag and pulls one of the lamps out, setting it atop the counter. "Do I open it? Is that all?"

"That's all. And get out of the way."

Using the rag like an oven mitt, she slowly pulls off the lid and steps back.

Magic explodes from the lamp, hitting Chelsea with a wave of air that makes her hair lift and her shirt flutter. Power shoots straight up to the ceiling, where the golden flame fans out above us. The magic is quickly sucked up by the building, soaking into the walls and ceiling before there's a brief pause.

Her gaze darts to me. "What next?"

"Give it a second."

One, two, three.

The building rumbles and Chelsea ducks down. "Is it going to collapse?"

"The magicks are talking to one another."

"It sounds like they're fighting." She glances up fearfully. "Like one of them just punched the other. Oops, sorry, Devlin."

I wave off her apology. "It's okay."

A moment later the rumbling stops. "Let's see if it worked," I whisper.

It takes another second or two, but the books begin to right themselves. The tome flying in circles stops and dives back onto a shelf. The ones trying lamely to get their covers to flap lift and, by magic, sweep up off the floor and find their way back to where they belong.

The whole place brightens as if it's taken on new energy.

Which I suppose it has—my energy.

Chelsea slowly looks around, watching in astonishment as the entire shop regains its composure, if you will.

She exhales a low breath. "Holy cow. I think you did it."

"It's but a small token of appreciation for your family."

She shakes her head. "You've done so much already. Blair loves you." Her eyes well with tears. "You've given her so much happiness."

She breaks off into tears. I rise and cross to the counter to give her a hug. She breaks down in my arms, and it takes all I've got not to crack, too.

I don't know what to say. Tell her that everything will be okay, and it's a lie. It doesn't feel like anything's going to be all right ever again. There's a hole in my heart that will never, ever be filled.

The giving of myself is the absolute very least that I can do for this family.

But instead of saying any of that, the only thing I can reassure her with is, "When the lamp's light is gone, use one of the others, and let me know when you're on the last. I'll refill them. I'll do whatever I can to keep the magic strong until…"

Until what?

I can't even think about it. Until I marry Blair? Until she wakes up?

I don't have answers. I don't have anything that I can give except my magic, and I'll give all of it, even if it kills me.

Which it just might.

DEVLIN

*I*t's been a few days since I first gave the lamp to Chelsea, and according to Clara, whom I see every day at the hospital, it's working. For now.

Using my magic to stabilize Castleview Books isn't a save-all. It's a Band-Aid on a wound that will eventually need stitches.

But if a bandage works for the moment, then I'm all in.

I'm back with Blair. The bruises that would be patching her face were healed by magic. She looks perfect, like Sleeping Beauty, and I'm not giving up on her.

I take her hand and squeeze it. "I know you're in there. Wake up. Please wake up. I can't..." I squash down a sob. "I just got you back. I can't lose you again."

I study her, looking for any sign that she can hear me—a twitch of her eyelid, a flexing of her fingers, but there's nothing.

A knock comes from the door. "Mr. Ross."

I look up to see Dr. Jones, who I like and despise at the same time. He's taken good care of Blair, but his bedside manner is lacking.

"Dr. Jones," I grind out.

"Can we talk?"

About the same thing that we discussed before? The last time we chatted, when Blair's parents were in attendance, out of respect for them, I didn't give this man a piece of my mind. But now we're alone. Now he's fresh meat.

I nod and release Blair's hand. She's hooked up to so many wires that I just want to rip them out. I give her one last look before stepping into the hallway.

I lean against the wall to keep myself upright. I've given so much magic that standing for long periods of time is grueling if not impossible. But I wouldn't take a moment of it back.

"Mr. Ross, I know this isn't easy, and I know that you aren't married to Blair, but that was your plan."

It does not escape my attention that he uses the past tense when talking about her future.

I fold my arms. "We wanted to be married as soon as possible."

He nods, his expression full of concern. False concern, if you ask me. "You and I have talked about this before, but there are things you need to seriously think about."

I exhale with a hiss.

"This is hard," he explains, sympathy in his eyes, "but I've seen cases like hers before. The chances that Blair will wake up are slim, so slim that the percentage is below one percent. You need to consider letting her go. You can spend a lifetime feeding her through a tube, but is that the life she would want?"

"You don't know what she would want," I growl.

He lifts his hands in surrender. "You're right. I don't. But is this what *you* want for her? A life hooked up? Because since she's not up and moving around, she's at risk of developing bedsores. Her muscles will atrophy because she's not using them. I know you have magic, and maybe some of the side

291

effects can be diminished, but they're still a possibility. Mr. Ross, her future is up to you, but I know what kind of life I would want for my loved one."

The nerve of this man. "One where they starve to death? You would have me commit murder," I say, glaring at him. "But I get it, it's not murder if your scans show that she's brain-dead, is it?"

His nostrils flare. "This is a decision for you and her parents."

"Doc, with all due respect, she's in there. You don't see it, but I know it. Blair is alive and she's trapped. She just needs to be unlocked. I don't know how. But that's the truth."

He shoots me a look like he feels sorry for my delusion. "Get back to me. I'm working this weekend."

He pats my shoulder as if that's supposed to ease the harshness of his words.

After he walks away, I scoff. What kind of medical ethics is this? Telling me to let Blair starve to death? I punch a fist into my hand. I'd like to punch a wall, but I don't have the strength.

I walk back into the room and sit down, my legs weak.

I refuse to consider a future without her in it. "Doctor just wanted to tell me how good you're doing. He said you're gonna be just fine." I take her hand and kiss the back of it. "Just fine, indeed."

As soon as I get home, Hands lays into me. *You need to shave. And take a shower. You smell terrible.*

I shake my head. "I don't care."

If Blair wakes up tomorrow, she won't recognize you.

"Yes, she will."

He points to a hall mirror, and I take a look. My hair's

shaggy, a patchy beard is clinging to my cheeks and my eyes are sunken in.

Okay, so Hands has a point. "Fine. I'll clean up."

After I get out of the shower and swipe a hand over the fogged-up mirror, the only thing that I can think is that a dead man is staring back at me—one who looks like all it will take is a strong wind to snap him in half.

Well, it's probably just about true. But somehow I find the strength to shave and put on a clean set of clothes.

I'm exhausted by the time I get back downstairs. Hands has cooked fresh trout and couscous. It smells delicious—the couscous is buttery, the trout is flaky, and I have no appetite. But I can't let Hands's food go to waste.

I sit at the table and take a small bite. I know it's good because Hands is a superb cook, but everything tastes like sawdust.

How was she today? he signs, taking a spot at the end of the table.

"The same." I move the food around on the plate with my fork, simulating eating. "The doctor approached me again about letting her go."

Maniac.

"I know. I get that he doesn't know her and so he's not invested, but I am. Her parents are; her family is."

It's too bad that your ability to see the future can't save her now.

"I know." Hands doesn't mean that in a bad way, and I don't take it like that. "But I don't have my power anyway. Blair still does."

Hands freezes while reaching for the salt. I assume to give it to me because Hands doesn't eat. *You can influence?*

"Yeah." I take a bite of the trout and force it down. "What?"

Could you influence her out of the coma?

What? I do a double take. "What did you say?"

Influence her out of the coma.

I drop the fork. Everything stops. The world tips on its side, and I'm falling off, crashing into stars—stars that could change my life.

I jump out of the chair, and it crashes to the floor behind me. "Oh my gods, Hands. You're brilliant! Why didn't I think of that? Influence Blair! I can influence her to come out." I look around for my jacket, find it and slip it on. "Thanks for the meal, but I've got to go. I've got to reach the hospital as soon as possible."

CLARA AND PHILLIP are with Blair when I arrive at the private room. Clara looks up. "I thought you were going home to get some rest."

"I did." My hands are twitching, I'm ready to jump in, but I don't want to give her parents false hope.

Phillip wrinkles his brow. "Everything all right?"

The energy that I've got left pulses through my body—it's antsy, jonesing to be released. "Can I be alone with her for just a moment?"

They exchange a look, and then Clara rises from the chair. "Of course."

"Thanks. There's something I need to say to her. It won't take long."

"We'll leave you alone." She ushers Phillip out the door. "We'll grab something to drink," she tells him.

As soon as they're gone, I nearly leap into the chair. I take Blair's hand and flare up her power.

Magic stirs in my heart, and I close my eyes, focusing it on reaching Blair. When I've done this in the past, all I've had to do was send a gentle (or in Storm's case, *not* so gentle) suggestion down a line of magic and straight into the person I was targeting.

But this is going to take more than a gentle push. This will take it all. I focus my magic on breaking through the barrier to her mind and nudging her.

Wake up. Wake up. Come back.

I keep sending the thought, watching and waiting, putting every bit of power that's in my body into nudging and nudging, pushing and pushing, wrapping my magic around her head like a pair of hands and diving deep into her mind, deeper than I had to go with Storm, diving like I'm trying to reach the bottom of the ocean and may not make it back up for air. It's the one shot I've got, so everything has to go into it.

I think about the doctor saying she's got less than a one percent chance of coming out of this, I think about a life of Blair never waking up, I think about how I want to see us married, with children, how I want to grow old with her, and how I want her to open a potion shop and really become the best version of herself.

It's because of her that I'm the best version of *myself*.

All these thoughts pour out of me along with the magic, and I'm still diving, still trying to reach the bottom of the ocean when—

Her eyelids flutter.

Was that real? She hasn't moved in so long that it feels like a mirage—an oasis resting deep in the desert, an illusion, but I'm praying that it isn't.

With one last push, I release the last drop of power I have, until—

Her pinkie twitches.

And I sever the connection. There's nothing left. I'm a dried-up husk. But for Blair, I will find the last bit of energy hiding inside me.

I take her hand. "Blair?"

Her fingers slowly curl around mine, and hope explodes in my chest.

"Blair?"

She blinks a few times. Her eyes open, and oh my gods, but it's a miracle!

She takes a good long look at me and then throws herself into my arms. She clutches onto me like I'm a life raft in the middle of the ocean. Never in my life have I experienced such relief.

It's feels like a house has been sitting on my shoulders and it's finally crumbled to the ground. I stroke the back of her head and hold her tight, cradling Blair like she's the most precious thing in the world, because she is.

She bursts into tears, and I pull back, wiping the streaks from her cheeks with my thumb. My heart's racing in my throat. Is she okay? "What's wrong? Are you in pain?"

She shakes her head, gulps down some air. "I was so scared. I was so afraid."

"Shh. You're safe now. Everything's going to be all right."

She hiccups and hugs me again, resting her cheek on my shoulder and whispering, "It was horrible. I couldn't reach you. All I wanted to do was see you and talk to you. I tried so hard, so many times. I tried to come back, but I couldn't." A shaky breath staggers from her lungs. "I thought I'd never be with you again."

I hug her tighter. "I felt the same way, but here we are, and everything's going to be all right." I stroke the back of her head and try to lighten the situation with, "This is nothing that a good nudging couldn't take care of."

She barks a laugh and pulls back, eyelids puffy, nose red— it's the most beautiful sight. Blair crying means she's alive, she's here with me.

A sly smile spreads across her face. "You nudged me."

"I did. You impressed?"

"I'm so much more than impressed. You are my hero."

I kiss the back of her hand. "I will take that compliment

happily every day for the rest of my life, and I will do everything in my power to live up to that."

Her brow quirks. "Are those going to be your wedding vows?"

I laugh. "Do you want them to be?"

"If they are, then I'm all in."

We laugh a moment and then slowly move in for a kiss. She pauses, pulls back. "My breath."

"Your teeth get brushed every day."

"Oh, that's right." She breaks into a smile. "Well, then, please kiss me. Kiss me forever and don't stop. I want to drown in you, Devlin Ross, and only you."

I kiss her as passionately as I dare, seeing as how she just woke up from a coma, and I'm sure she needs to be examined. But this kiss is everything. It's about a future that lays before us like a yellow brick road, it's about hope and it's all about love.

When we break apart, I caress her cheek, and she tilts her face into my touch. "I love you so much," she whispers.

"I love you more."

"Doubtful. I love you to infinity," she boasts.

I chuckle. "I love you to infinity plus one."

She closes her eyes and smiles, and that's when I remember. "Your parents! They just went down the hall. I need to tell them. And the nurses!" I turn my head toward the door and shout, "She's awake!"

When no one comes, I rise, my legs still weak. I kiss her hand again. "Stay right where you are. Don't move." I release her to take one step away and then turn back around. "You promise not to go anywhere, right?"

She lifts the arm with the IV stuck inside her. "Trust me, I'm not going anywhere."

"Just being sure. I love you, Blair Thornrose."

She grins. "I love you, too, Devlin Ross."

I open the door and take one last look at her. "Be right back."

Then I race down the hall, shouting, "She's awake! Get the doctor!"

A nurse starts to rush past me to check on Blair, and I grab her by the shoulders. "Did you see which direction her parents went?"

She points down the hall. "That way."

Everyone I see, I tell them that Blair's awake. They don't know me. They don't know Blair, but I don't care. My world is restored. Blair is alive! She didn't die and she's awake!

I'm just about to round a corner when her parents whip around it. "She's awake," I exclaim, throwing my arms up.

Clara presses her palms to her cheeks. "Thank the gods!"

Phillip hugs her. "It's a miracle!"

I stop, out of breath, and place both hands on my hips. Panting, I reply, "Yes, it is."

I'm about to turn and go back to Blair's room, but I can't move. My energy's vanished. All of it. I used too much magic. I used every single ounce that was within me, and with it went my life force.

My legs aren't responding. They're not listening to me, and before I'm able to stop, my knees buckle. I reach for the wall as I fall to floor.

My last thought as darkness falls on me is, *At least I saw her one last time before I died.*

39

$\mathcal{D}$evlin gave too much. He gave all of himself and so much more. And now he's paying for it.

I was lost, so lost in my own head that I almost didn't feel him nudging me. It was so subtle, so quiet that I nearly missed it.

It was a dim light shining like a beacon, and when I saw it, I reached for it, but it was just beyond my grasp. It took all my focus to grab it, and when I did, it pulled me in, wrapped around me and nudged me awake. It influenced me back to life, like a breath of air from God had been blown into my lungs.

And the darkness swept past and the sounds got louder, and that pinkie finger that I'd been trying to move finally twitched and my eyes were open and there sat Devlin!

And everything was perfect. I was back. He was there.

Then he collapsed.

He gave too much of himself. He gave it all, not leaving anything for himself to draw from.

We've switched places. How ironic is this? By saving me, he put himself in mortal danger.

And now Devlin is at my parent's house, in my bed, sleeping. There was no point in keeping him at a human hospital. There was nothing that they could do anyway.

My parents, myself and my sisters stand around him, and we've got one shot to do this and do it right.

"Place your hands on him," Nana directs.

Oh yeah, Nana. She hasn't gone anywhere. She actually kept the house together while I was asleep. I prefer to think of myself as asleep rather than in a coma. Who doesn't like a good *Sleeping Beauty* reference?

We do as she says, placing our hands on Devlin. He's cold, but he still has a pulse. He's lost so much weight these past weeks. It breaks my heart. I've lost weight, too. I'm wearing the engagement ring on my middle finger. Once I get back to my regular weight, it won't slip off my ring finger anymore. I can't wait for that day.

"Now," Nana tells us, "give him your power. Just a little. Give him some magic."

Yes, all of us are pitching in because, as you know, we don't have much magic left. But we give what we can to him, and within seconds his body is glowing. The hollows of his cheeks fill out. The circles under his eyes lighten, and he lifts a hand and touches his head.

"I know y'all didn't just give me every ounce of power you have to save my life," he says with smirk.

My heart leaps with joy. "No," I tell him, tears spilling down my cheeks. "We only gave you half."

His eyes pop open. He sees me and he tugs me into a hug, pulling me down onto the bed. "I thought I'd lost you again."

"Never," I whisper.

My dad squeezes his shoulder. "I'm glad you're back, son."

"Me too," Nana announces.

I stifle a laugh. Everyone tells Devlin that they're happy he's back, and Mama says, "We'll leave you two alone."

I sit on the bed, and he sits up, placing his back on the headboard. He glances up and around. "So this is your room. The very secret and very elusive boudoir of one Blair Thornrose."

"Do you like it?"

He cocks his head and studies the space. "I'm thinking it needs boy band posters."

I tip my face to the ceiling and laugh. "You know, you're right. It could use some." My gaze drops back to meet his, and we smile wearily at one another. Devlin slides a hand up my cheek, and I lean into his touch. "How dare you leave me right after I woke up."

He laughs weakly. "I was trying to help your family."

"It worked, from what they've said. You have saved us."

"For now."

"For now."

We stare at each other another moment, and that's when pressure builds in my chest. My rib cage expands, and it feels like my heart's about to push through my sternum. The intensity climaxes until it releases like liquid spilling out of a popped water balloon.

Immediately after, a tingle worms its way into my chest. It's a very familiar magic, one that I've been missing for some time.

I suck air, mouth open. "Our powers switched back."

Devlin cracks a smile. "So they did."

I think we realize at the same time, just like on the night he proposed, why our powers hadn't returned earlier, and for that I'm beyond grateful.

If I had been in charge of my influence when I was hit by that truck, I might never have woken up.

Devlin needed to have my gift this entire time.

He opens his arms, and I fall on top of him. He grunts as if in pain.

I sit up, afraid that I've crushed some vital part of him. "Did I hurt you?"

He shakes his head. "Darlin', I will take a little pain from you any day." I slowly lay down on top of him, and Devlin smooths my hair. "You know what's ironic?"

"What's that?"

"Everything that's happened—us getting together, you accepting my proposal—all of it is because our powers switched, a thing that neither of us wanted."

I smile. "What we both thought was the worst thing that could ever have happened to us, became the best thing."

"It sure did."

He takes my hand and threads his fingers through mine. "And just think—you were so mad about it all."

"I was."

"And look where we are—if that one moment had never happened, we wouldn't be here. We wouldn't be engaged. You'd still *pretend* hate me."

I giggle. "But I'd be secretly pining for you the whole time."

"Just like I would be for you."

I lift my head and rest my chin on my hands, which are folded on his chest. "But you did too much, Devlin. You gave too much, and because of it, I could have lost you."

"I did it to help your family."

"No more helping my family like that. You almost got yourself killed."

"Worthy cause."

He takes my face in his hands and pulls me into a kiss. It tastes like a lifetime of *I missed yous.*

I never want this kiss to end. I want it to last forever. I want this moment with Devlin to last forever.

"What was it like?" he asks when we separate.

I sigh and rest my head on his chest. "I could hear everything. I heard when you went outside the room with my parents and the doctor told you to let me go."

Devlin's body tenses beneath me. "For the record, I would have brought you back to my house and hired a full-time nursing staff to look over you."

"I know you would have."

He rubs his fingers down my arm. "So. Think your power is still a curse?"

"Ha ha. No. I don't. Not anymore."

"Good."

"And what about yours?" I sit up and look into those green and gold eyes.

"What I think, is that there is sometimes more to the story than the snippet of vision that I receive."

"Like..."

"Like the outcome." He smirks. "This outcome was a helluva lot better than I thought it would be."

"That's an understatement."

He's quiet for a moment. "Hey, where's your ring?"

I lift my hand and show him the sparkling gems on my finger.

"We can get it sized," he tells me.

"No. I'll gain the weight back. I don't want this ring out of my sight for any reason at all. I've spent too long loving and hating you to have you take this away from me to get it made smaller."

"You've heard of something called magic, right?"

I laugh and drop my face to his chest. "I forgot. You know, when your family's pretty much depleted and your business is on the fritz, it's easy to forget about something called magic."

"Speaking of"—he takes my hand—"when do you want to get married?"

"Honestly?"

"Absolutely."

I frown.

"What?"

"You're not just trying to get married quickly so that you can save my family's business, right?"

"How did you know my evil plan?" he jokes.

I grin. "You're so transparent."

"So are you." We kiss and when he pulls back he murmurs, "I'm serious. When do you want to get married?"

I think about it a moment, and then I answer.

40

*I*t's been a month since I awoke, and it's my wedding day.

Sounds like we're doing this shotgun style, doesn't it? We just got engaged and are already getting married. But don't worry, there's not a bun in this oven, just a woman who really really really wants to start spending the rest of her life with the man she's loved (secretly and begrudgingly) for the past ten years.

And I'm so ready for it.

A knock comes from the door. "Come in."

Addison appears. She's wearing a beautiful high-waisted lavender gown that reveals her tiny baby bump. It's adorable. I love it. Can't wait to be an aunt.

"Do you have everything?" she asks.

"Of course she does," Chelsea responds, handing me my shoes. "Dallas and I are here."

Dallas grabs a white cowboy hat from the bed and puts it on. "Yeah, Addison, we've got this."

"They're taking good care of me," I assure her. "And please thank Feylin again for allowing us to marry in the castle."

"Of course. Let me see you."

I take one last look in the full-length mirror and exhale. My gown, against Mama's most motherly desire for me, is midnight blue. It's the dress that I was wearing the night that Devlin proposed. This dress has had one great thing happen in it, and several bad things—Storm's explosion, Cathy, the truck.

So I wanted to give it another good memory, because I deserve it. I deserve to not be pinned down by a memory that I had no control over. I'd rather live in good ones, so I'm giving that to this dress, and after our wedding, I have a feeling it's going to become my lucky gown.

Or maybe that's just me hoping. But everyone needs hope, right?

"Do you have your something old?" Addison asks.

Chelsea pulls out a broach that belonged to Nana. "Right here."

She pins the pearls on me.

"Great!" Addison does a little fist pump. "What about something new?"

"Shoes." I show her my feet and the fresh heels I'm wearing. "What do you think?"

"Oh, I love that they're so pearly," she says as Dallas flits around me, fluffing out my veil. "Something blue is your dress."

I turn this way and that. "Yes."

"And something borrowed?"

"The pin," Chelsea says.

"Nana's dead," I tell her. "It can't be borrowed because she's not going to need it anymore."

She grimaces. "Good point."

Addison's brows lift. "So you don't have anything?"

"No, I've got...no. I don't have anything." How do I not have anything borrowed? How did we forget this? I quickly scan the room. What can I take with me? The footstool? No, obviously not. The mirror? The bed?

I need to just stop.

"I was afraid of that," Addison says, pulling something out from behind her back.

It's the rose bouquet from when she married Feylin, and the roses are as perfect as if they haven't aged a day. There's a single golden rose nestled in the middle of all the red ones, but that's another story for another time.

I can't believe it. "You kept this?"

"Of course I did." She waves me away like *why wouldn't I?* "Here. Take it. Unless you don't want to."

"No, of course not. I'm not married to my bouquet. I mean" —I sink onto one hip—"I'm not *marrying* my bouquet. But I love yours, thank you!"

She gives me a warm hug before pushing the flowers into my hands. "Here." She touches the ends of my hair. "You look beautiful."

I do a mock curtsy. "Thank you, Your Highness."

"Stop it. I may be a queen here, but I'm always just your sister, who loves you."

I fan my face to keep from tearing up. "Stop it. I don't need to cry and ruin my makeup."

"Yeah, I'm pretty sure Devlin would dump you if that happened," Dallas says sarcastically.

"One day," I tell her, "you'll fall in love, and you'll talk differently about this."

She rolls her eyes. "I doubt it."

"Me too," Chelsea says. "I seriously doubt I'll be falling in love with anybody anytime soon. So, hurry up and save our magic for now, Blair! We need you."

I burst into laughter. My sisters mean well, and I wouldn't know what to do with myself if I didn't have them.

"All right." I take one last look in the mirror. "Who's ready to get married?"

"You are," they shout.

We burst into laughter, and Addison takes me by the arm. "Come on. I'll walk you to Dad."

The four of us head out of the room and I exhale. My heart's fluttering against my chest. My stomach's tight. I never thought that I'd be nervous doing this—then again, I never thought that I'd be marrying Devlin, so there's that—but I am unequivocally nervous. *So* nervous.

I take a deep breath as I walk down the stairs. Addison leads me to the door that signals the entrance to the garden. Last year she got married here, in the exact spot where Devlin and I are about to tie the knot. This place holds good memories for my family. I hope to add more to it.

My sisters drop me off beside my dad.

"Good luck," Dallas says.

I shoot her a look. "What's that supposed to mean?"

She shrugs. "It means good luck. Don't trip."

"I wasn't even thinking about that until you said something," I hiss.

Chelsea pats my arm. "Ignore her. She's young. Stupid."

"I am not."

Addison ushers them both through the door. "Come on. Let's get in our seats."

They shuffle off, Dallas still snipping at Chelsea. Chelsea was only kidding. My younger sister will get over it soon enough.

Devlin and I decided against bridesmaids and groomsmen. We wanted it to be just us, and let our families enjoy the ceremony.

My dad looks great. His hair is combed to one side, and he's beaming at me. His tie's crooked, so I fix it and press down his lapel.

"Never thought I'd see the day you married Devlin Ross." He puffs out his chest with a deep breath. "Though I always liked him."

"Even when he'd bring two dates to a dance?"

"It just showed me that he wasn't serious about them. Besides"—insert stern fatherly glance here—"he always asked you to dance, which said even more, I suppose."

The music begins and Dad leads me outside. It's a gorgeous day in the fae garden, as it should be. Guests fill every seat. There are witches and wizards, werewolves and vampires. Magicals have come from all over to witness my marriage.

"Psst."

I glance over at Nana, who's sitting in a seat. She's actually sitting in an entire row filled with other ghosts, who are all smiling and giving me thumbs-up.

Once her existence was out in the open, it didn't take long before other spirits started coming out of their proverbial closets. For all the people that pretended to be so offended and terrified at the ball the night Nana showed herself, almost half of them were being haunted by their own relatives.

Can you believe that?

I suppose it's no surprise, because folks like to point fingers a lot, even when they're doing the same thing that they're pointing the finger for in the first place.

"Knock 'em dead, kid," Nana says.

"Thanks," I whisper.

For some reason I don't think brides are supposed to talk when they're walking down the aisle. That seems like something that would only happen in a romantic comedy.

Devlin's been standing with his back to me, but just now he turns around and I'm knocked over by how handsome he looks. He must think the same thing about me because he clutches his heart with both hands and pretends to stagger back.

I grin and press the bouquet to my nose bashfully. He is so beautiful. His hair is raked back from his forehead. It's thick and wavy. His golden skin is nearly glowing, and he looks like his handsome old self.

After his collapse, my family wouldn't take any more of his magic for the store unless he limited what he gave us.

So he did.

Me being back helped him make that decision, and I'm more than grateful that he didn't kill himself trying to save my family.

A life without Devlin is no life at all. Now that I've gotten him and I'm swimming in the ocean that is Devlin, able to see him whenever I want, talk to him, cuddle with him, I honestly don't know how I survived this long without him. He is everything to me, and always has been.

I'm pretty sure that I'm everything to him, too.

Just kidding, I *know* that I am.

In the front seat sits Hands. Beside him is Lilly, Devlin's grandmother. She smiles warmly at me. Hands gives me the okay sign, and I wink in return.

And then Dad delivers me to Devlin and he takes my hand, kissing it like a gentleman.

"Sorry," he tells the priest, "I couldn't wait for 'man and wife' to kiss her."

The crowd laughs. I laugh. He's just the most charming fellow. He knows it, too.

"You look beautiful," he whispers.

"So do you."

"Thank you. So. You ready to get married?"

"More than ready."

As soon as we say, "I do," a heaviness fills the air. Magic imbues my body from head to toe—the family's magic. Two daughters down, five to go, and our power won't be secure until each of us is wed.

But for now, we're safe.

And then the ceremony is over. I'm being kissed and everyone's dancing and celebrating.

My heart is so full that it could explode. It *might*. I don't know. *Maybe*. Actually it better not. That sucker better keep on ticking for another hundred years. I want to suck every drop of life from this existence with my brand-new husband that I can.

After my family's many congratulations and our guests shower us with so much love, the sun begins to set and fairy lights flare to life around us, suspended in the air by magic. A breeze moves through the trees, and Devlin eyes me from the other side of the makeshift dance floor, where he's talking to Feylin. When Addison joins them, he excuses himself and approaches where I sit, basking in all the joy.

"Dance?"

I grin. "Aren't you tired of dancing?"

"Not with you." He extends his left hand that now sports a wedding band. "I'll never get tired of dancing with you."

I let him pull me to standing, and we move slowly, my cheek on his shoulder and Devlin holding me to him. He chuckles.

"What is it?"

He sighs happily. "I was just remembering that tango we did to make Storm jealous and how I was ready to rip your clothes off by the end of it."

"You can rip my clothes off tonight."

"It would be my pleasure, and I'm sorry to bring up Grayson."

Storm is currently sitting in a cell, all his money unable to buy him out of the Castleview jail. That's because Devlin has about as much money and can hire just as good of lawyers as Storm.

"You know, there's one thing that bothers me," I tell him.

"Now what could be bothering you on a night as perfect as this one?"

"I never found out what kind of supernatural Storm is."

"What? You don't know?"

I lift my head and study him. He is genuinely baffled that I have no clue. "No. Do you?"

He chuckles. "Of course I do."

"How do you know?"

"Isn't it obvious?"

I scoff. "If you know, then what is he? Not that it matters, because the type of supernatural a person is, isn't important. It's what's on the inside that counts, but Storm's insides aren't any good, so maybe his outside is better."

"Well said."

"It wasn't, but thank you. So. What is he?"

Devlin's lips pull back into a seductive smile. "What will you give me if I tell you?"

I throw out my arms dramatically. "The world."

"I don't want the world. I only want you."

"Then you have me. So?"

He grimaces. "I'm not sure it's my place to tell."

I tickle his side. "Devlin Ross, if you don't tell me right now, I'll scream."

"Fine. Fine. Storm Grayson is half wizard."

"That much I guessed. What else?"

He clears his throat. Devlin's really milking this suspense. I just about want to tickle it out of him. "The other half of him is fae."

My jaw drops. "How did I not ever think that?"

"I don't know. Why didn't you?"

"I should have. All the signs are there except for Feylin inviting him to the castle and loudly proclaiming it."

"They sure are." He lifts my hand over my head and spins

me. When I fall back onto him, he says, "So. Are you ready to go to bed?"

I tug my teeth over my bottom lip. His gaze flicks to my mouth. "I'm ready to be your wife."

"Then let's go to bed."

EPILOGUE

5 MONTHS LATER

"We came as soon as we heard," I tell Mama, dropping my purse on a chair. "How is Addison?"

"The doctor's with her now," she says, nodding to the closed door.

"And Feylin?"

"He's inside."

I exhale. "Good."

Devlin slides up behind me and wraps a hand around my waist. "Is there anything you need, Clara?"

She shakes her head. "No. Just for my grandbaby to be born, safe and sound."

The castle is buzzing with activity. Servants are running this way and that. My sisters are pacing the halls, and so is my dad, who stops moving every once in a while to toss a football to Ryals, who's excited to be getting a new baby brother or sister.

Though Feylin is technically Ryals's cousin, he and Addison officially adopted him as their son, and they couldn't have asked for a better child—and he couldn't have gotten better parents, in my humble opinion.

"What can I do?" I ask Mama.

She shakes her head. "Just wait. Like the rest of us."

I glance around the hall nervously. My big sister's having a baby. A baby! I say a silent prayer that the delivery goes off without a hitch.

"Do you want to sit?" Devlin asks, pointing to a couch.

"I can't." My nerves are jumping. "I won't be calm until I get word that there's a healthy mama and baby."

As if on cue, the door to Addison's room opens and Feylin pops his head out. He's wearing scrubs and a cap. He looks like a human surgeon.

We all hold our breath. Okay, *I* hold my breath.

"Addison's doing great." His gaze sweeps the hall. "And it's a girl!"

A gush of air swooshes from my lungs in relief. "Yay!"

My family shouts in happiness. We hug one another as servants clap and congratulate Feylin.

Mama sighs blissfully and Nana floats up beside her, shrugging. "I knew everything would be fine. She's my grand-daughter. Of course it's all fine."

Mama rolls her eyes. "When can we see them?" she asks Feylin.

"In just a few minutes."

Dad and Devlin approach Feylin and give him all the manly congratulations, hand shaking and back patting. Then he turns to Ryals. "You've got a little sister. What do you think of that?"

Ryals throws his arms up in the air and cheers. His happiness is contagious, and it's impossible not to smile.

It's a few minutes before we're able to see Addison and the baby. We don't barge in all at once; we go in a few at a time.

When Devlin and I enter the room, Addison's lying in the

bed cradling a tiny bundle. Feylin's sitting beside her smiling down at the baby girl.

Addison lifts her to me. "Do you want to hold her?"

"Yes, of course."

She passes the baby to me, and I gently take her, being reminded of what it was like to hold my littlest sisters after they had been born, and feeling love bloom in my heart for this beautiful, innocent creature.

The baby is perfect, her eyes open and blinking, adjusting to this new life. "Welcome, baby."

I show her to Devlin. He nods to them. "She's beautiful, Addison, Feylin."

My sister beams. "Thank you."

"Hey there, little girl," I whisper. "Welcome to our family."

I brush a finger over her tiny chin and she yawns. It's the sweetest sight in the world.

"What are you going to name her?" Devlin asks.

The brand-new parents exchange a look. "We're still working that out," he admits sheepishly.

Addison gives her husband a look full of love. "We're taking our time. The right name will come along."

"Yes, it will," Devlin says.

"Do you want to hold her?" I ask.

He reaches for the baby. "I would love to."

My husband holds the baby gently, and there's just something about seeing a man with a child in his arms. Well, at least there is for me. To watch someone so strong cherish and protect something so tiny warms every inch of my body.

"We don't want to tire y'all out," Devlin tells them, handing the baby back to me.

"We just wanted to say hello," I confirm, placing her in Feylin's arms. "And tell you how happy and proud we are."

Addison grins. "Thank you."

We go out and spend a few minutes with my family. We're all together, and this feels right. My husband is hanging out with my parents and talking to my sisters. My older sister just had a baby.

This is it. This is family.

When Devlin and I leave, my parents are still fussing over the baby, as they should. They'll stay the night to make sure that Addison and Feylin are okay and don't need anything. Not that the fae servants couldn't do that, but you know—there's something different about a mother watching over her child, and I know my mama wants to be with that grandbaby as much as possible.

"I'm so happy for them," I tell Devlin.

"Me too."

It's a warm night. It's humid, which is to be expected, and my skin's sticky, but I don't mind. Tonight I will endure all the humidity that the Southeast has to offer, because my heart has wings.

"You know," Devlin starts, "we could have kids."

I laugh. "Of course we could."

"No, I mean, *now*. Whenever you want."

He gestures toward the town that unfolds in front of us. Teenagers are hanging out by the fountain. The windows of Castleview Books are dark. Business has bounced back and we're doing well.

Devlin's been keeping himself busy testing the artificial womb. So far, it's all going great. If things keep progressing, he'll be able to roll it into hospitals by the end of the year.

Lit torches float above us, suspended by magic. They cast amber light on the streets of the town that we call home.

"I love you, Devlin," I say.

He tugs me in and kisses the top of my head. "I love *you*."

We're almost to the house when he pauses, and I stop, watching him. He's staring at the ground, stock-still. Having been around him enough times, I know when he's experiencing a vision.

When it's over, he exhales and presses a hand to his heart. "Whew. That was trippy."

"Everything okay? Did you see a new invention?"

"No." One side of his mouth turns up into a smile. "I saw us."

He never sees us. "Seriously?"

"As a heart attack."

I drag a finger down the buttons of his shirt. "And what did you see?"

"Well, I saw us, as I said, and I saw *you* with your own potion shop."

"Really?"

"Uh-huh."

A potion shop. The idea of owning one has never crossed my mind until now, and now that it has, I want one. To be able to create potions to help people with skin conditions and hair tonics, and whatever else I can make—the ideas are limitless.

I clap my hands. "I love that! Yes! Let's do it."

He kisses me and I wrap my arms around his neck, pushing up on my toes and bending one leg at the knee, lifting it up, just 'cause.

When the kiss breaks, he says, "That's not all I saw."

"What else?"

"I saw us—with a family of our own."

My heart swells. "How many kids?"

He squints. "Not sure. Maybe a dozen?"

"Stop it! Honestly?"

"Honestly?" He tips his face up to the sky for a moment before dropping his lips back on mine and murmuring, "As many as you want."

"You're not going to give me an answer?"

"As we both know, sometimes one vision doesn't give all

the information that you need. More could come after, so I'm gonna let the number be a surprise."

I scoff. "You are the worst, you know that?"

"I know. But you love me."

We kiss again. "I do love you. Forever and ever."

Thank you so much for reading HOW TO OUTWIT A WIZARD. I hope you loved Blair and Devlin as much as I do. Their story was a joy to write.

If you haven't read the first book in the seres, HOW TO FAKE IT WITH A FAE, you don't want to miss it. Every book in the series is a standalone, but each book does build on the last. Scan the code below to start reading.

If you'd like to remain up-to-date on my release schedule, including when Chelsea's book is dropping, click **HERE** to grab your scene and receive my newsletter.

You can also touch base with me by joining my Facebook group, Amy Boyles's Cozy Coven. Click HERE to join.

Made in the USA
Las Vegas, NV
22 October 2024

10300398R00194